THE CRYPTID CLUB

A NESSIE SITUATION

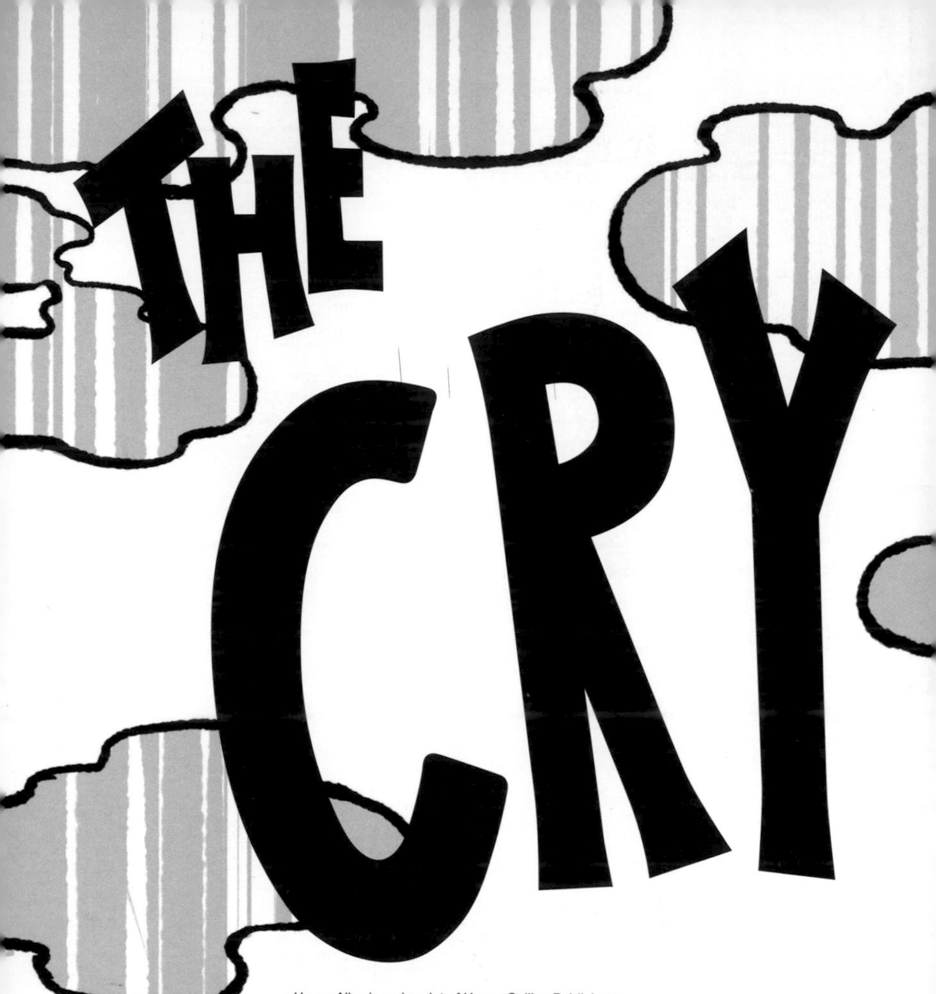
THE
CRY

HarperAlley is an imprint of HarperCollins Publishers.

Cryptid Club #2: A Nessie Situation

www.harperalley.com

Library of Congress Control Number: 2022932405
ISBN 978-0-06-306082-1 — ISBN 978-0-06-306081-4 (pbk.)

Typography by Joe Merkel
22 23 24 25 26 RTLO 10 9 8 7 6 5 4 3 2 1
❖
First Edition

PUD CLUB

A NESSIE SITUATION

HARPER
alley

An Imprint of HarperCollins Publishers

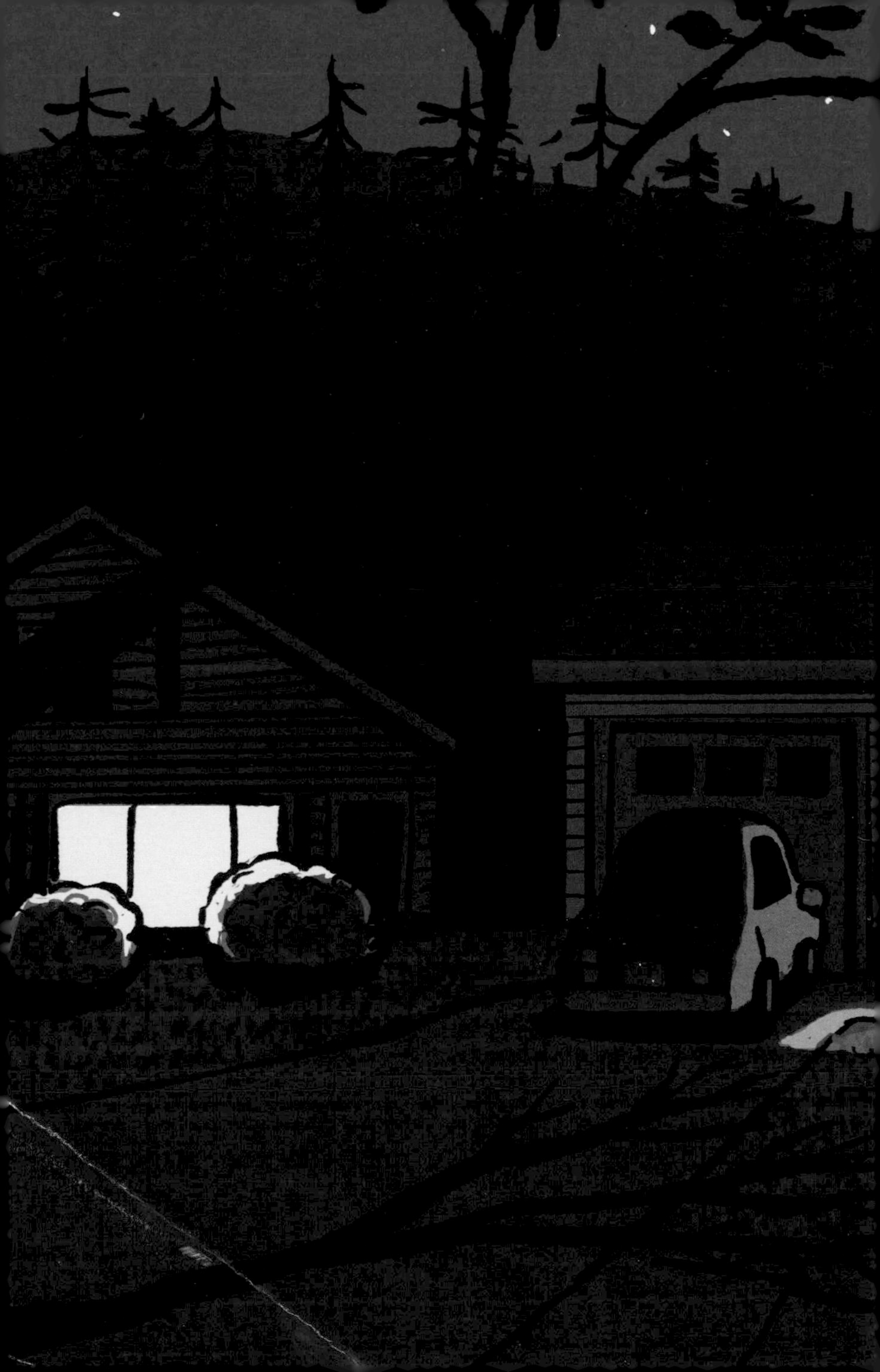

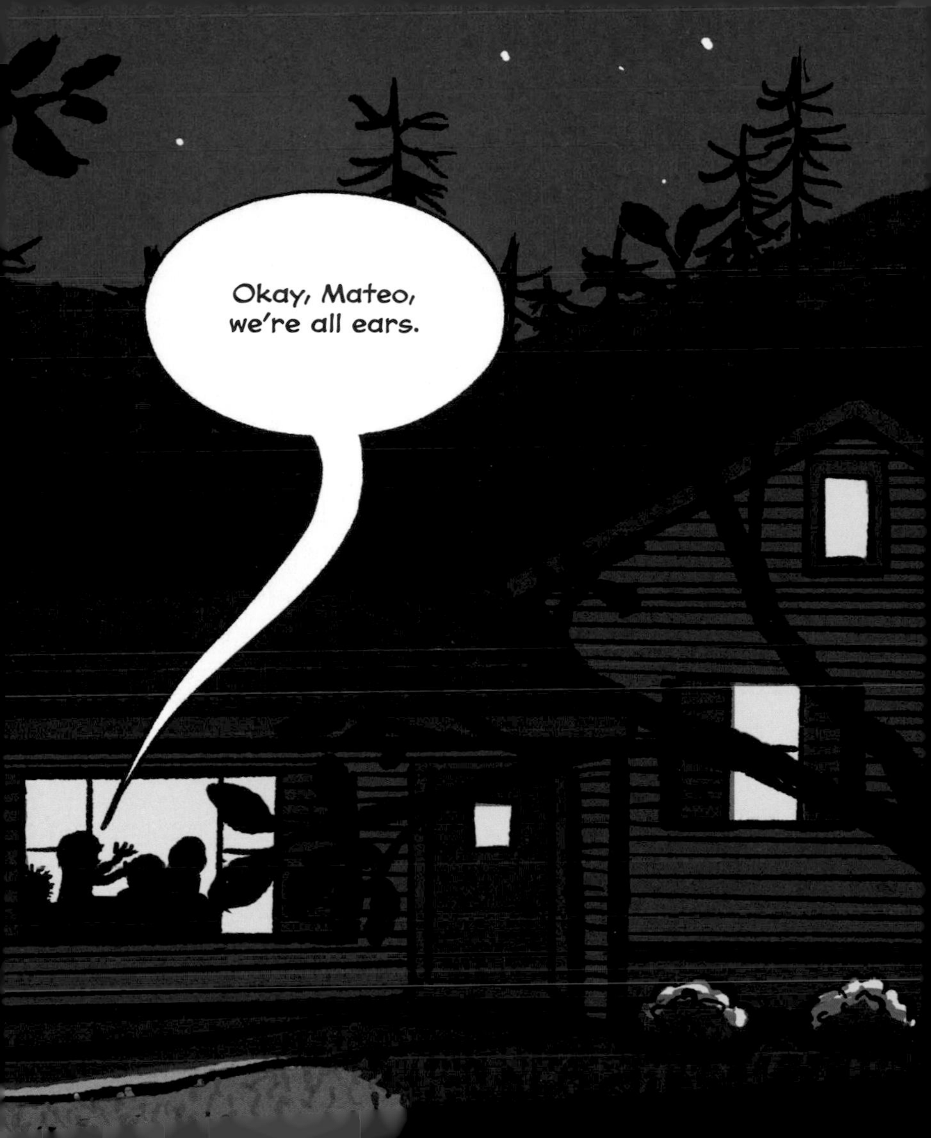
Okay, Mateo, we're all ears.

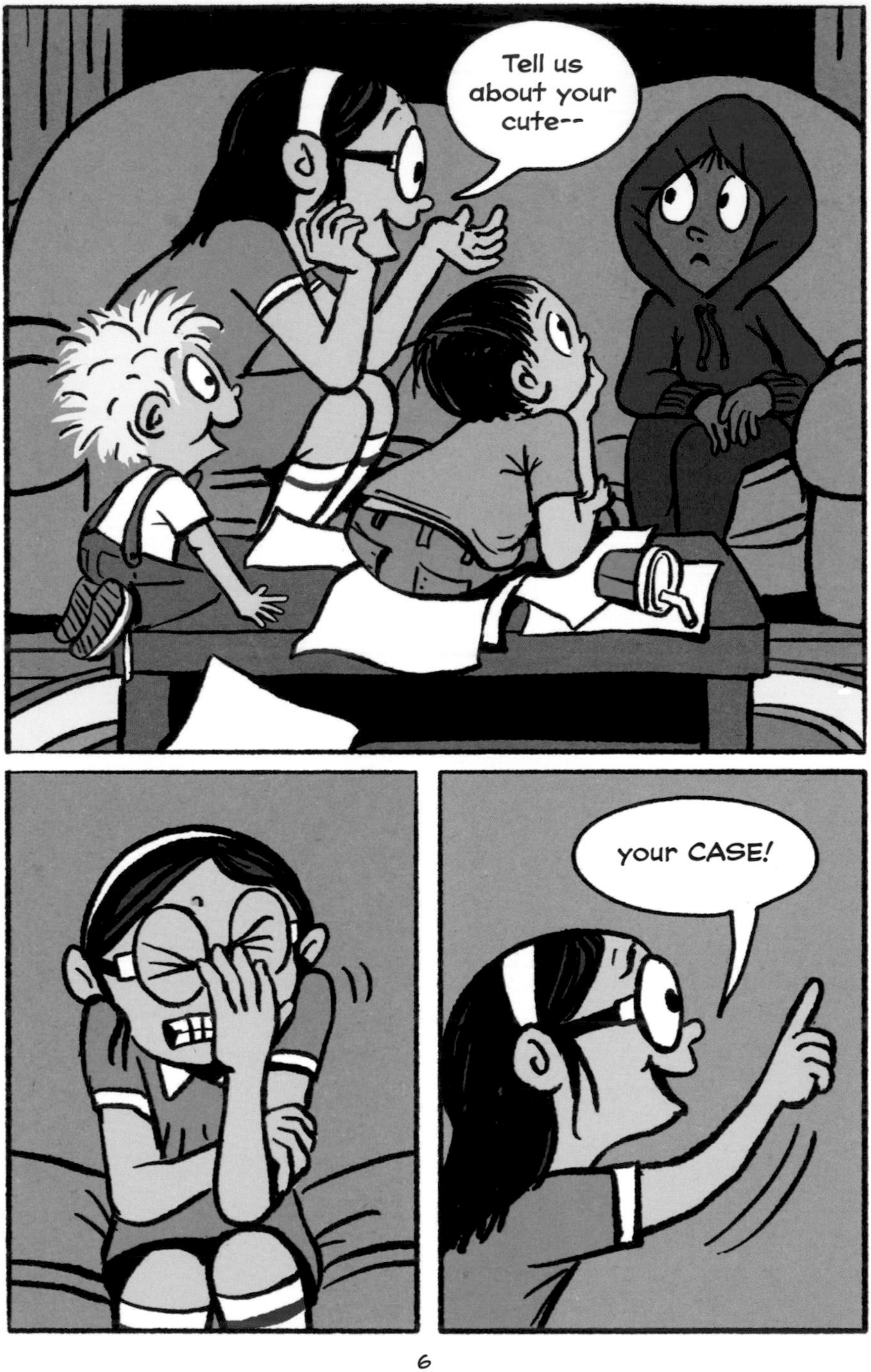
Tell us about your cute--
your CASE!

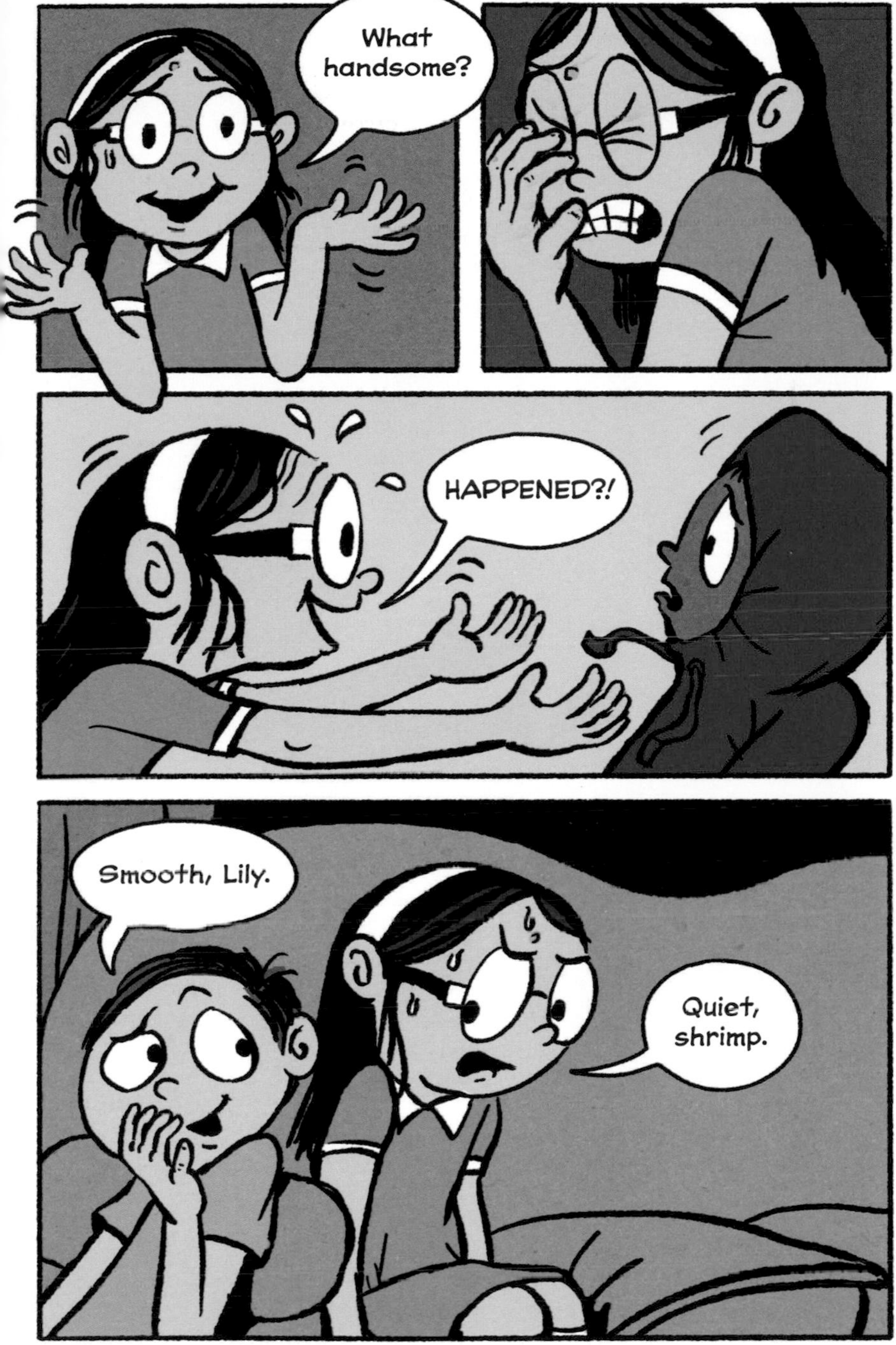
What handsome?
HAPPENED?!
Smooth, Lily.
Quiet, shrimp.

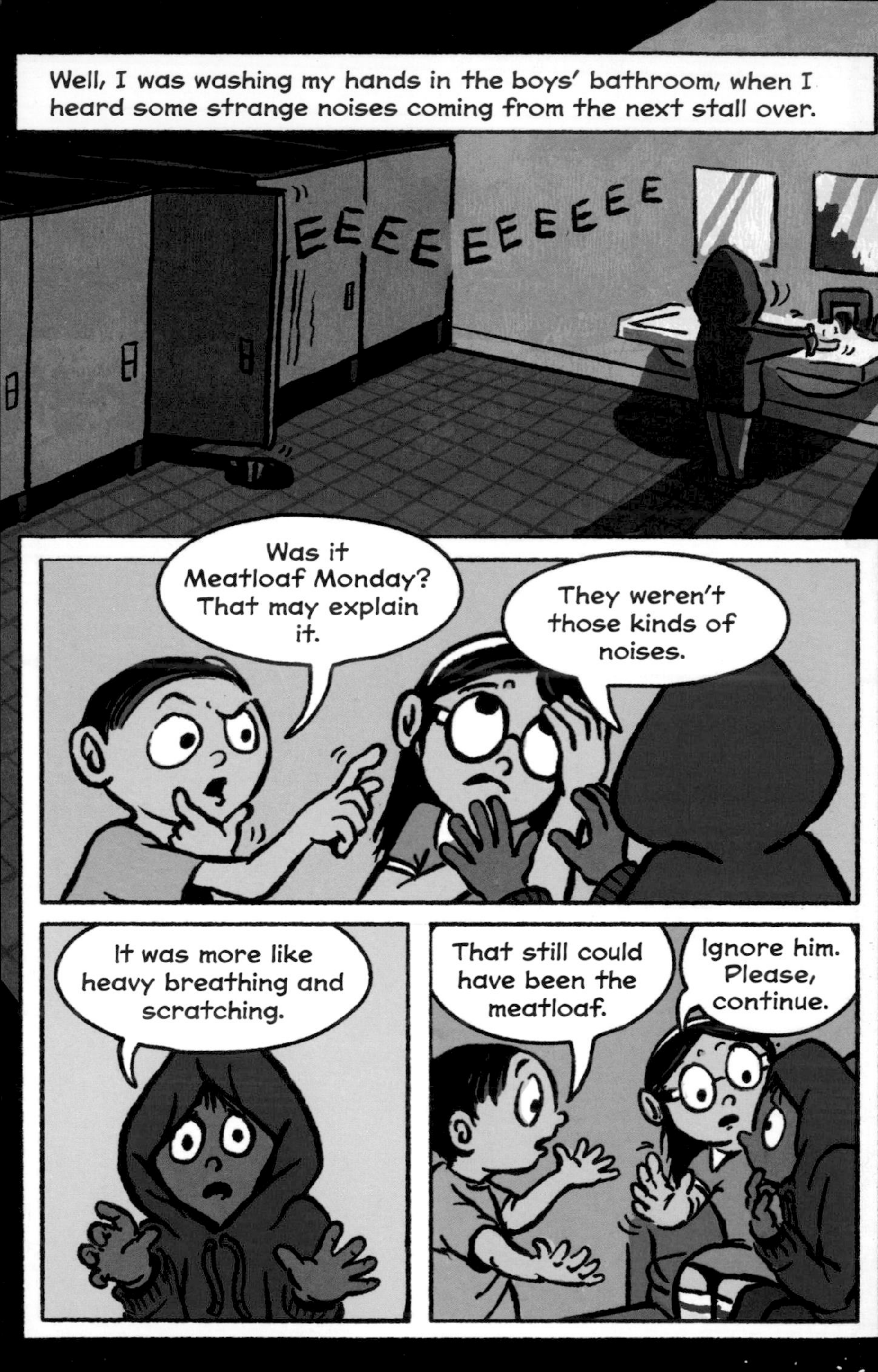
Well, I was washing my hands in the boys' bathroom, when I heard some strange noises coming from the next stall over.
EEEEEEEEEEEE
Was it Meatloaf Monday? That may explain it.
They weren't those kinds of noises.
It was more like heavy breathing and scratching.
That still could have been the meatloaf.
Ignore him. Please, continue.

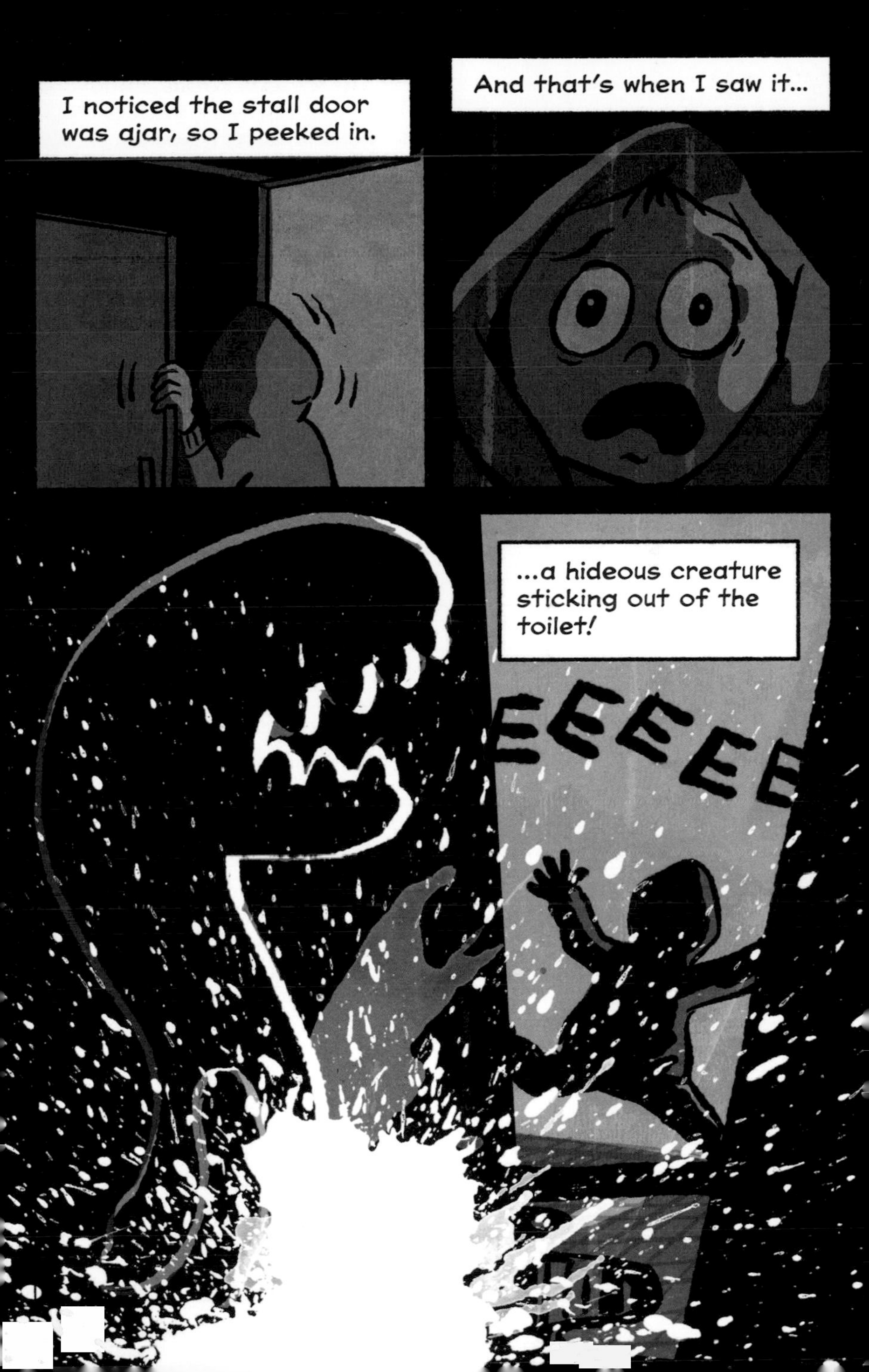
I noticed the stall door was ajar, so I peeked in.
And that's when I saw it...
...a hideous creature sticking out of the toilet!
EEEEE

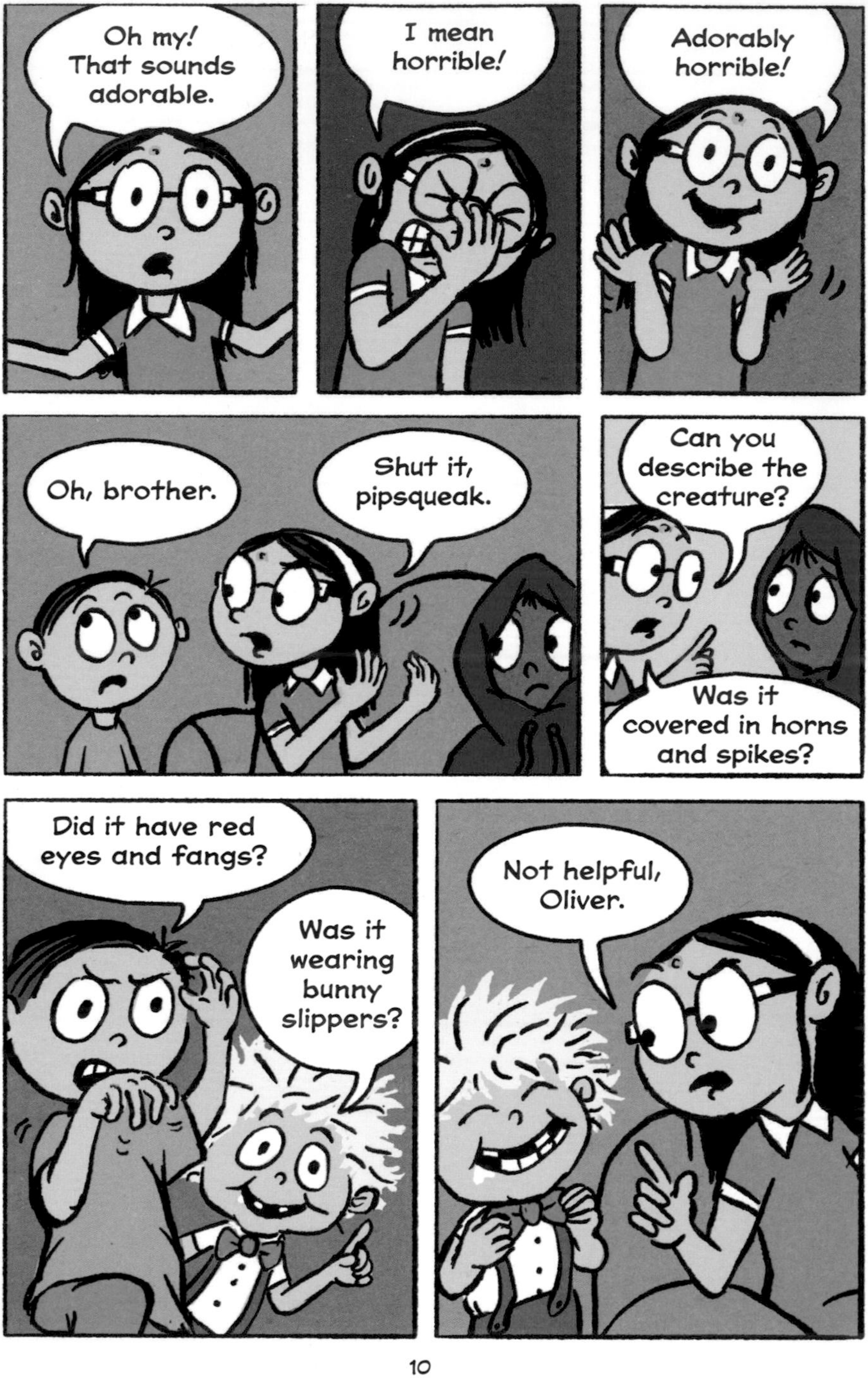
Oh my! That sounds adorable.
I mean horrible!
Adorably horrible!
Oh, brother.
Shut it, pipsqueak.
Can you describe the creature?
Was it covered in horns and spikes?
Did it have red eyes and fangs?
Was it wearing bunny slippers?
Not helpful, Oliver.

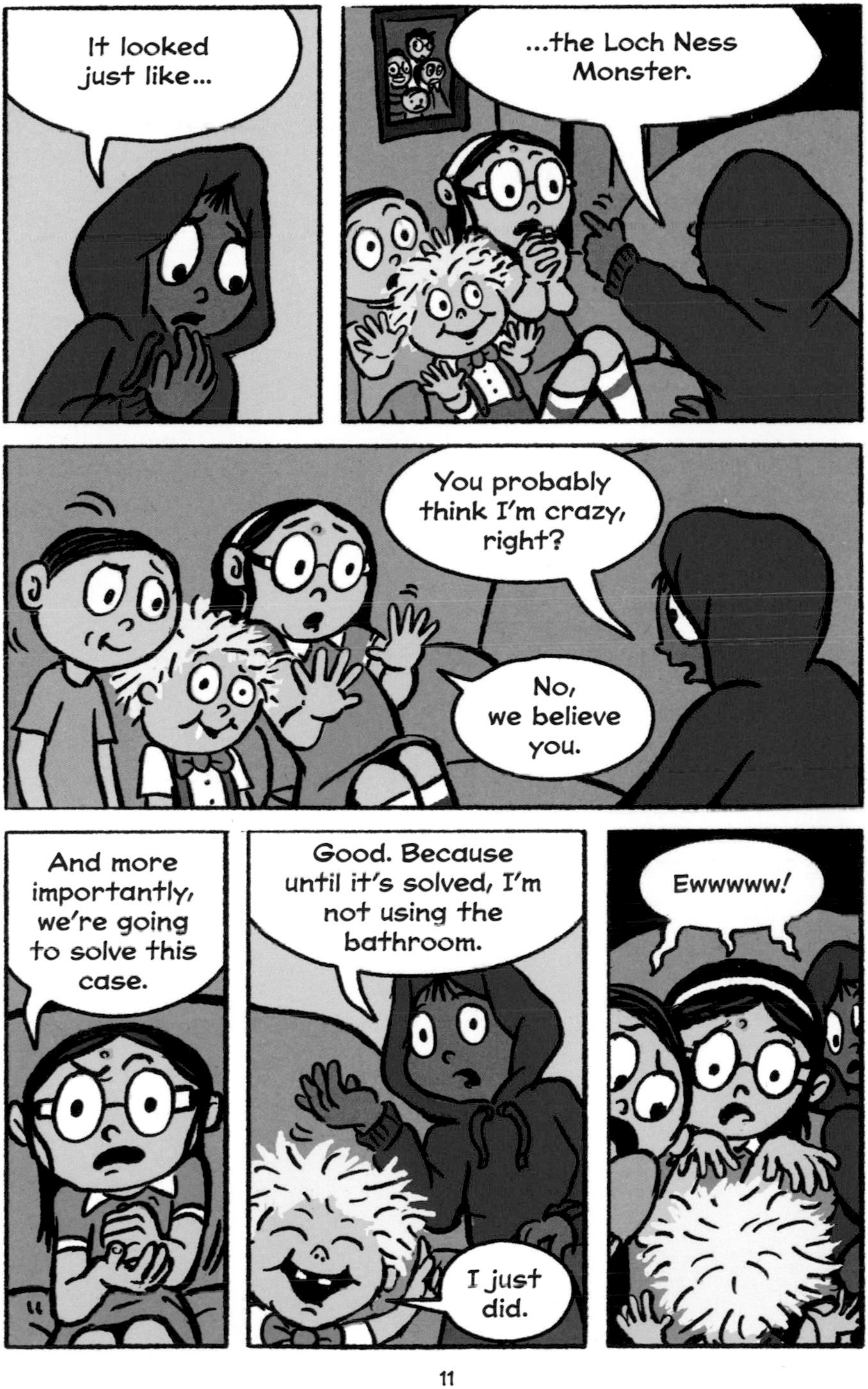
It looked just like...
...the Loch Ness Monster.
You probably think I'm crazy, right?
No, we believe you.
And more importantly, we're going to solve this case.
Good. Because until it's solved, I'm not using the bathroom.
I just did.
Ewwwww!

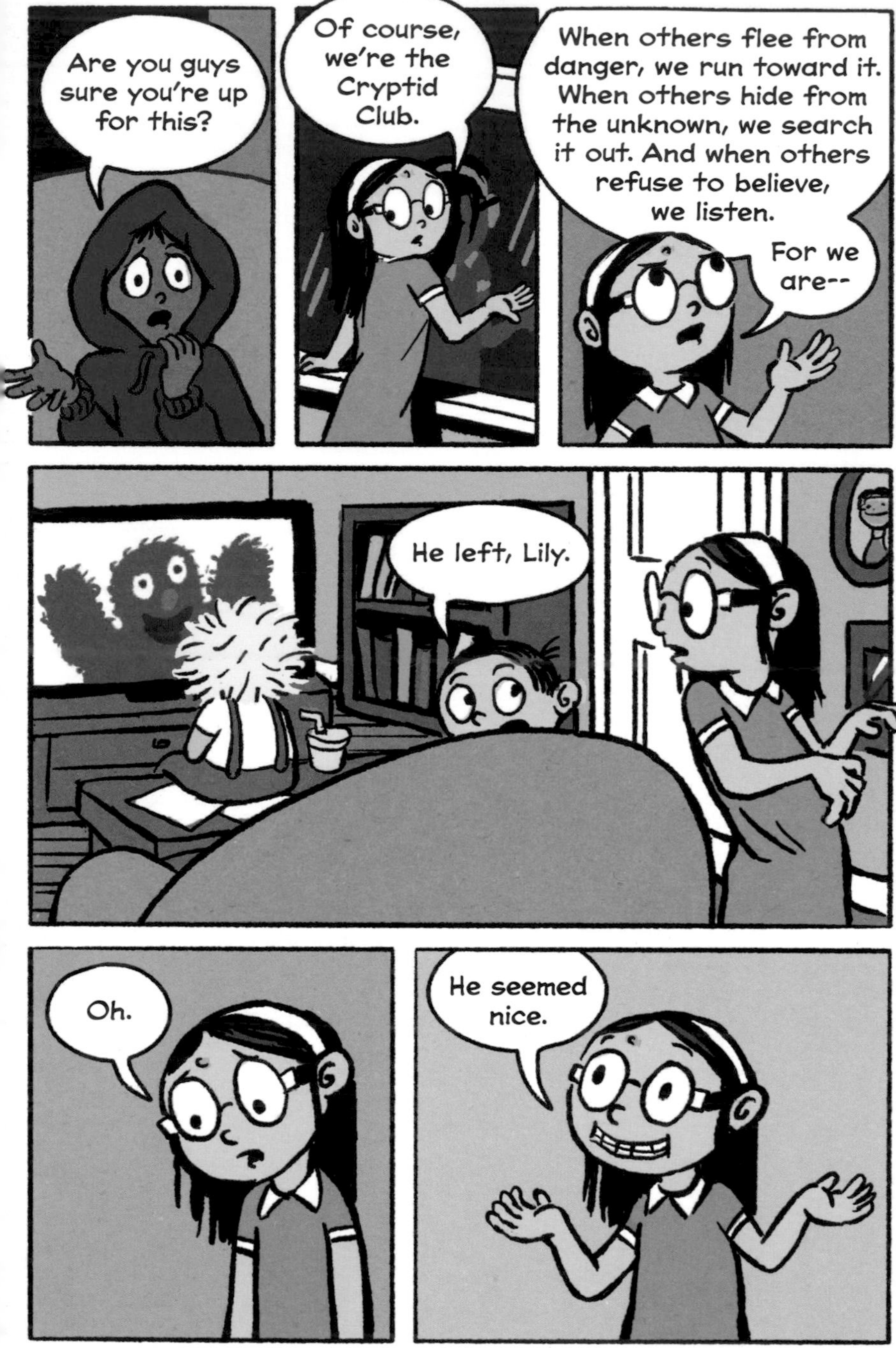
Are you guys sure you're up for this?
Of course, we're the Cryptid Club.
When others flee from danger, we run toward it. When others hide from the unknown, we search it out. And when others refuse to believe, we listen.
For we are--
He left, Lily.
Oh.
He seemed nice.

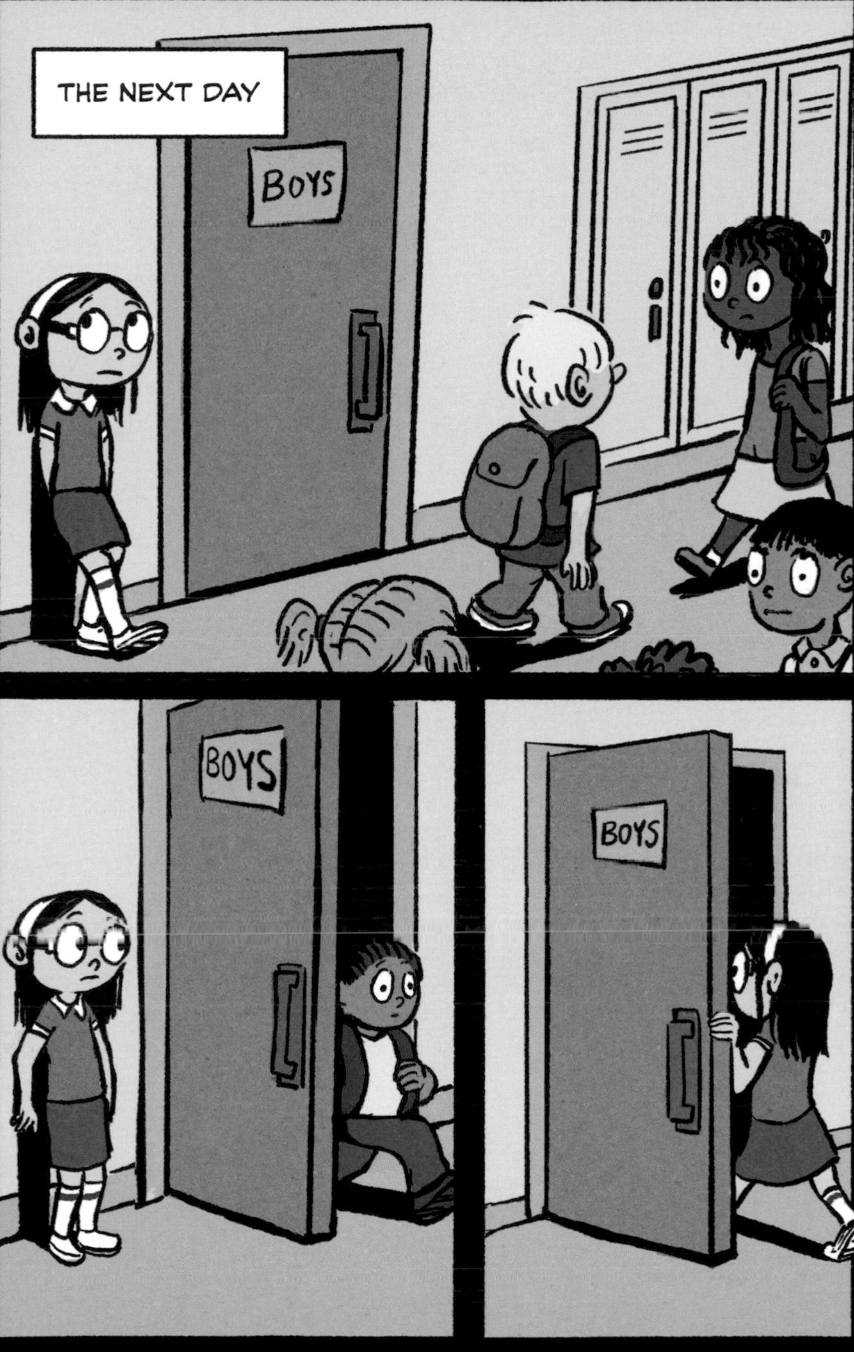
THE NEXT DAY
BOYS
BOYS
BOYS

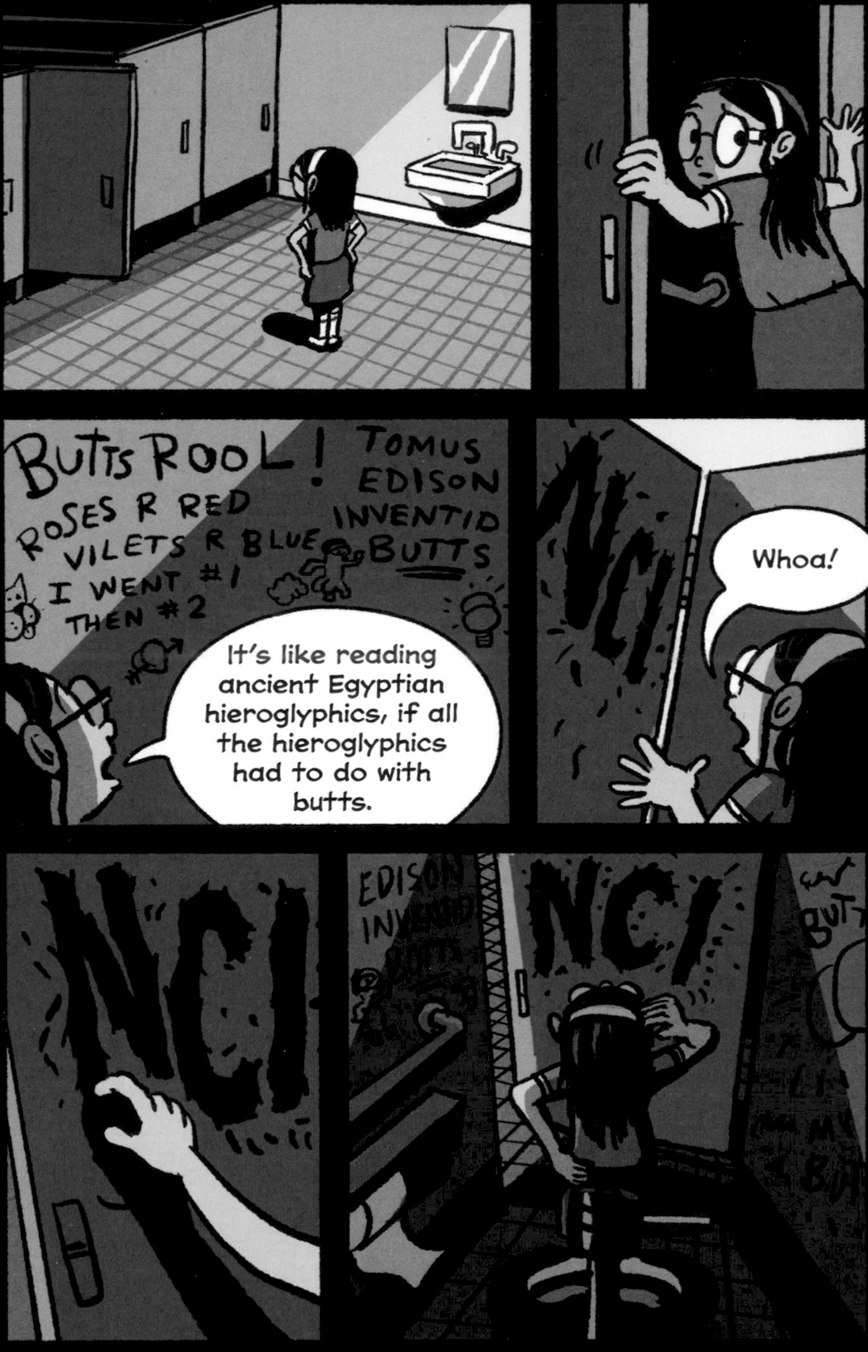
BUTTS ROOL!
TOMUS EDISON INVENTID BUTTS
ROSES R RED VILETS R BLUE I WENT #1 THEN #2
It's like reading ancient Egyptian hieroglyphics, if all the hieroglyphics had to do with butts.
NCI
Whoa!
NCI
EDISON INVENTID
NCI

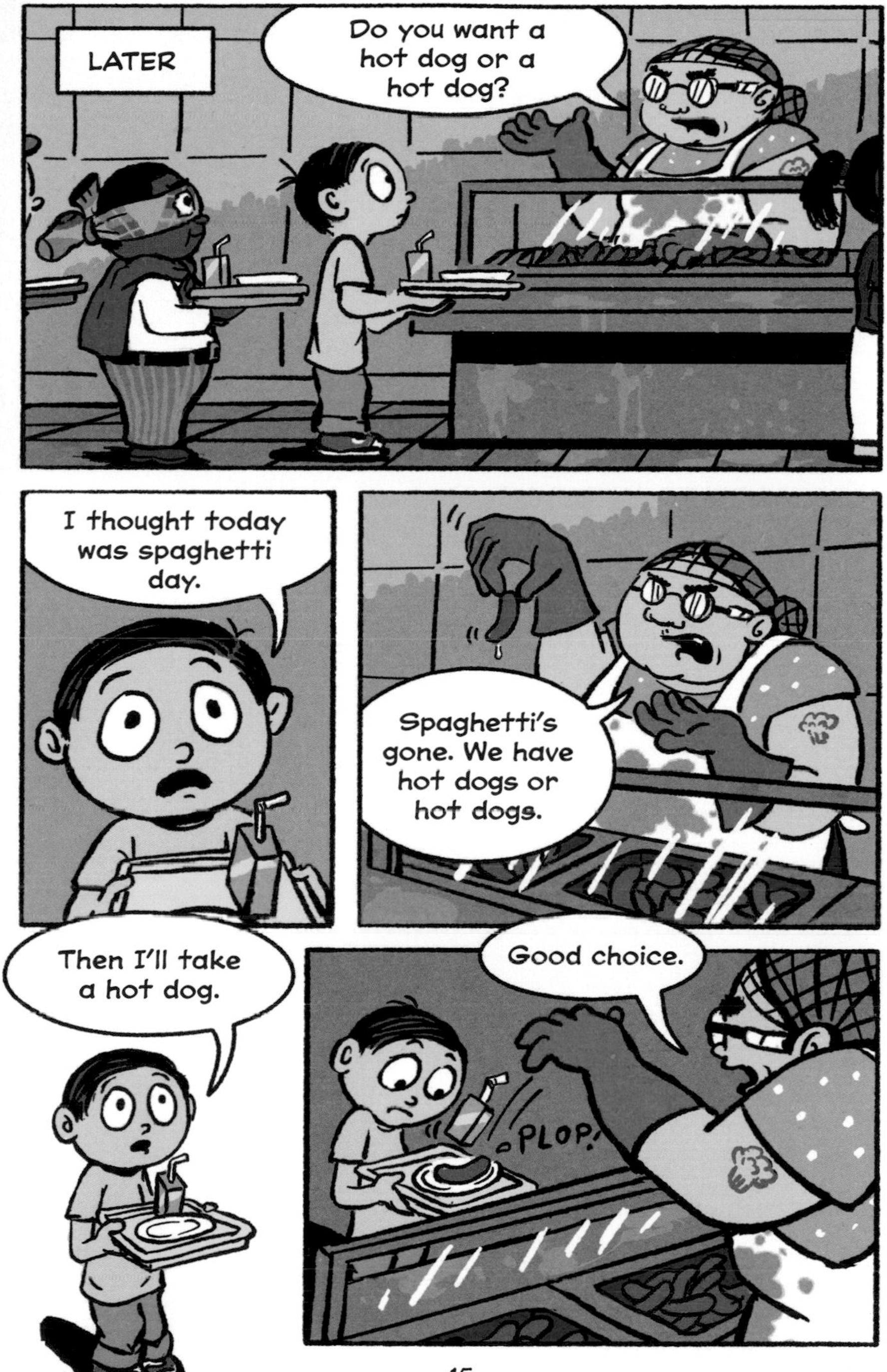

LATER
Do you want a hot dog or a hot dog?
I thought today was spaghetti day.
Spaghetti's gone. We have hot dogs or hot dogs.
Then I'll take a hot dog.
Good choice.
PLOP!

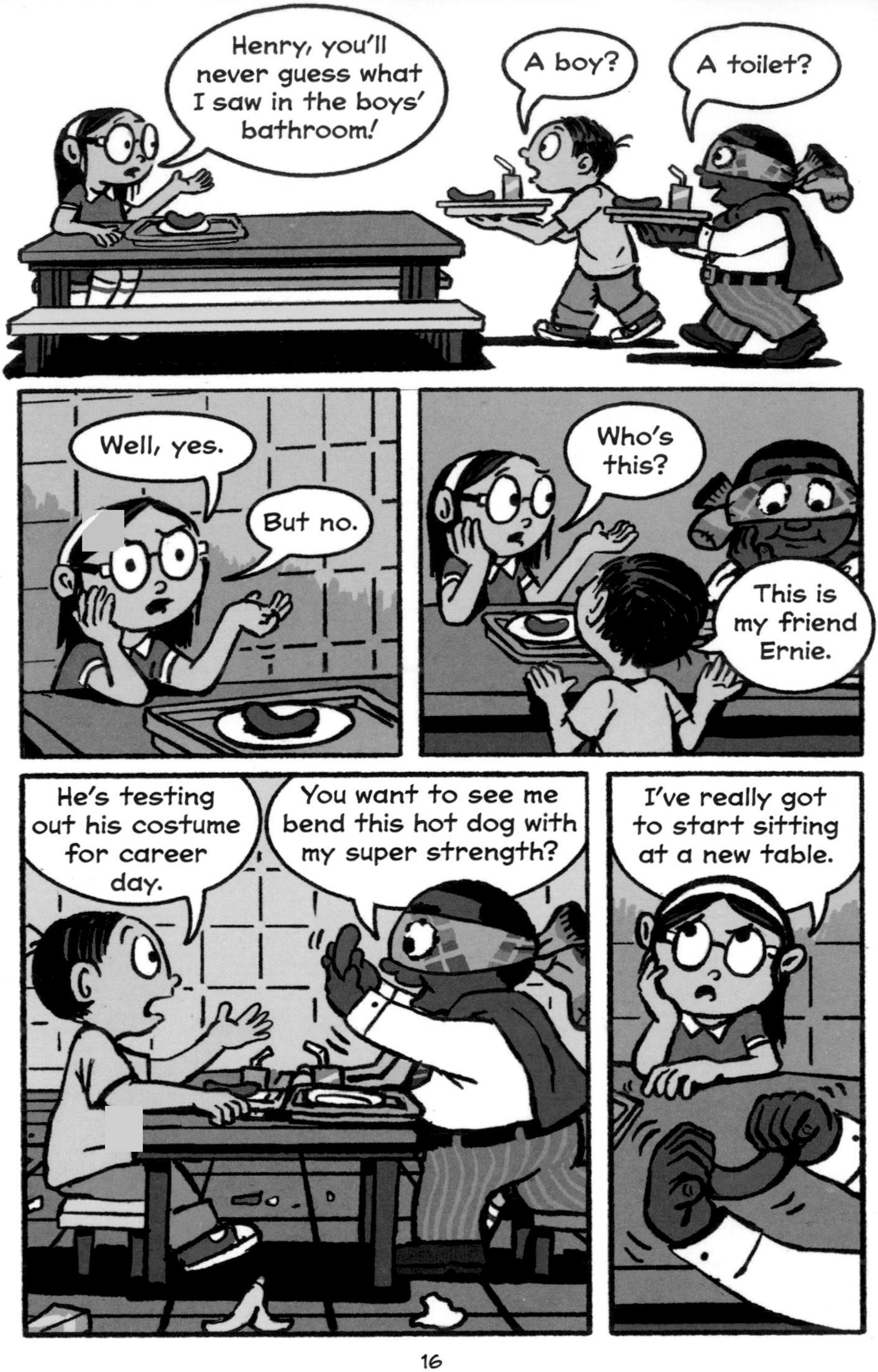
Henry, you'll never guess what I saw in the boys' bathroom!
A boy?
A toilet?
Well, yes.
But no.
Who's this?
This is my friend Ernie.
He's testing out his costume for career day.
You want to see me bend this hot dog with my super strength?
I've really got to start sitting at a new table.

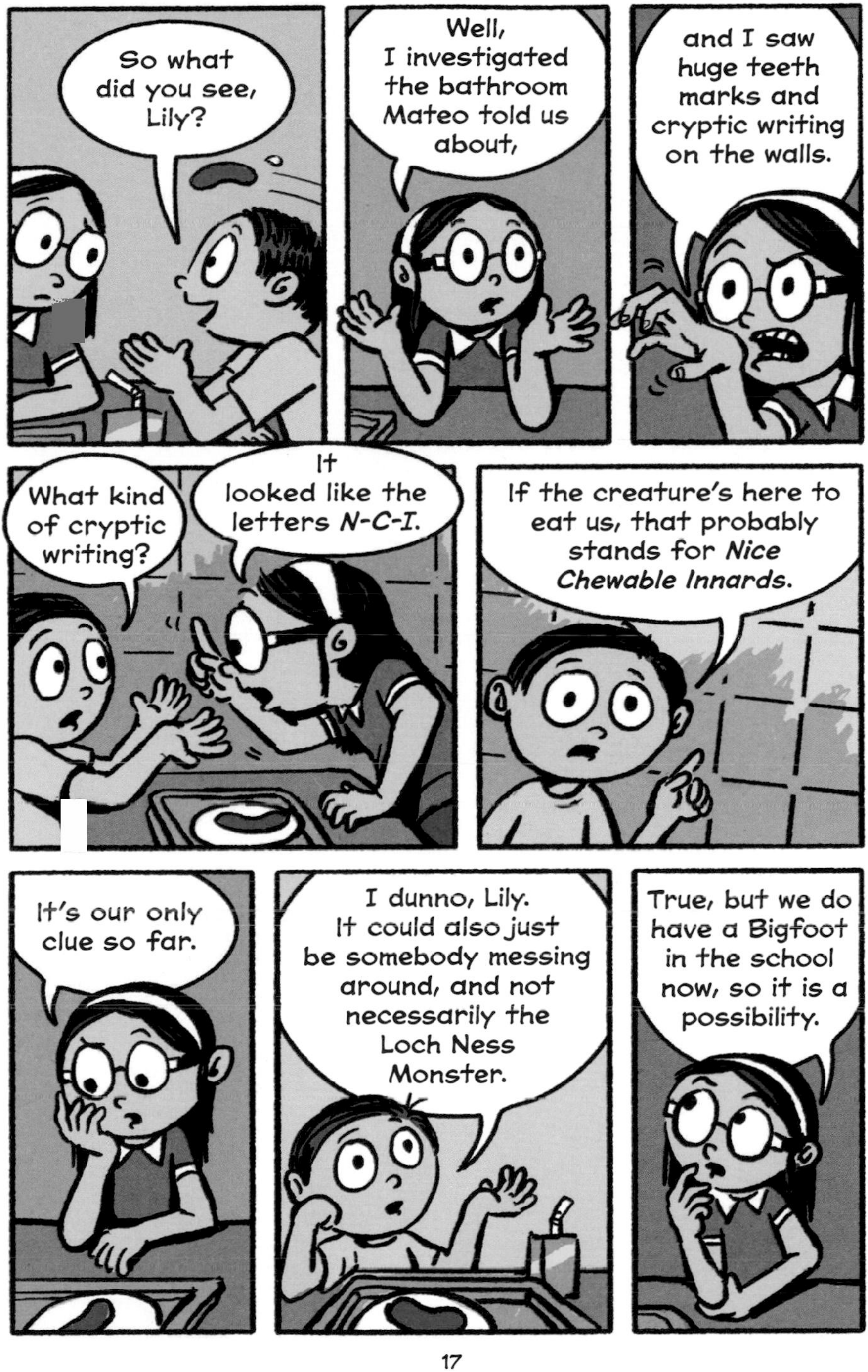
So what did you see, Lily?
Well, I investigated the bathroom Mateo told us about,
and I saw huge teeth marks and cryptic writing on the walls.
What kind of cryptic writing?
It looked like the letters *N-C-I*.
If the creature's here to eat us, that probably stands for *Nice Chewable Innards*.
It's our only clue so far.
I dunno, Lily. It could also just be somebody messing around, and not necessarily the Loch Ness Monster.
True, but we do have a Bigfoot in the school now, so it is a possibility.

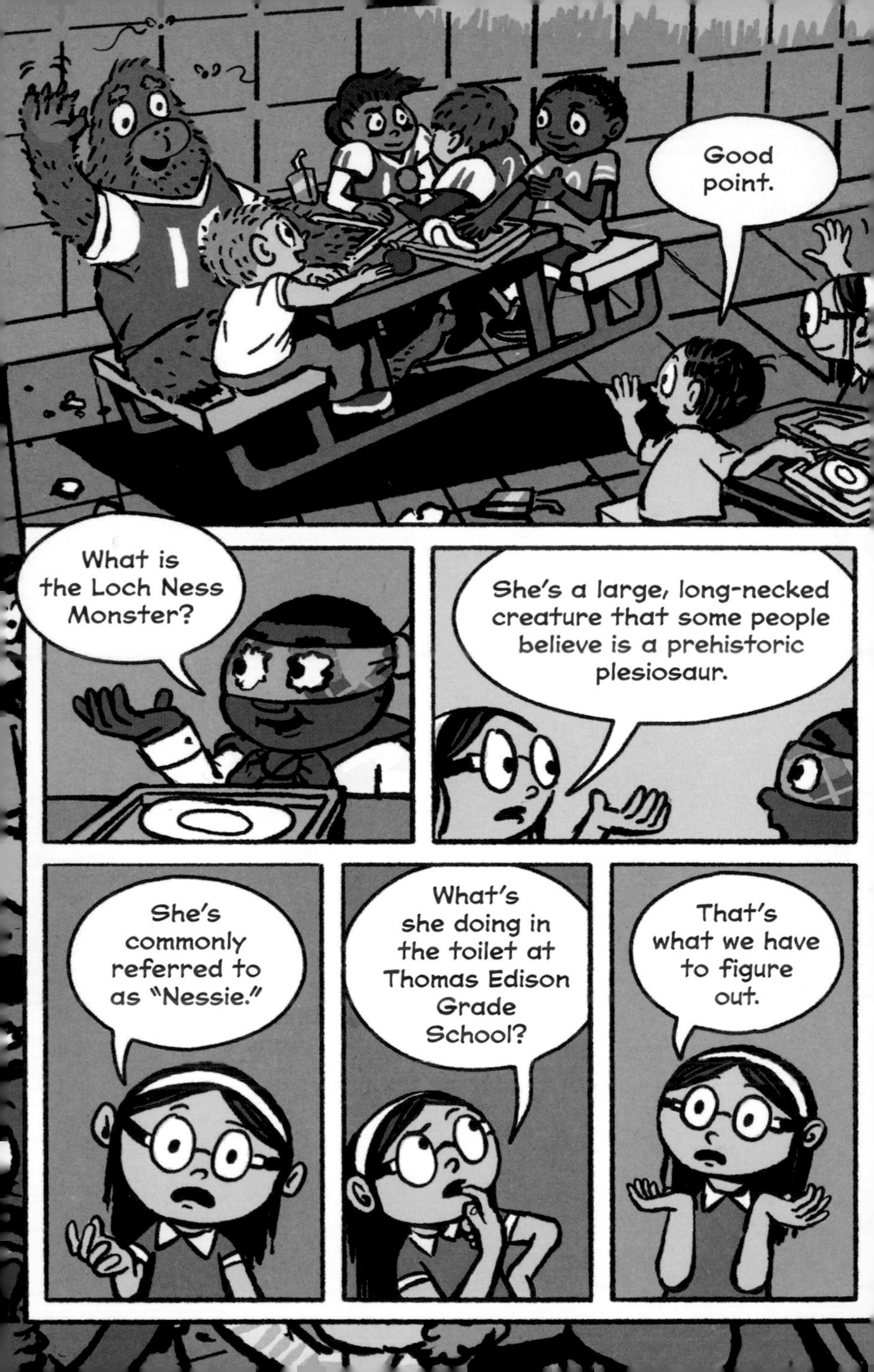
Good point.
What is the Loch Ness Monster?
She's a large, long-necked creature that some people believe is a prehistoric plesiosaur.
She's commonly referred to as "Nessie."
What's she doing in the toilet at Thomas Edison Grade School?
That's what we have to figure out.

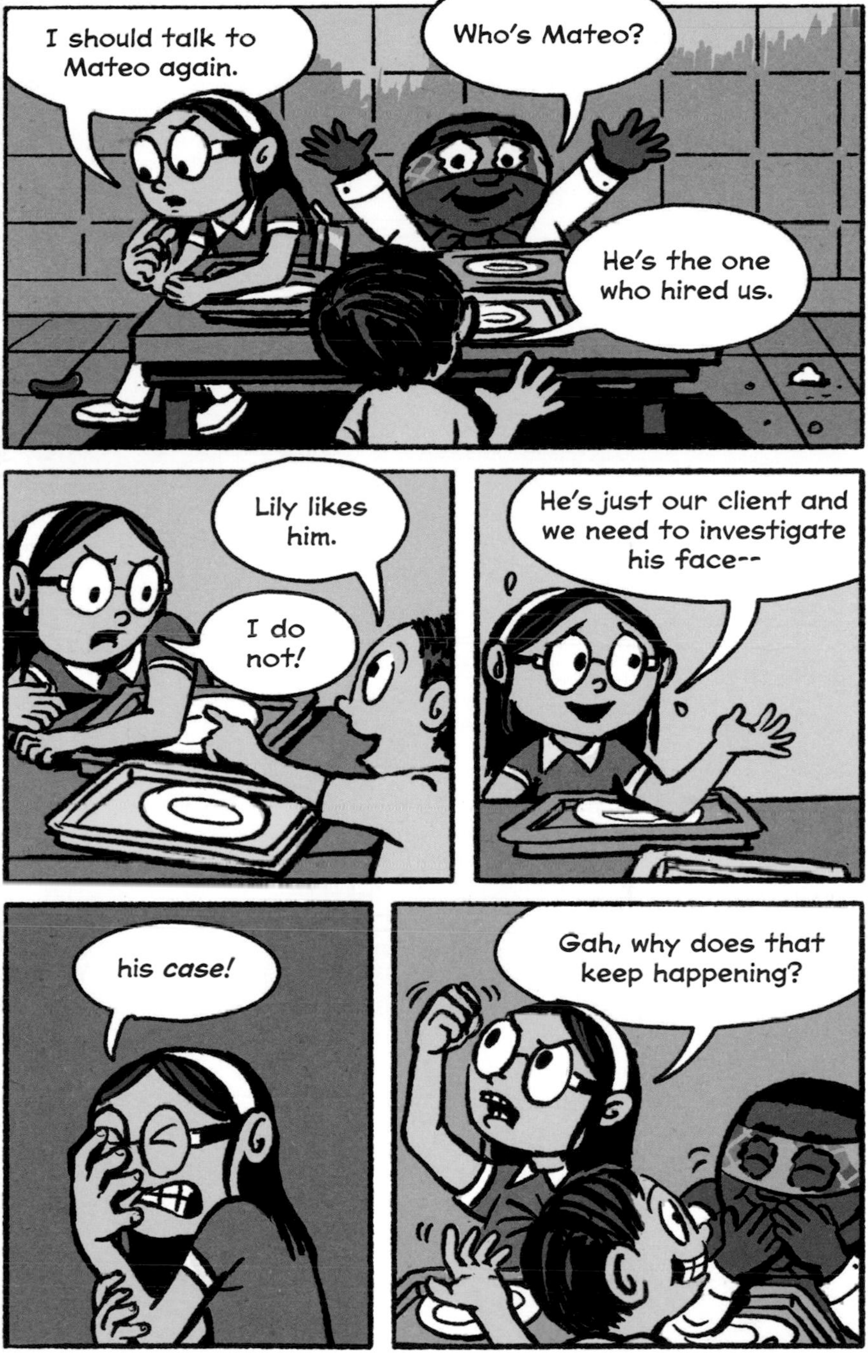

I should talk to Mateo again.
Who's Mateo?
He's the one who hired us.
Lily likes him.
I do not!
He's just our client and we need to investigate his face--
his *case!*
Gah, why does that keep happening?

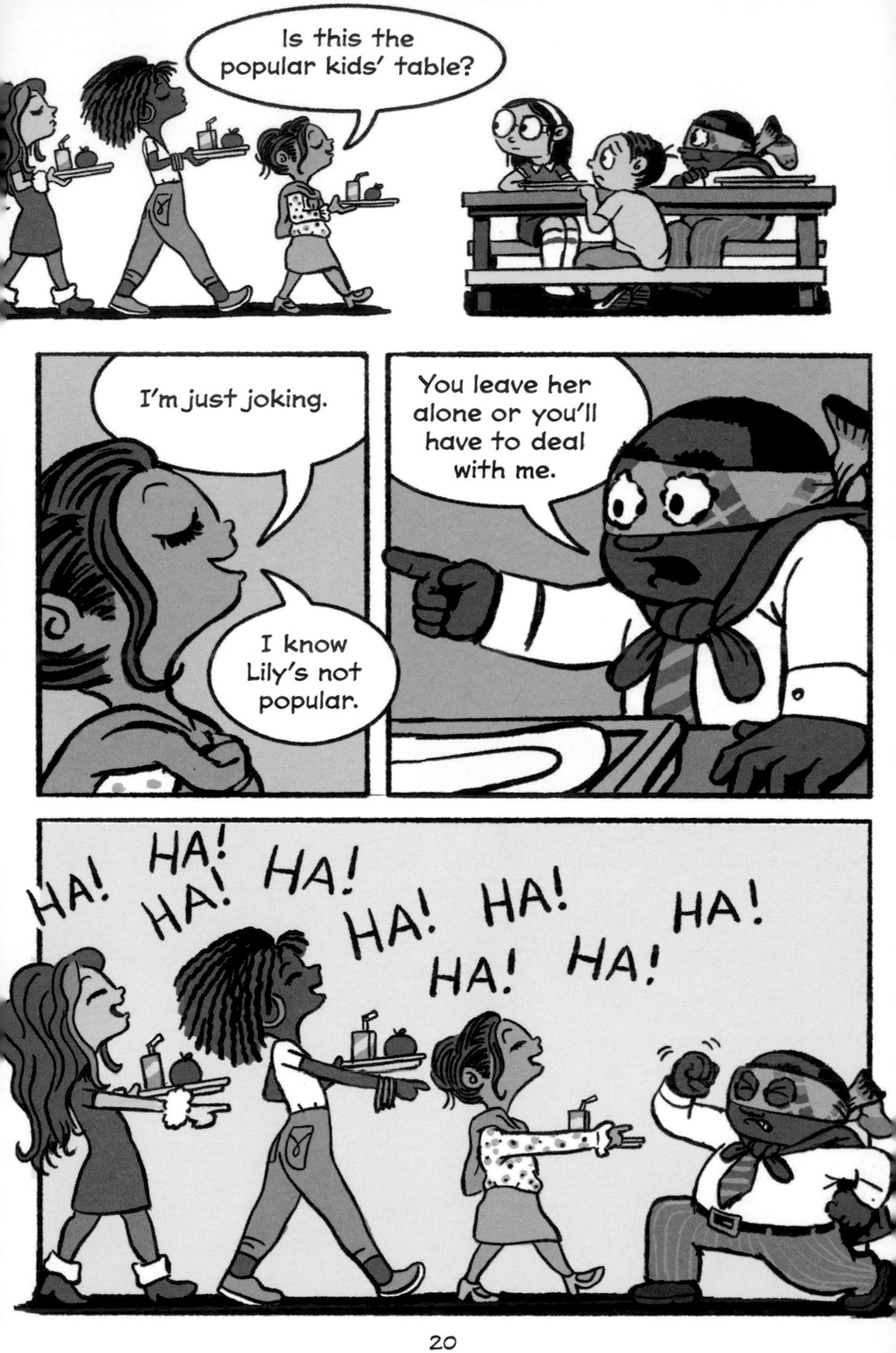
Is this the popular kids' table?
I'm just joking.
I know Lily's not popular.
You leave her alone or you'll have to deal with me.
HA! HA! HA! HA! HA! HA! HA! HA! HA!

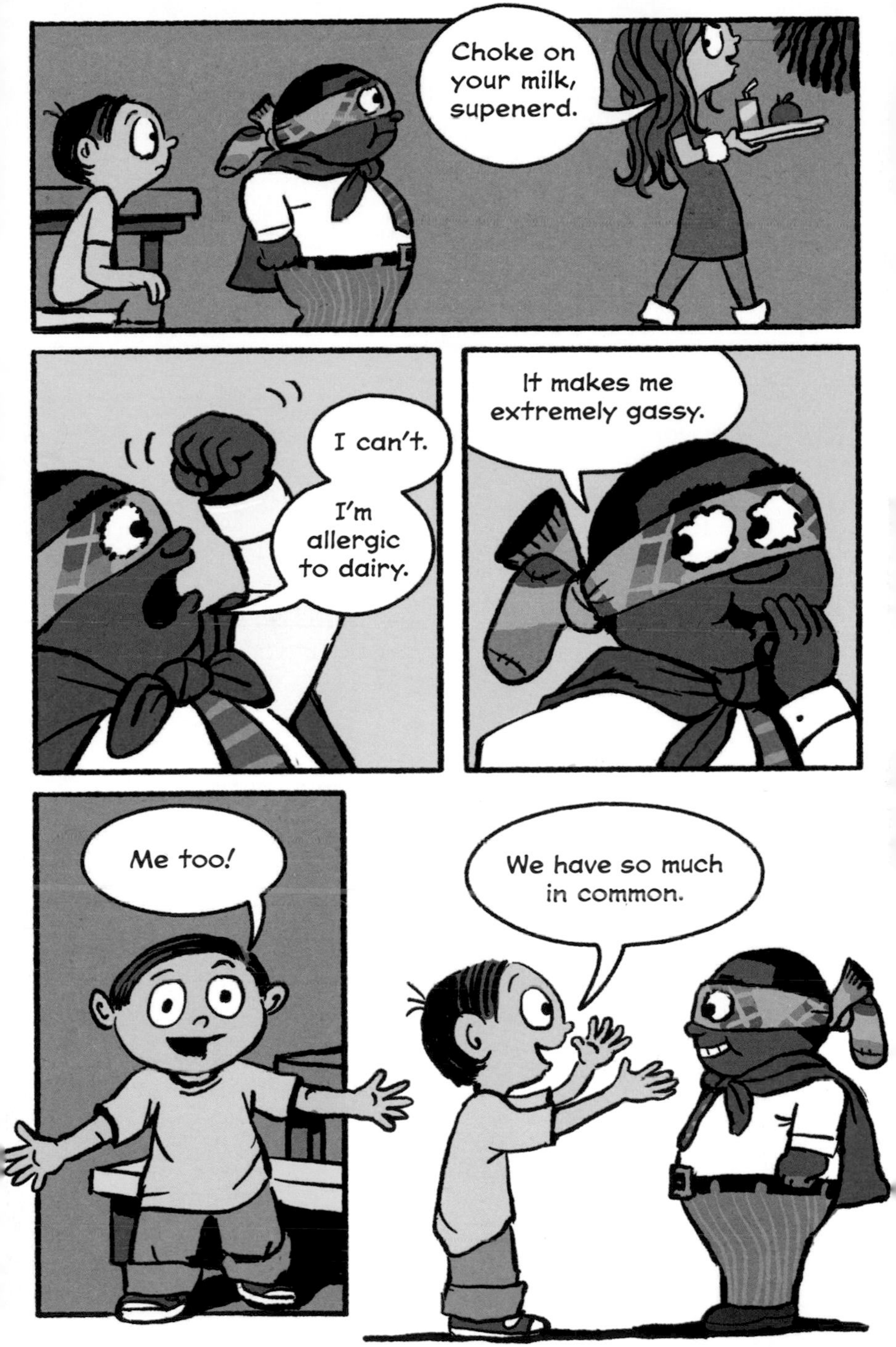
Choke on your milk, supenerd.
I can't.
I'm allergic to dairy.
It makes me extremely gassy.
Me too!
We have so much in common.

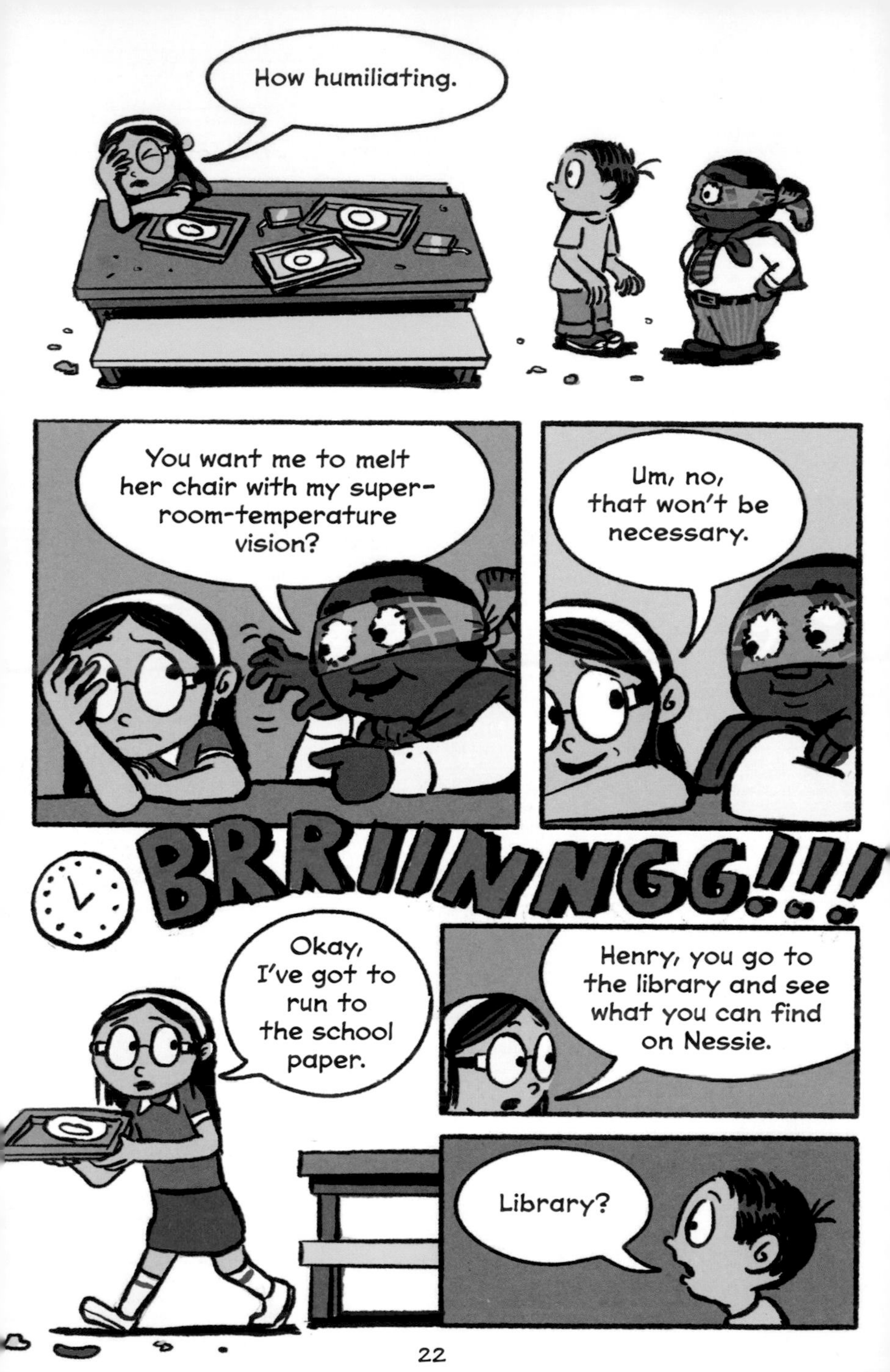
How humiliating.
You want me to melt her chair with my super-room-temperature vision?
Um, no, that won't be necessary.
BRRIINNGG!!!
Okay, I've got to run to the school paper.
Henry, you go to the library and see what you can find on Nessie.
Library?

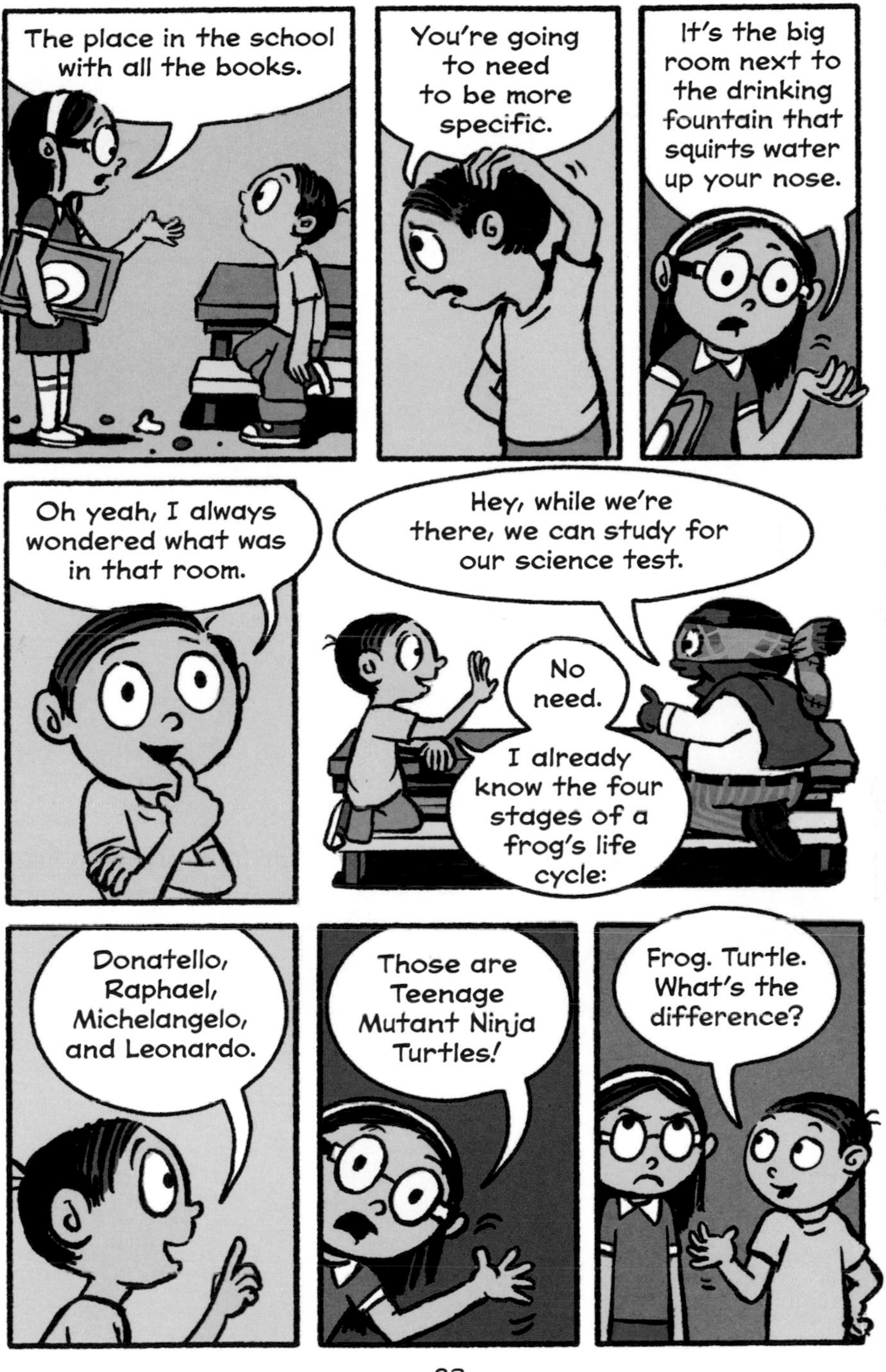
The place in the school with all the books.
You're going to need to be more specific.
It's the big room next to the drinking fountain that squirts water up your nose.
Oh yeah, I always wondered what was in that room.
Hey, while we're there, we can study for our science test.
No need.
I already know the four stages of a frog's life cycle:
Donatello, Raphael, Michelangelo, and Leonardo.
Those are Teenage Mutant Ninja Turtles!
Frog. Turtle. What's the difference?

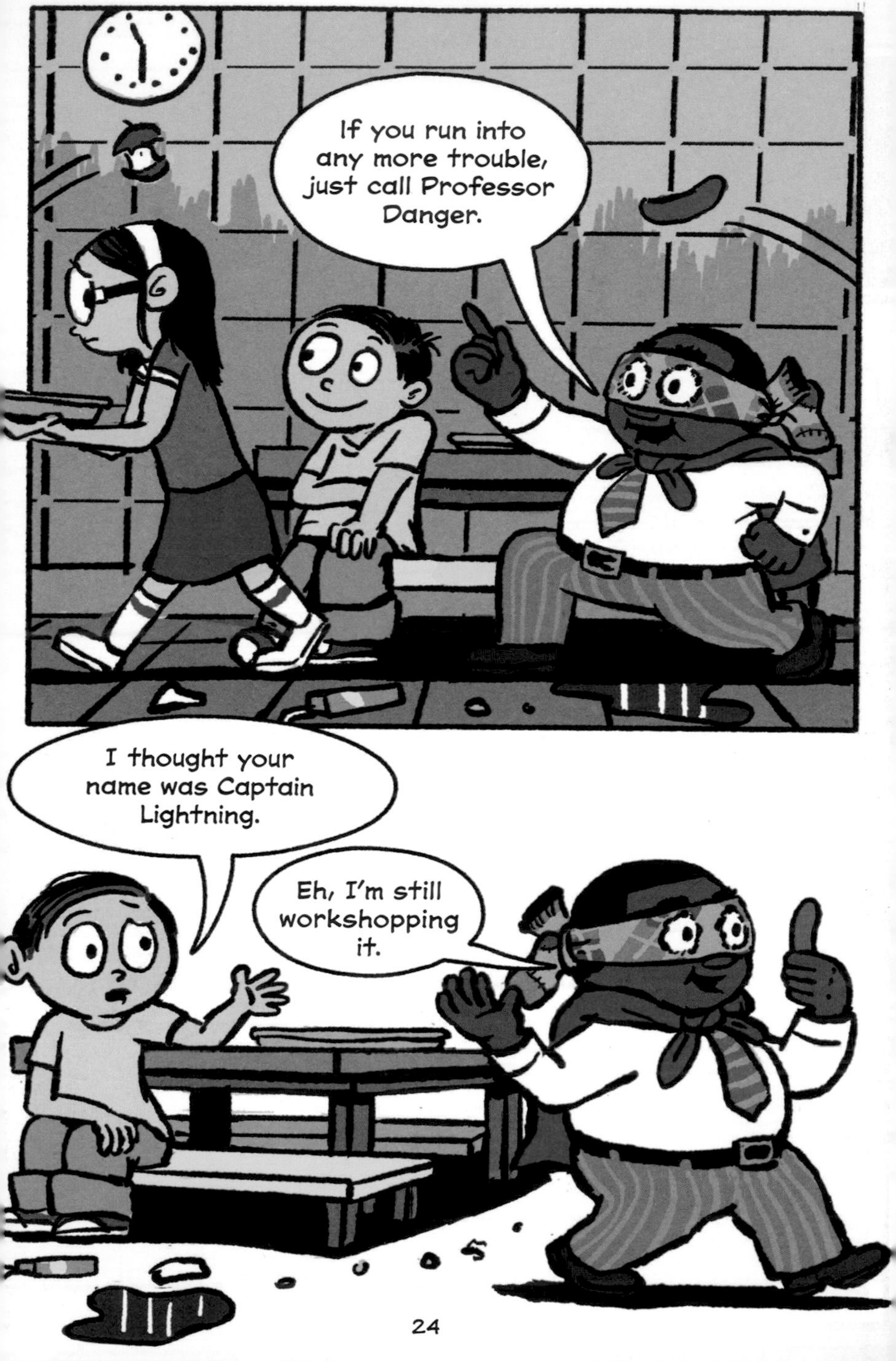
If you run into any more trouble, just call Professor Danger.
I thought your name was Captain Lightning.
Eh, I'm still workshopping it.

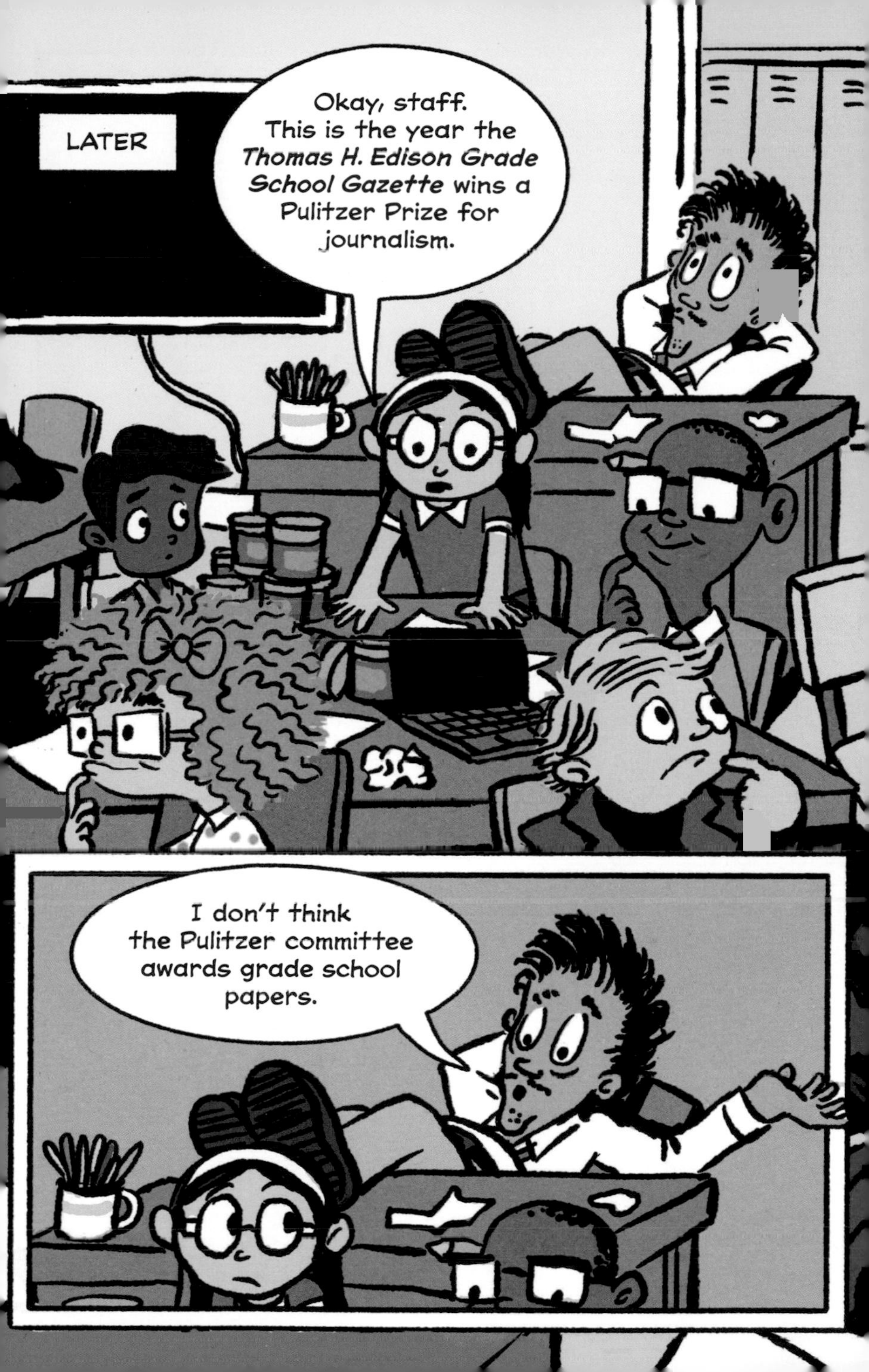
LATER
Okay, staff. This is the year the *Thomas H. Edison Grade School Gazette* wins a Pulitzer Prize for journalism.
I don't think the Pulitzer committee awards grade school papers.

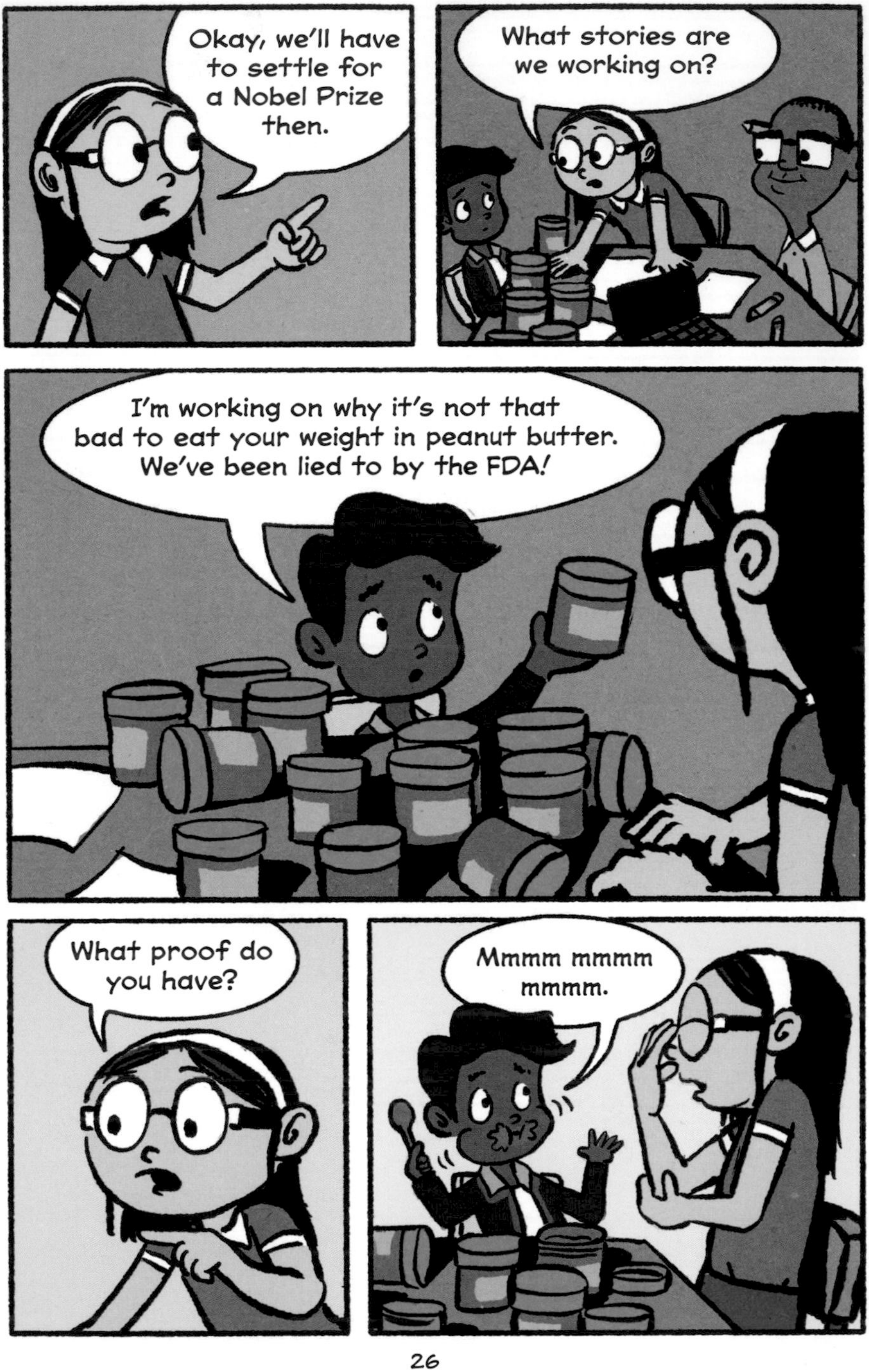
Okay, we'll have to settle for a Nobel Prize then.
What stories are we working on?
I'm working on why it's not that bad to eat your weight in peanut butter. We've been lied to by the FDA!
What proof do you have?
Mmmm mmmm mmmm.

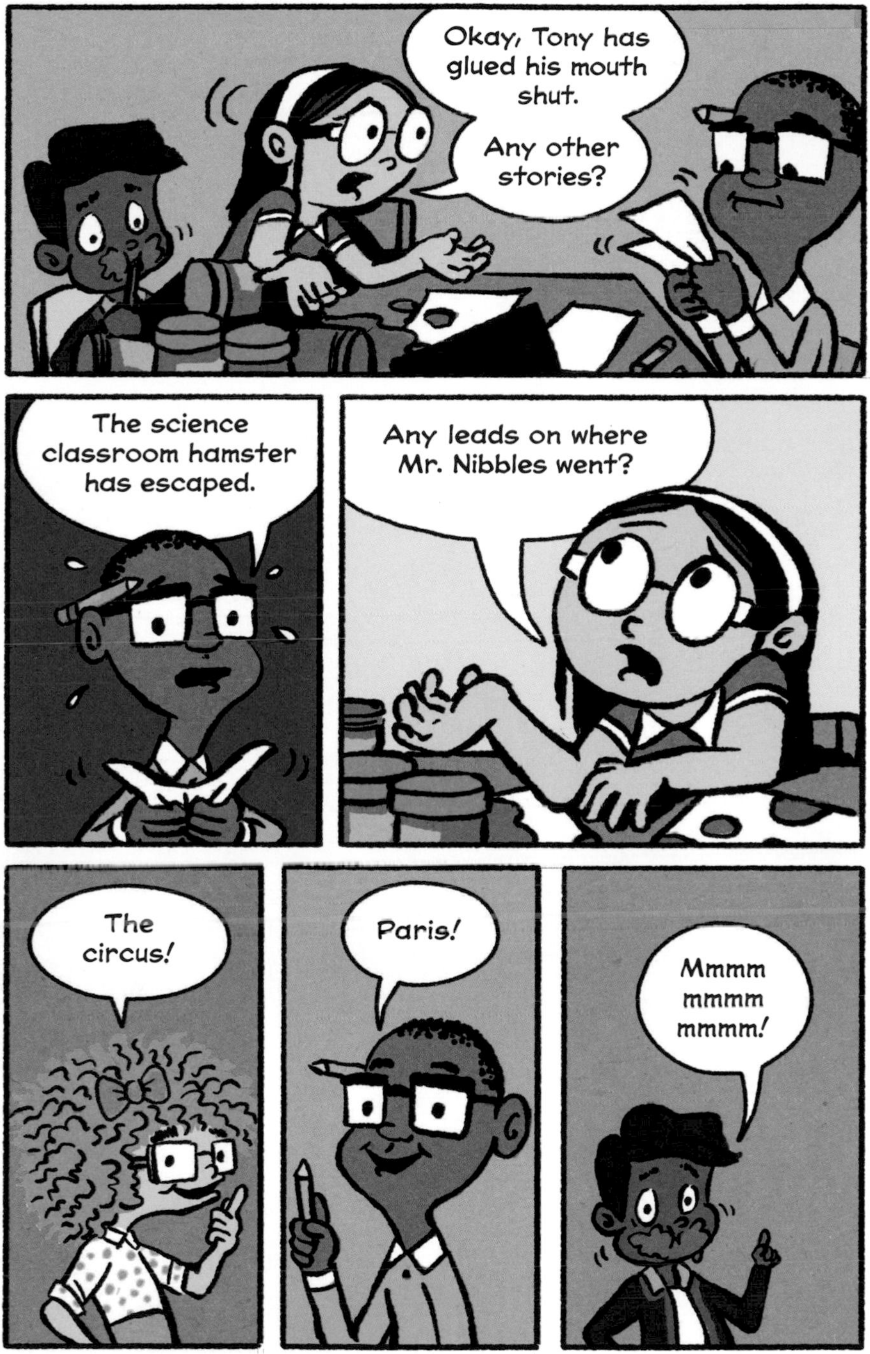
Okay, Tony has glued his mouth shut.
Any other stories?
The science classroom hamster has escaped.
Any leads on where Mr. Nibbles went?
The circus!
Paris!
Mmmm mmmm mmmm!

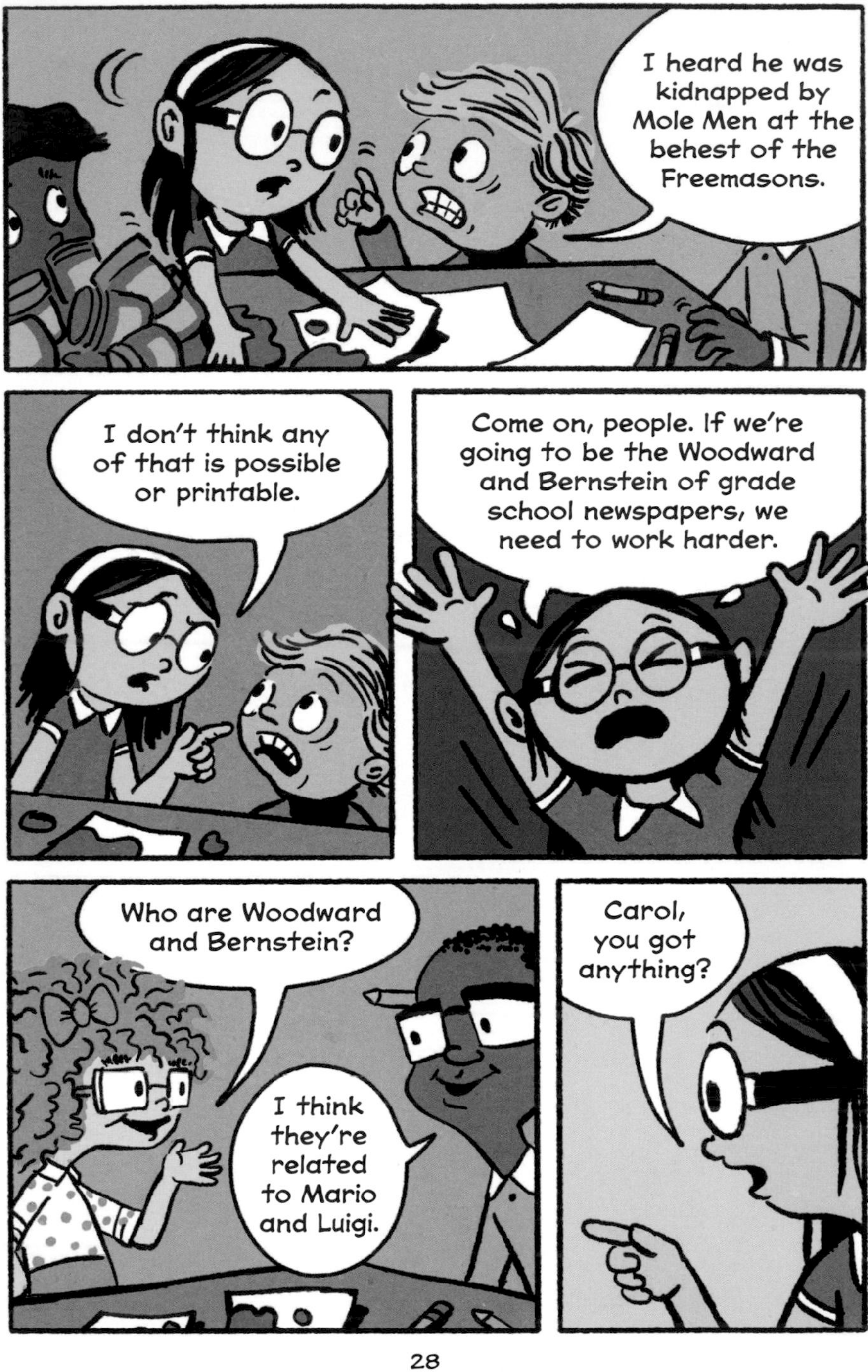
I heard he was kidnapped by Mole Men at the behest of the Freemasons.
I don't think any of that is possible or printable.
Come on, people. If we're going to be the Woodward and Bernstein of grade school newspapers, we need to work harder.
Who are Woodward and Bernstein?
I think they're related to Mario and Luigi.
Carol, you got anything?

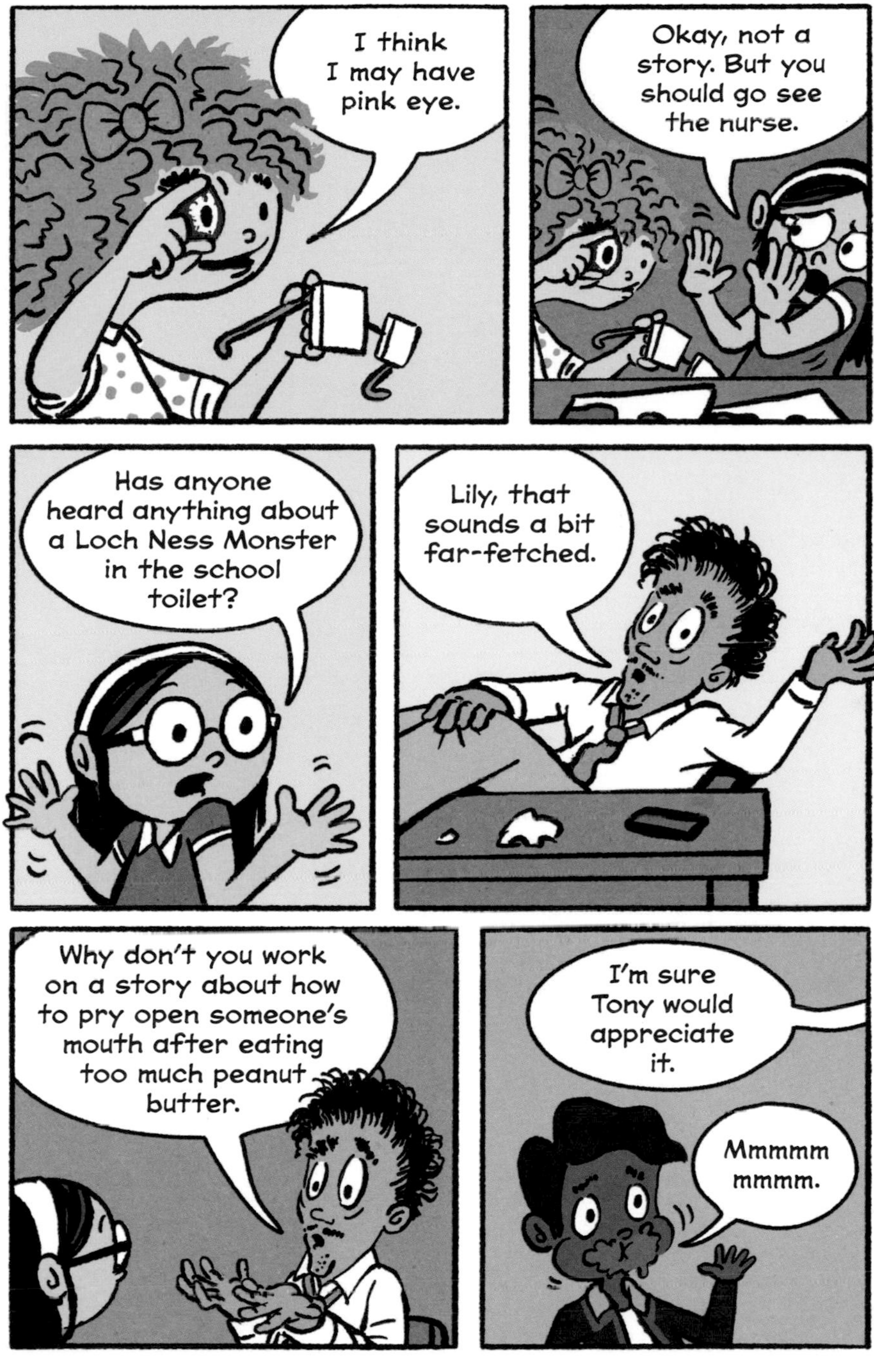
I think I may have pink eye.
Okay, not a story. But you should go see the nurse.
Has anyone heard anything about a Loch Ness Monster in the school toilet?
Lily, that sounds a bit far-fetched.
Why don't you work on a story about how to pry open someone's mouth after eating too much peanut butter.
I'm sure Tony would appreciate it.
Mmmmm mmmm.

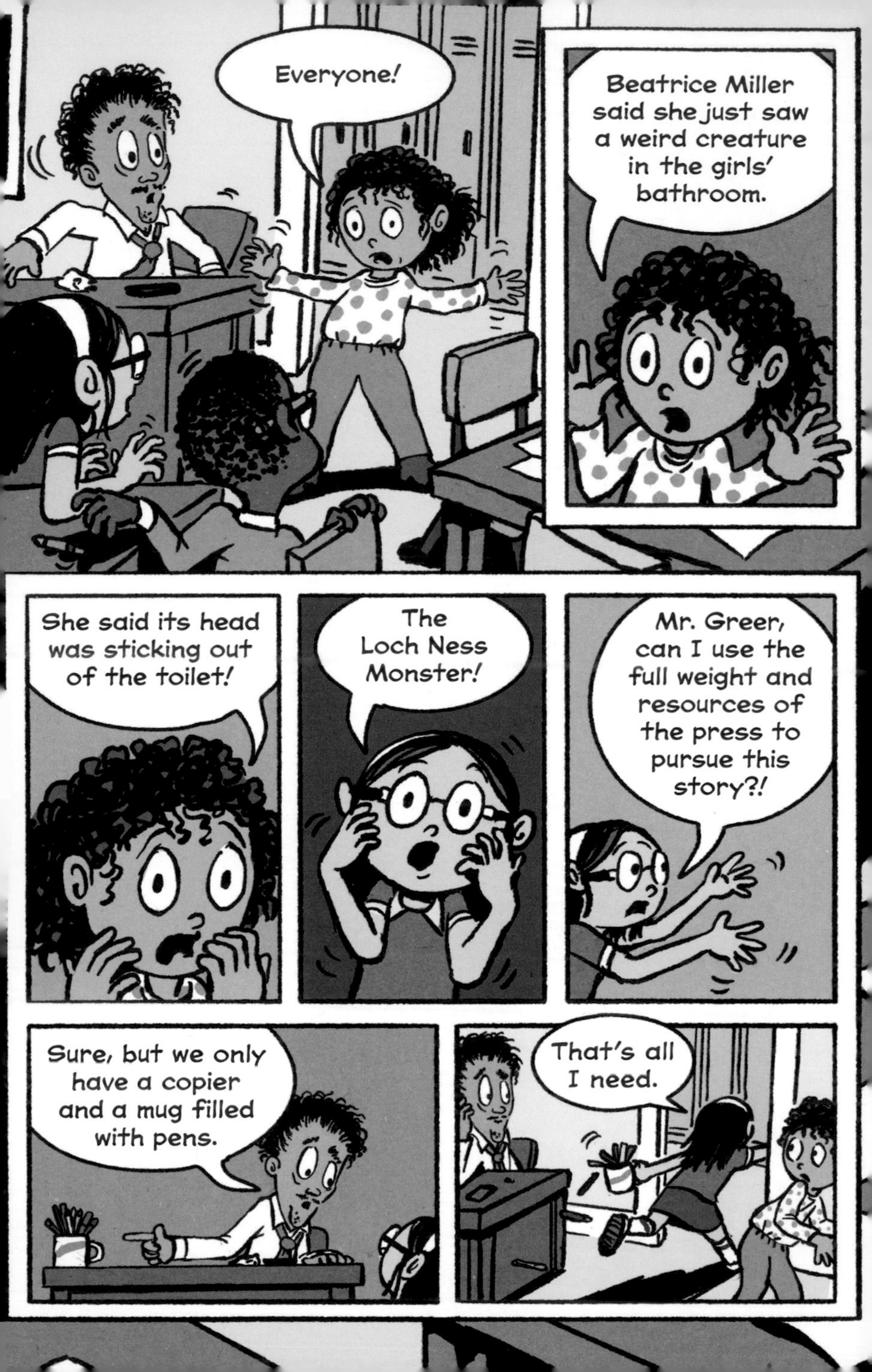
Everyone!
Beatrice Miller said she just saw a weird creature in the girls' bathroom.
She said its head was sticking out of the toilet!
The Loch Ness Monster!
Mr. Greer, can I use the full weight and resources of the press to pursue this story?!
Sure, but we only have a copier and a mug filled with pens.
That's all I need.

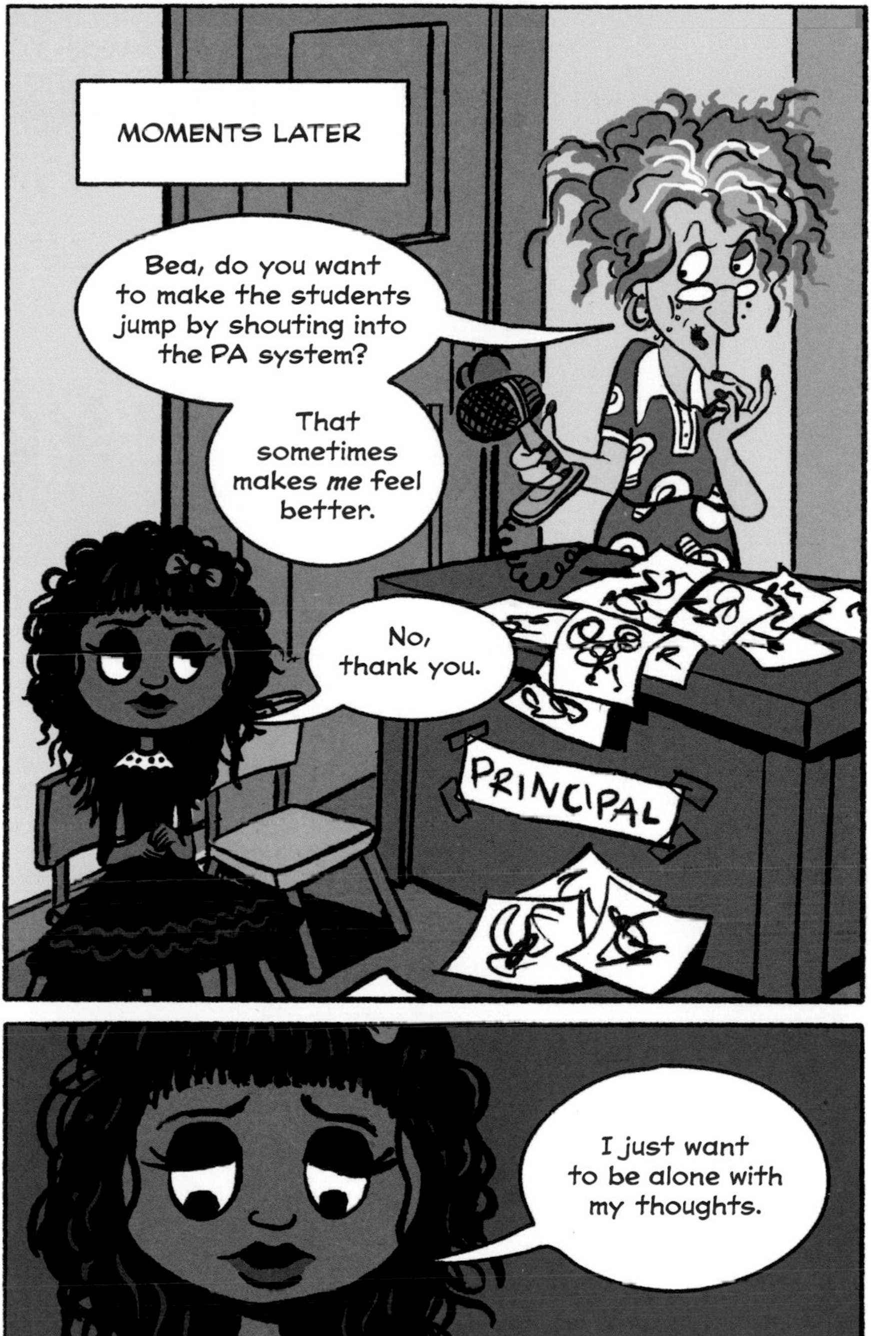
MOMENTS LATER
Bea, do you want to make the students jump by shouting into the PA system?
That sometimes makes *me* feel better.
No, thank you.
PRINCIPAL
I just want to be alone with my thoughts.

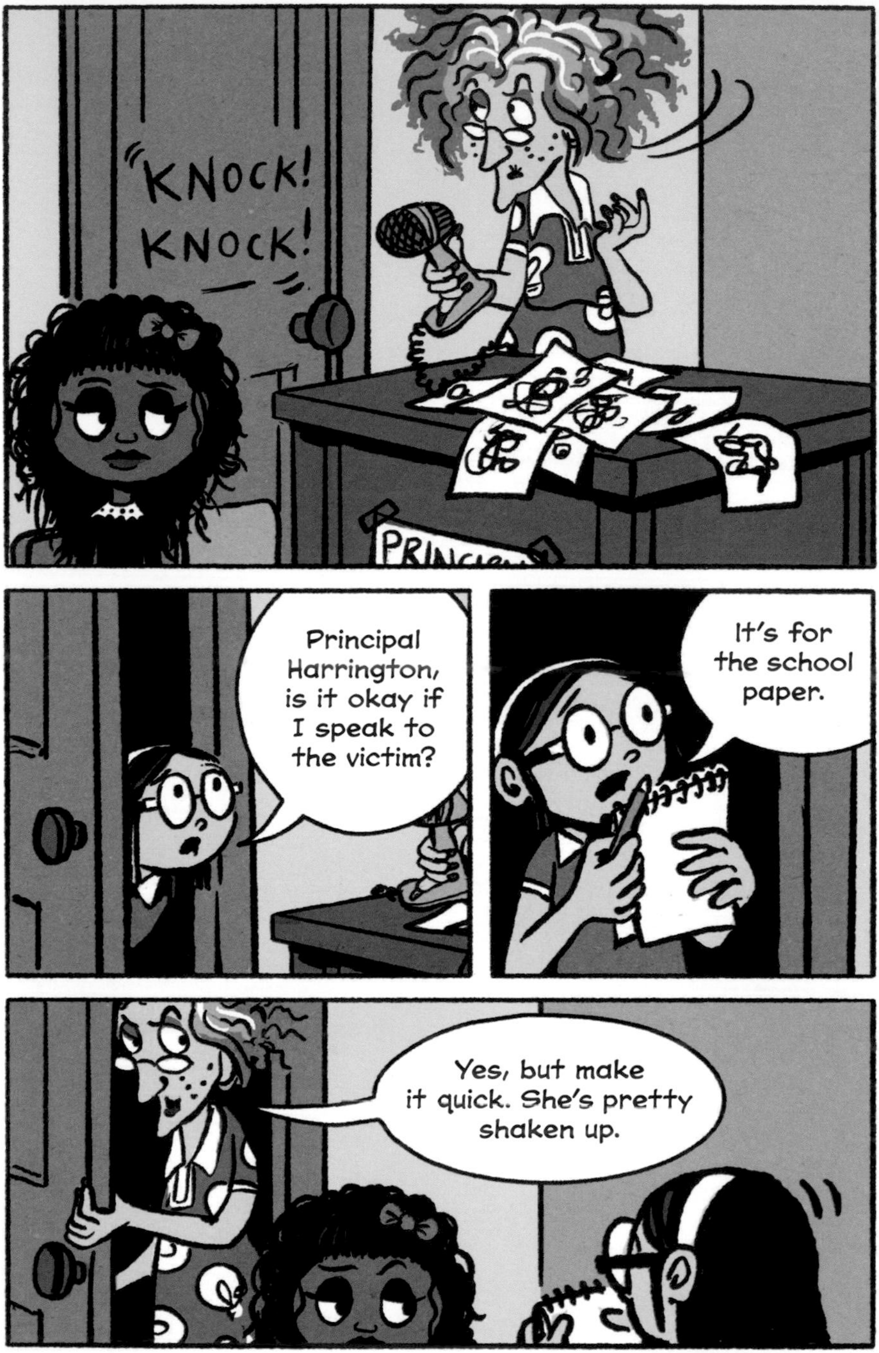
KNOCK! KNOCK!
PRINCI
Principal Harrington, is it okay if I speak to the victim?
It's for the school paper.
Yes, but make it quick. She's pretty shaken up.

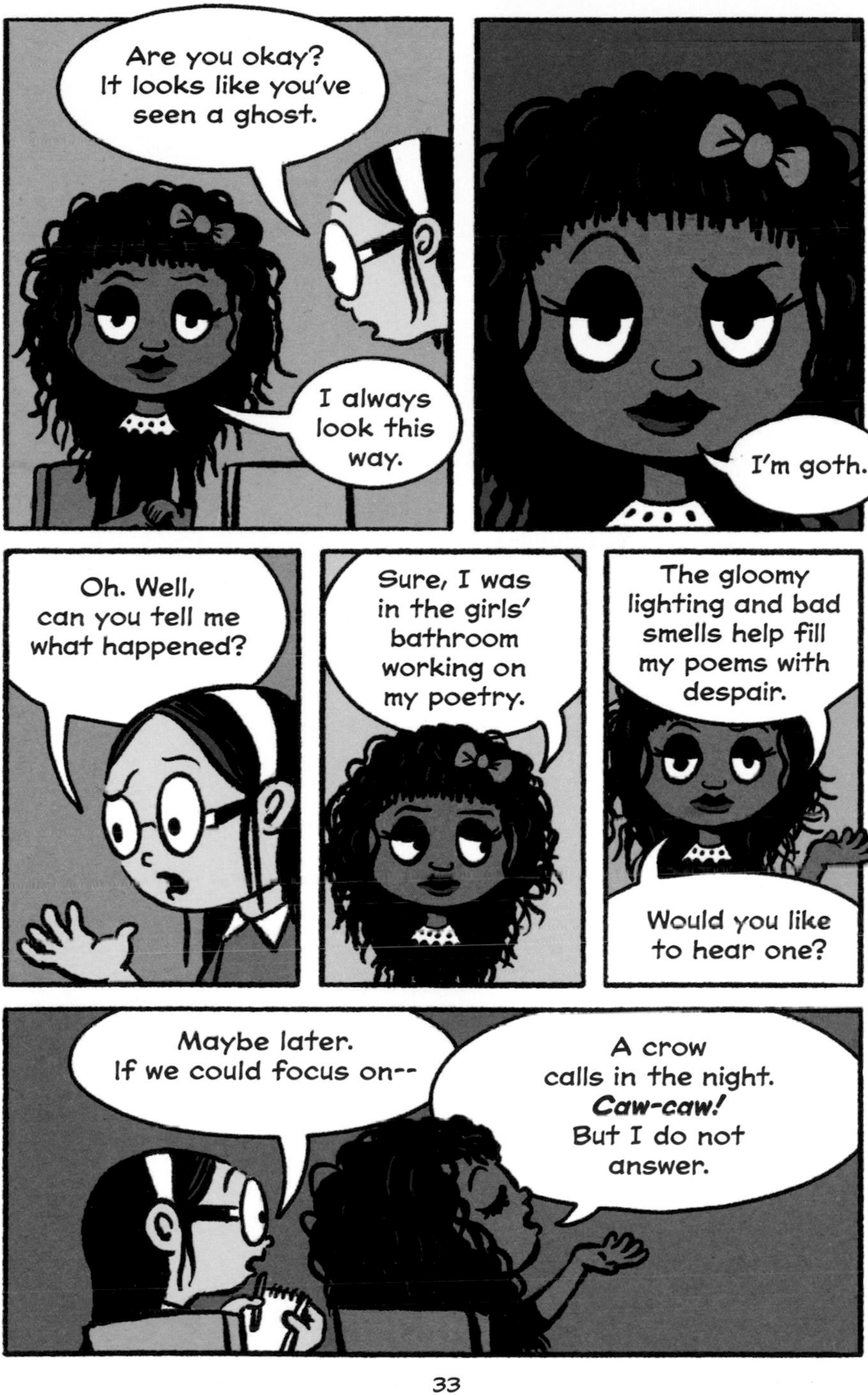
Are you okay? It looks like you've seen a ghost.
I always look this way.
I'm goth.
Oh. Well, can you tell me what happened?
Sure, I was in the girls' bathroom working on my poetry.
The gloomy lighting and bad smells help fill my poems with despair.
Would you like to hear one?
Maybe later. If we could focus on--
A crow calls in the night. Caw-caw! But I do not answer.

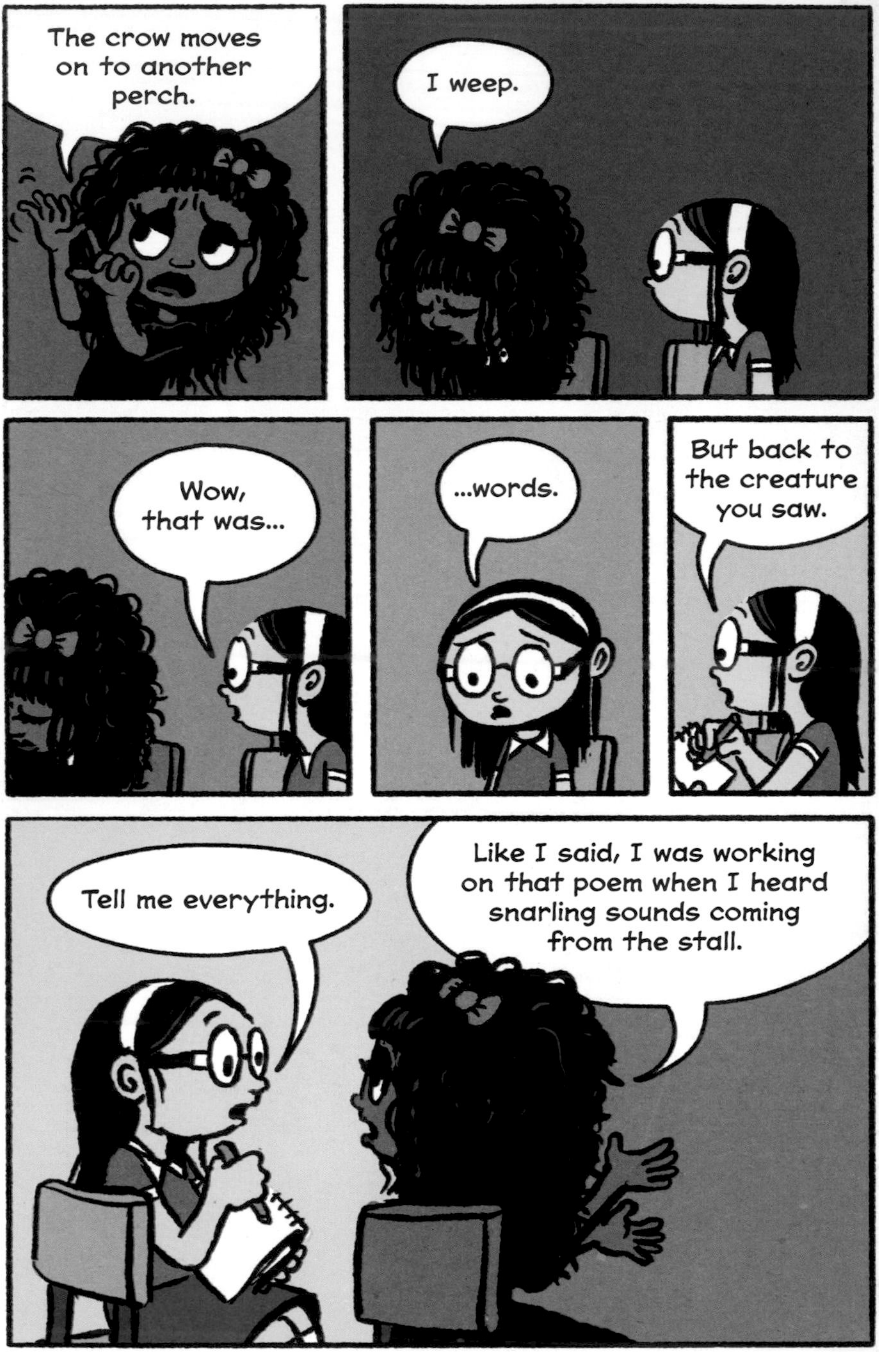
The crow moves on to another perch.
I weep.
Wow, that was...
...words.
But back to the creature you saw.
Tell me everything.
Like I said, I was working on that poem when I heard snarling sounds coming from the stall.

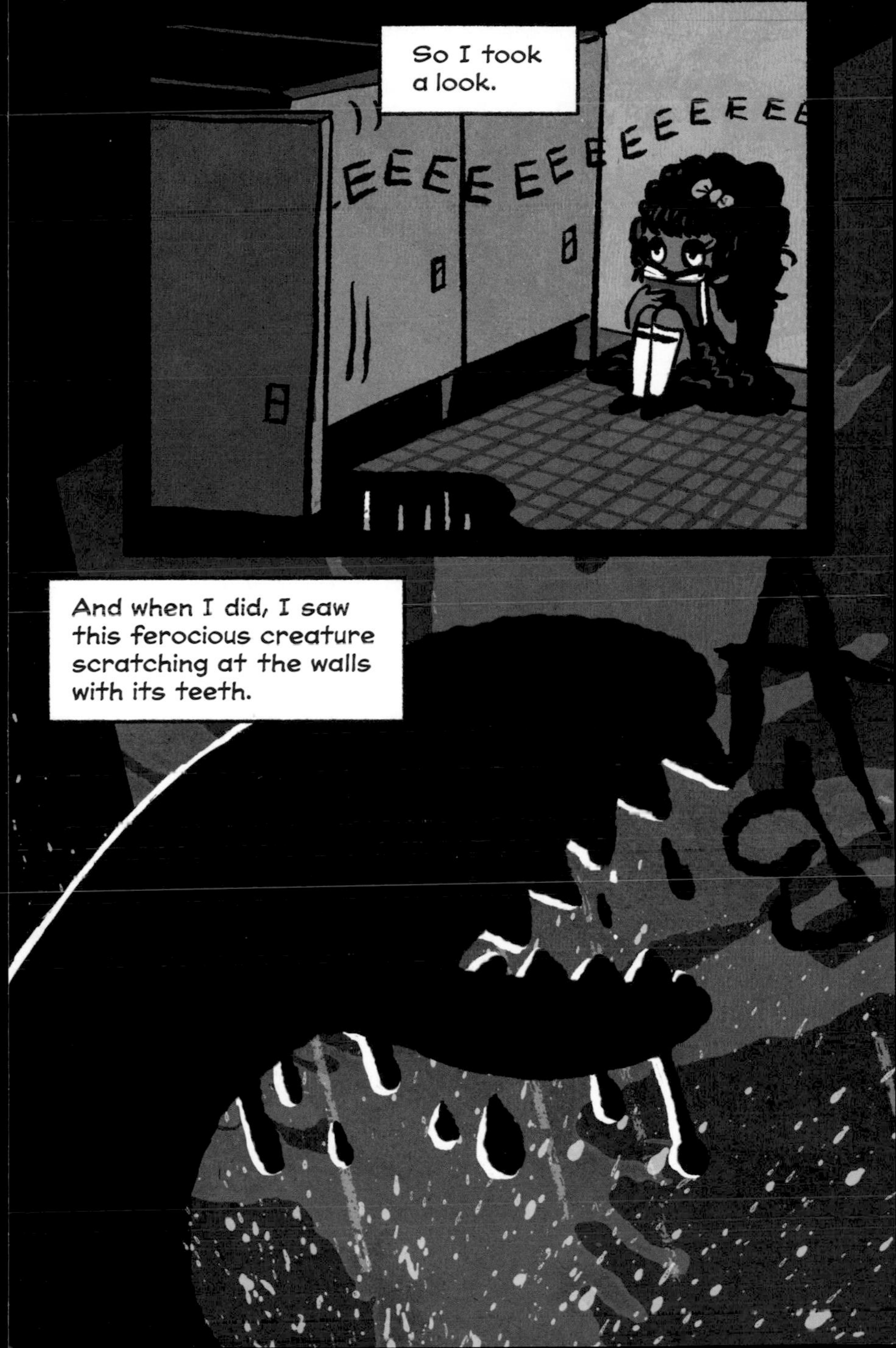
So I took a look.
EEEEEEEEEEEEEEEEE
And when I did, I saw this ferocious creature scratching at the walls with its teeth.

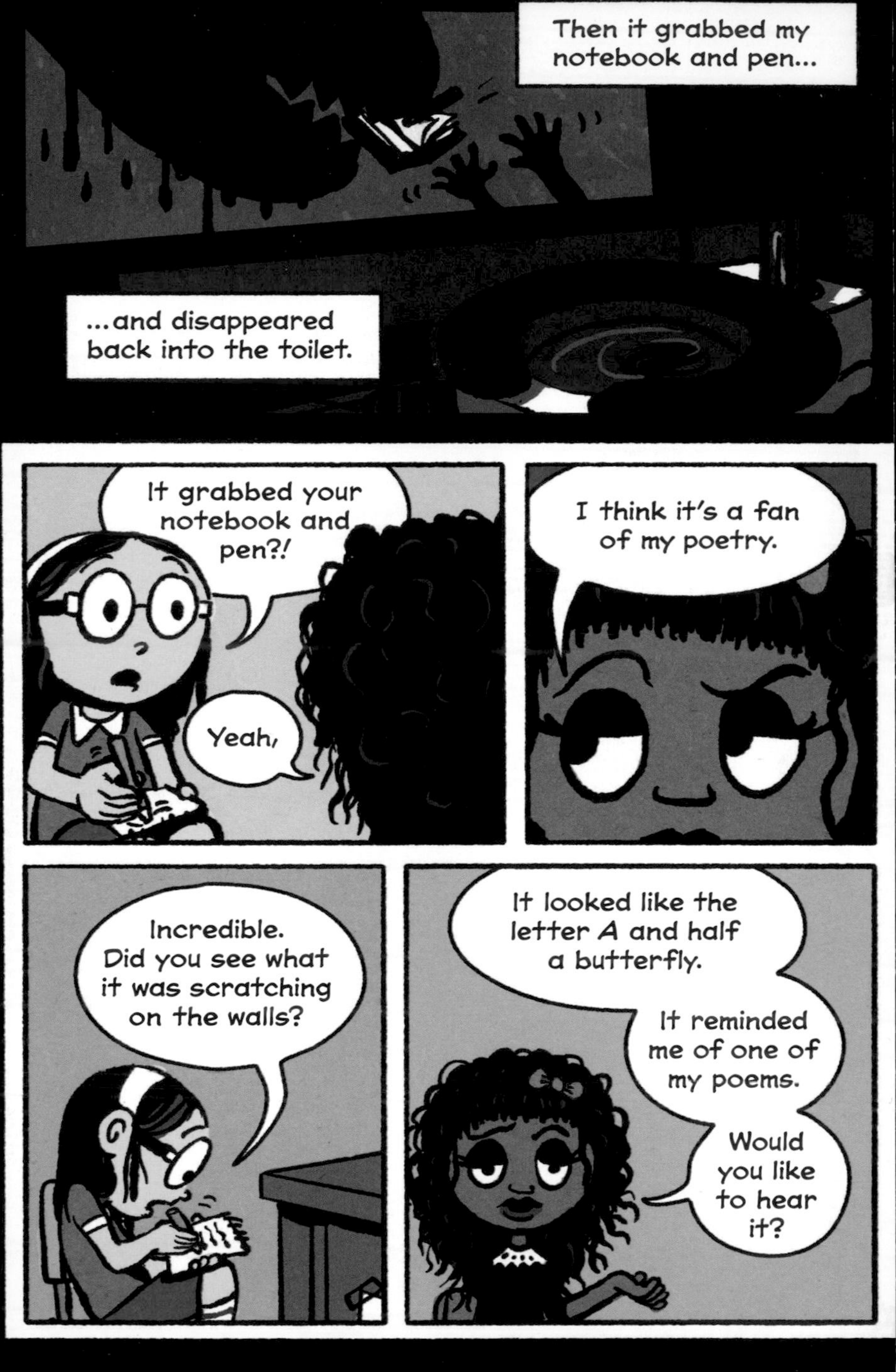
Then it grabbed my notebook and pen...
...and disappeared back into the toilet.
It grabbed your notebook and pen?!
Yeah,
I think it's a fan of my poetry.
Incredible. Did you see what it was scratching on the walls?
It looked like the letter *A* and half a butterfly.
It reminded me of one of my poems.
Would you like to hear it?

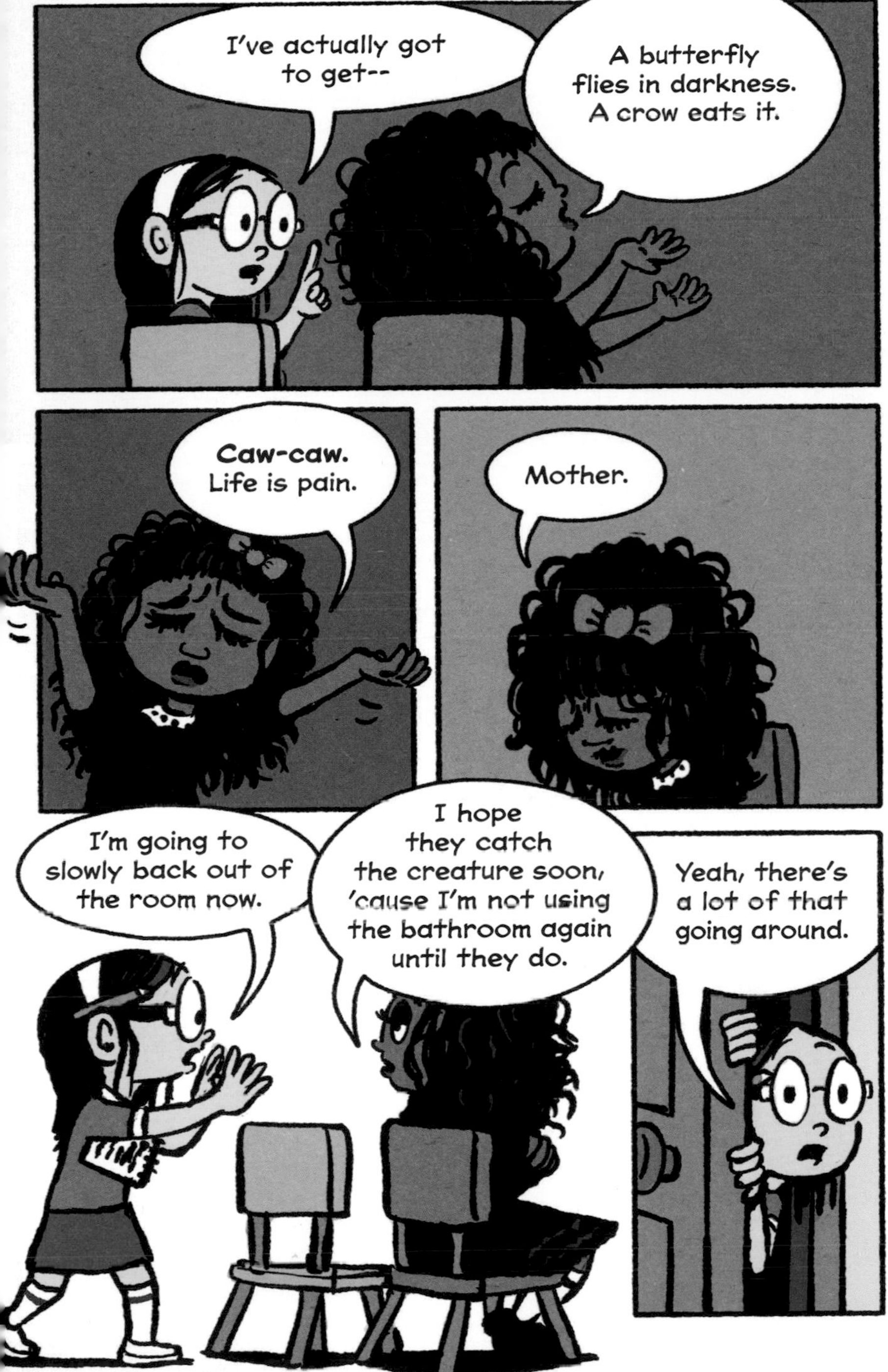
I've actually got to get--
A butterfly flies in darkness. A crow eats it.
Caw-caw. Life is pain.
Mother.
I'm going to slowly back out of the room now.
I hope they catch the creature soon, 'cause I'm not using the bathroom again until they do.
Yeah, there's a lot of that going around.

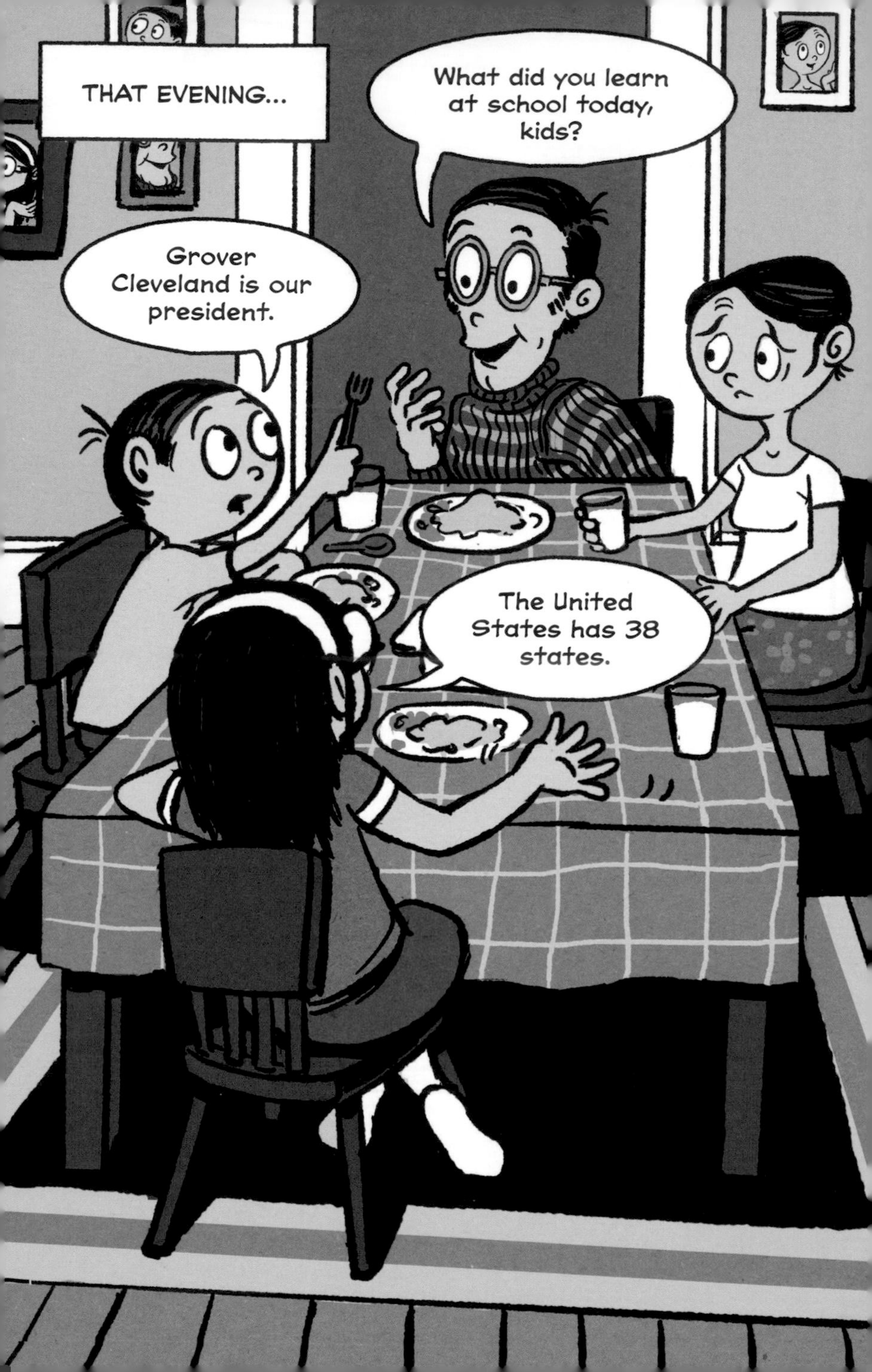
THAT EVENING...
What did you learn at school today, kids?
Grover Cleveland is our president.
The United States has 38 states.

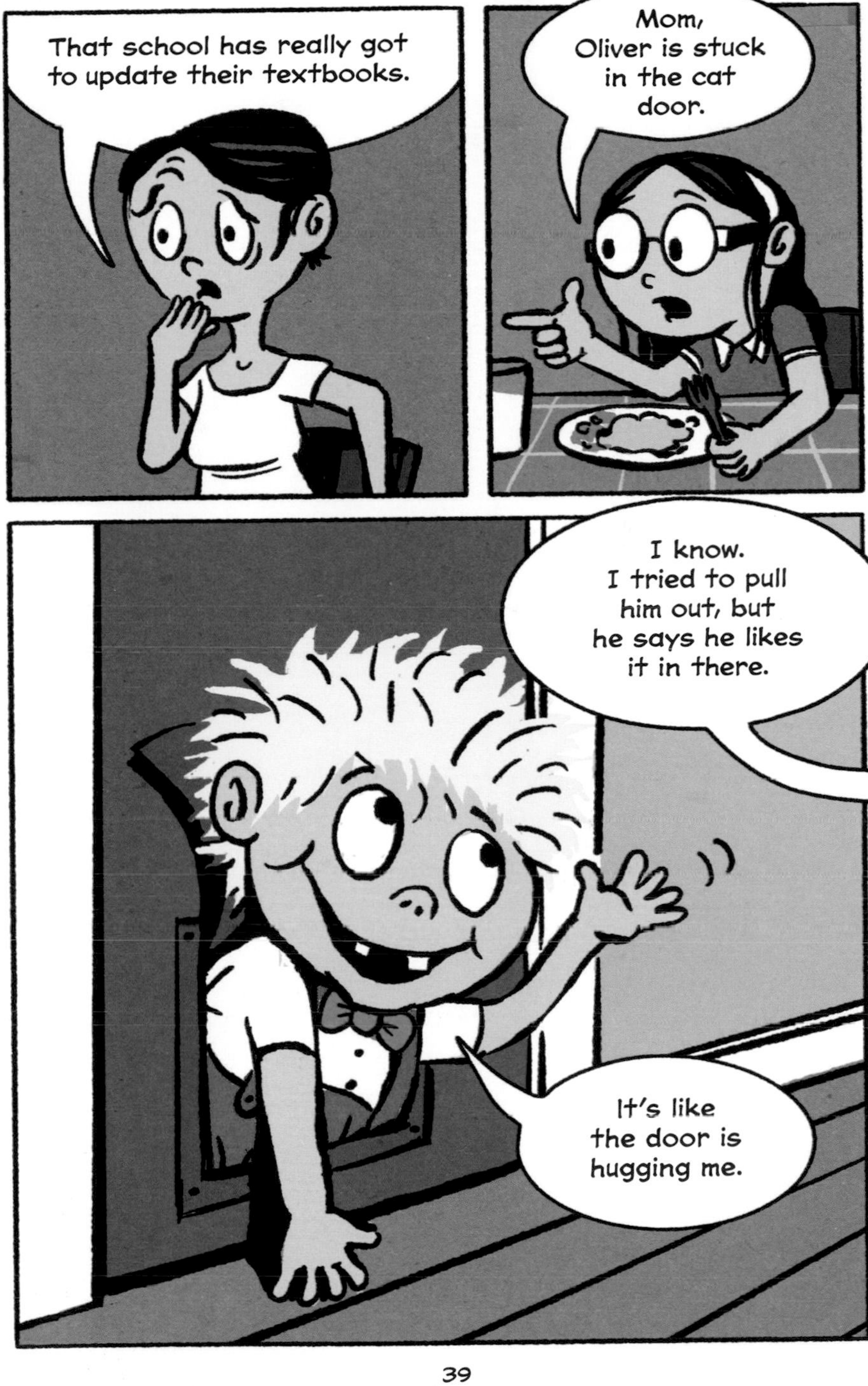
That school has really got to update their textbooks.
Mom, Oliver is stuck in the cat door.
I know. I tried to pull him out, but he says he likes it in there.
It's like the door is hugging me.

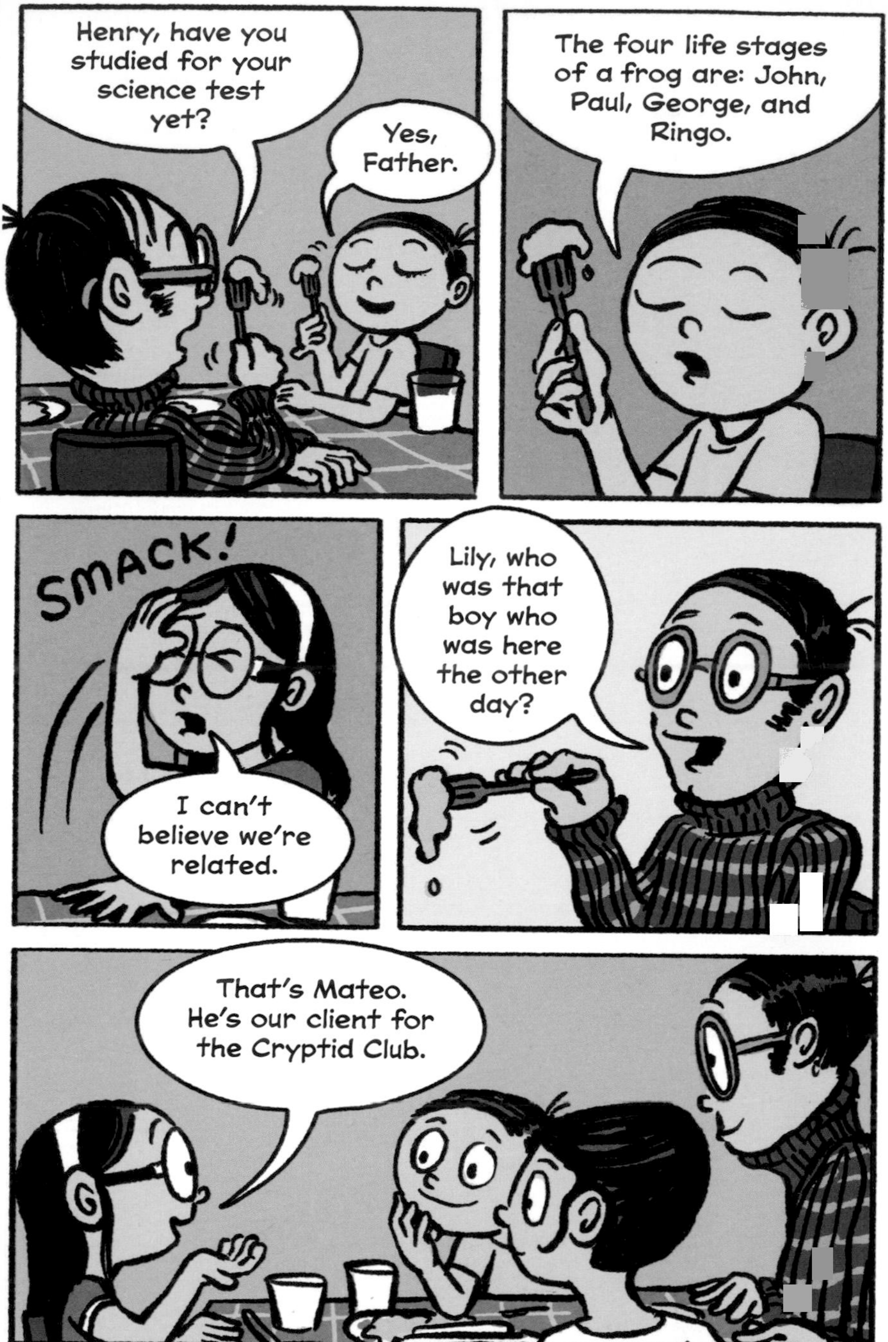

Henry, have you studied for your science test yet?
Yes, Father.
The four life stages of a frog are: John, Paul, George, and Ringo.
SMACK!
I can't believe we're related.
Lily, who was that boy who was here the other day?
That's Mateo. He's our client for the Cryptid Club.

Oh yes, the Cryptid Club. Such an interesting extracurricular activity.

You know when I was your age, I played baseball.

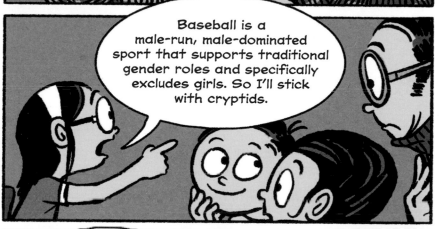

Baseball is a male-run, male-dominated sport that supports traditional gender roles and specifically excludes girls. So I'll stick with cryptids.

They're more progressive.

You walked right into that one, dear.

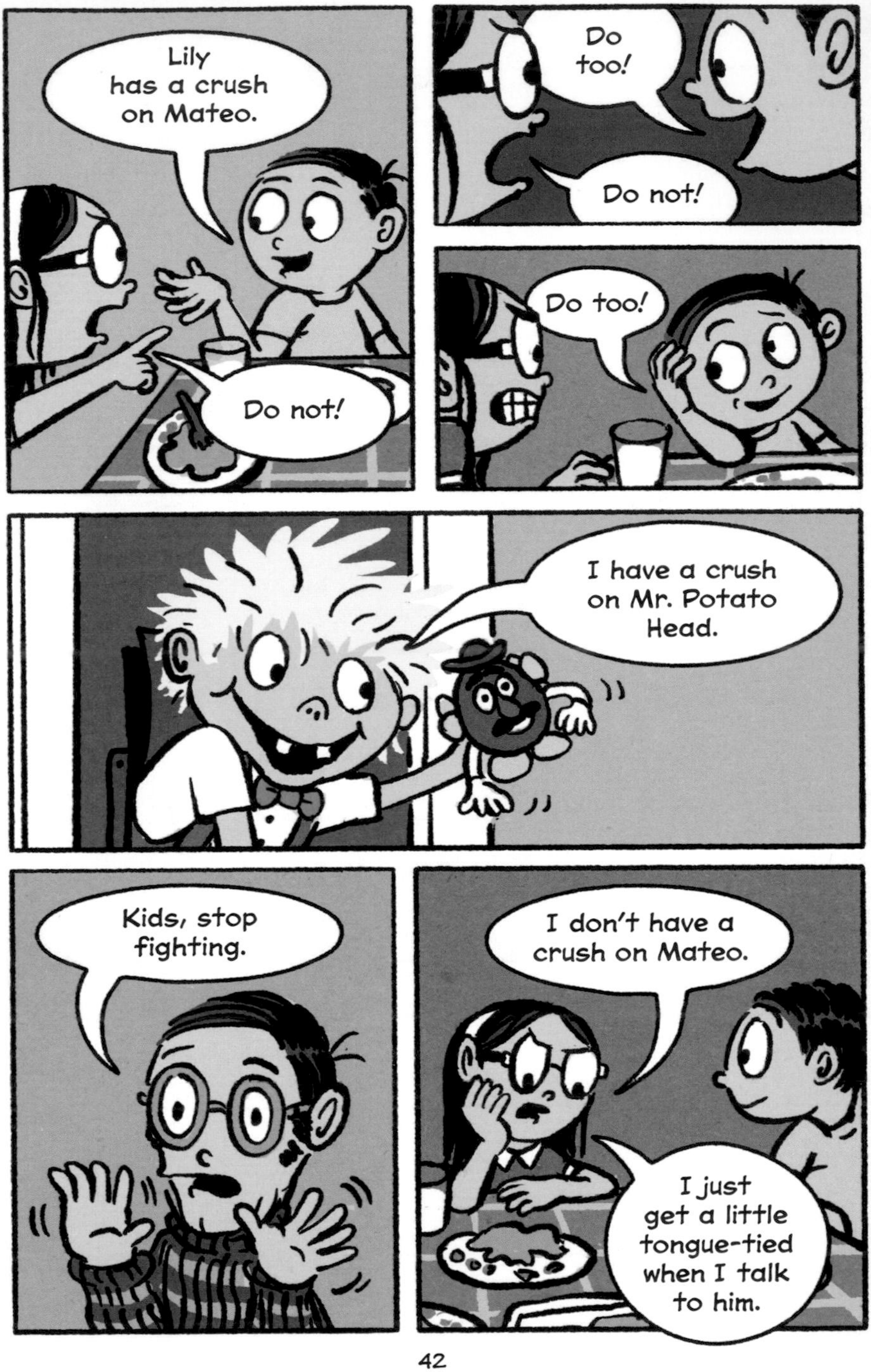
Lily has a crush on Mateo.
Do not!
Do too!
Do not!
Do too!
I have a crush on Mr. Potato Head.
Kids, stop fighting.
I don't have a crush on Mateo.
I just get a little tongue-tied when I talk to him.

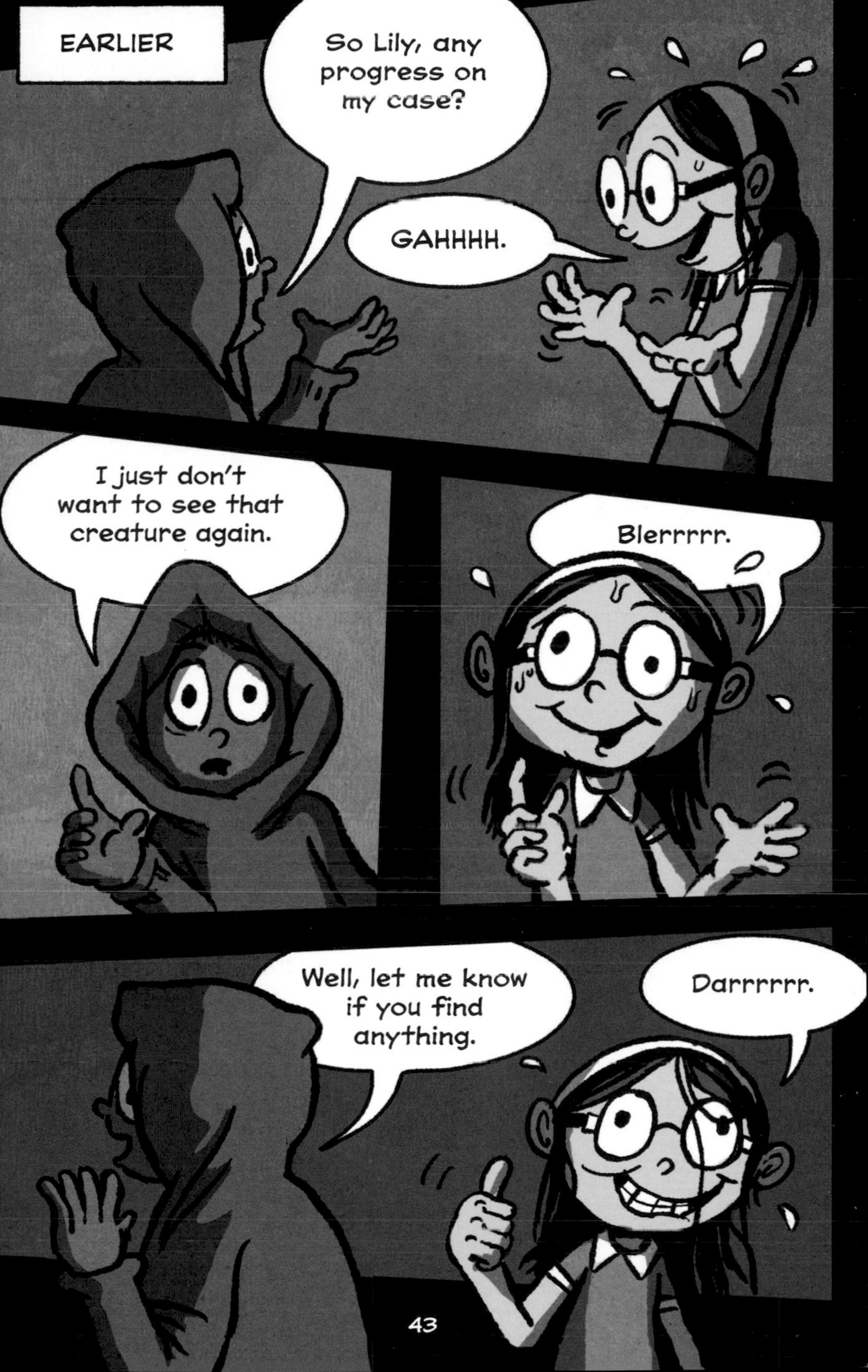
EARLIER
So Lily, any progress on my case?
GAHHHH.
I just don't want to see that creature again.
Blerrrrr.
Well, let me know if you find anything.
Darrrrrr.

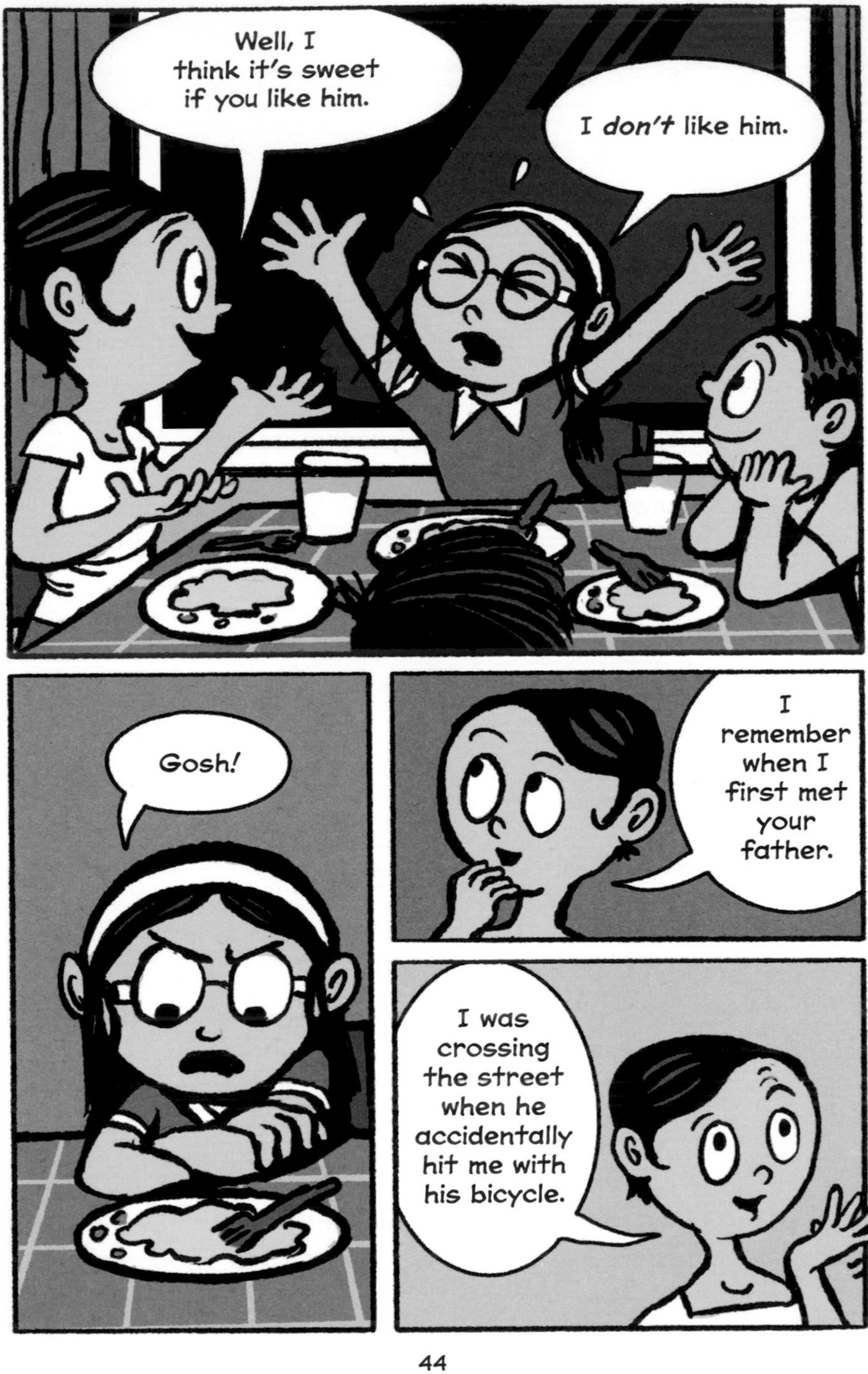

Well, I think it's sweet if you like him.
I *don't* like him.
Gosh!
I remember when I first met your father.
I was crossing the street when he accidentally hit me with his bicycle.

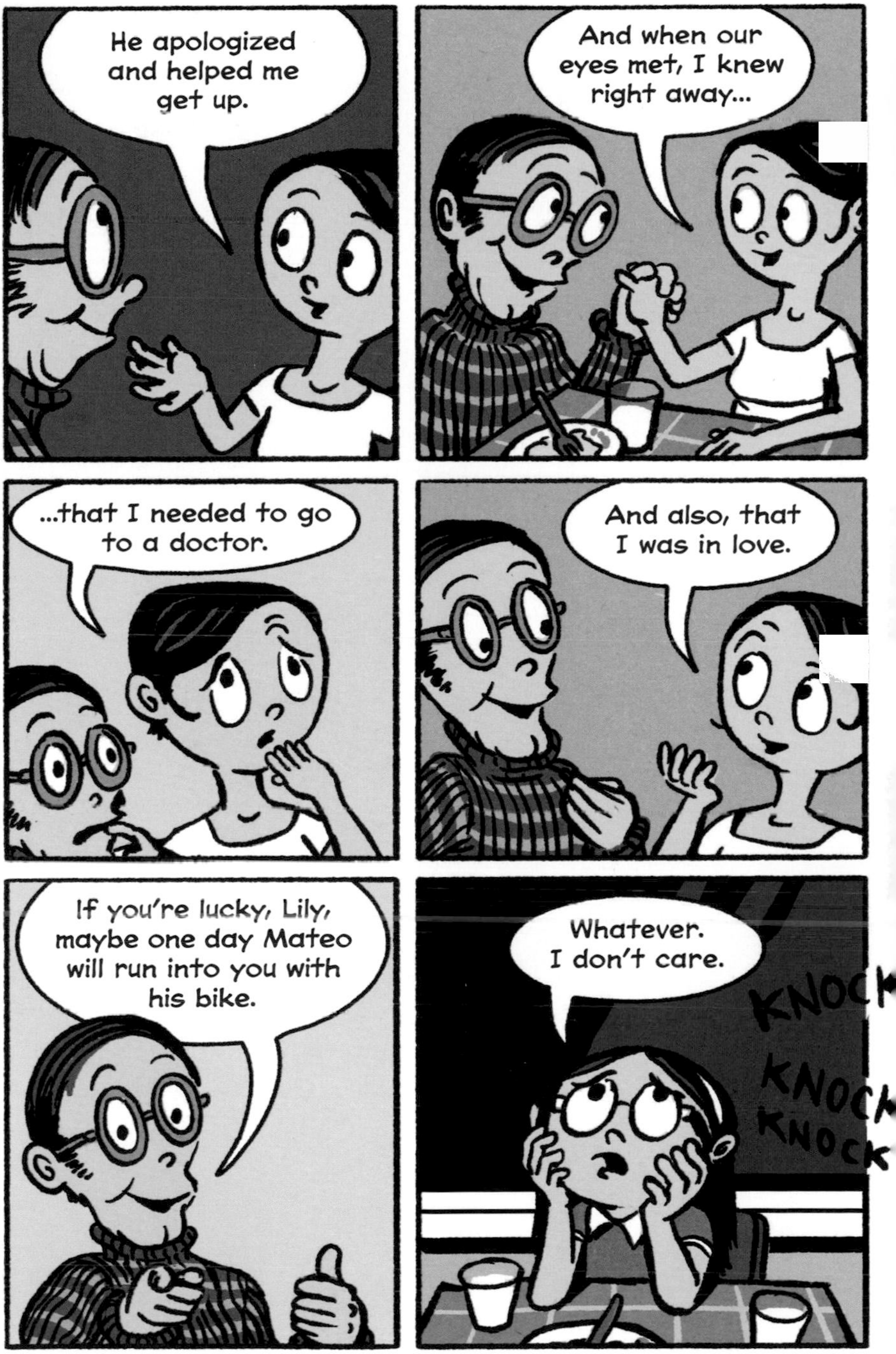
He apologized and helped me get up.
And when our eyes met, I knew right away...
...that I needed to go to a doctor.
And also, that I was in love.
If you're lucky, Lily, maybe one day Mateo will run into you with his bike.
Whatever. I don't care.
KNOCK
KNOCK
KNOCK

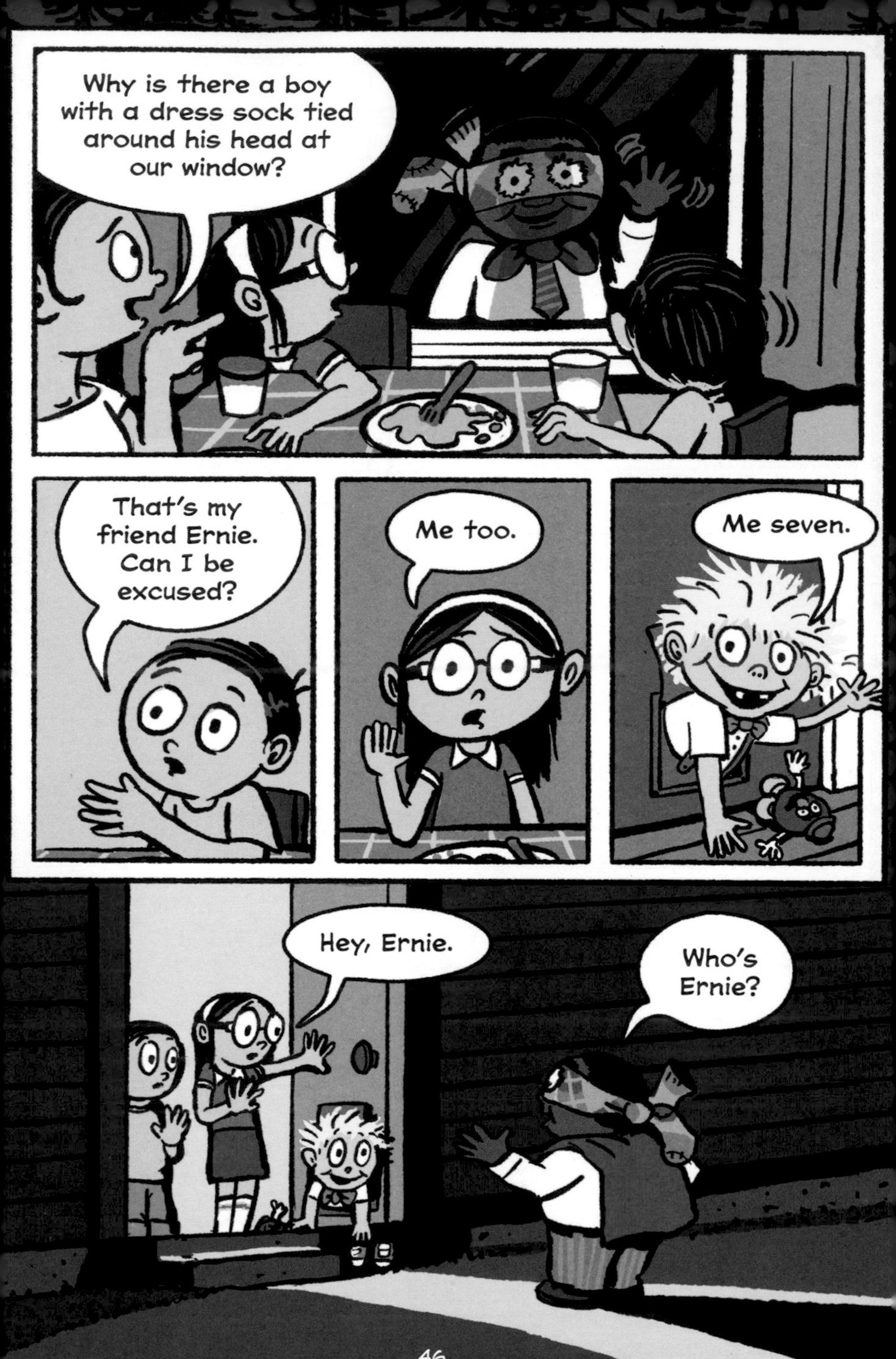
Why is there a boy with a dress sock tied around his head at our window?
That's my friend Ernie. Can I be excused?
Me too.
Me seven.
Hey, Ernie.
Who's Ernie?

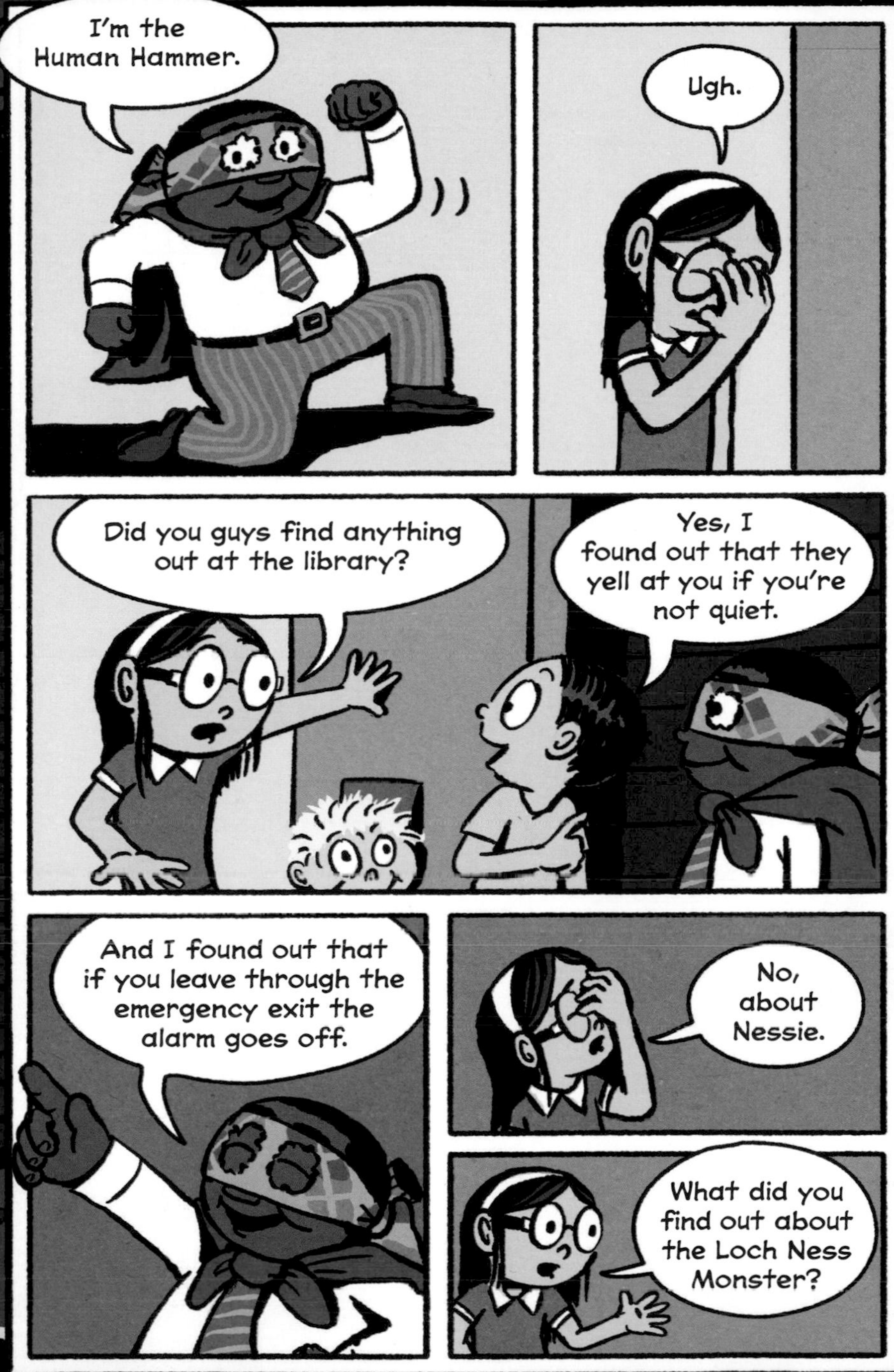
I'm the Human Hammer.
Ugh.
Did you guys find anything out at the library?
Yes, I found out that they yell at you if you're not quiet.
And I found out that if you leave through the emergency exit the alarm goes off.
No, about Nessie.
What did you find out about the Loch Ness Monster?

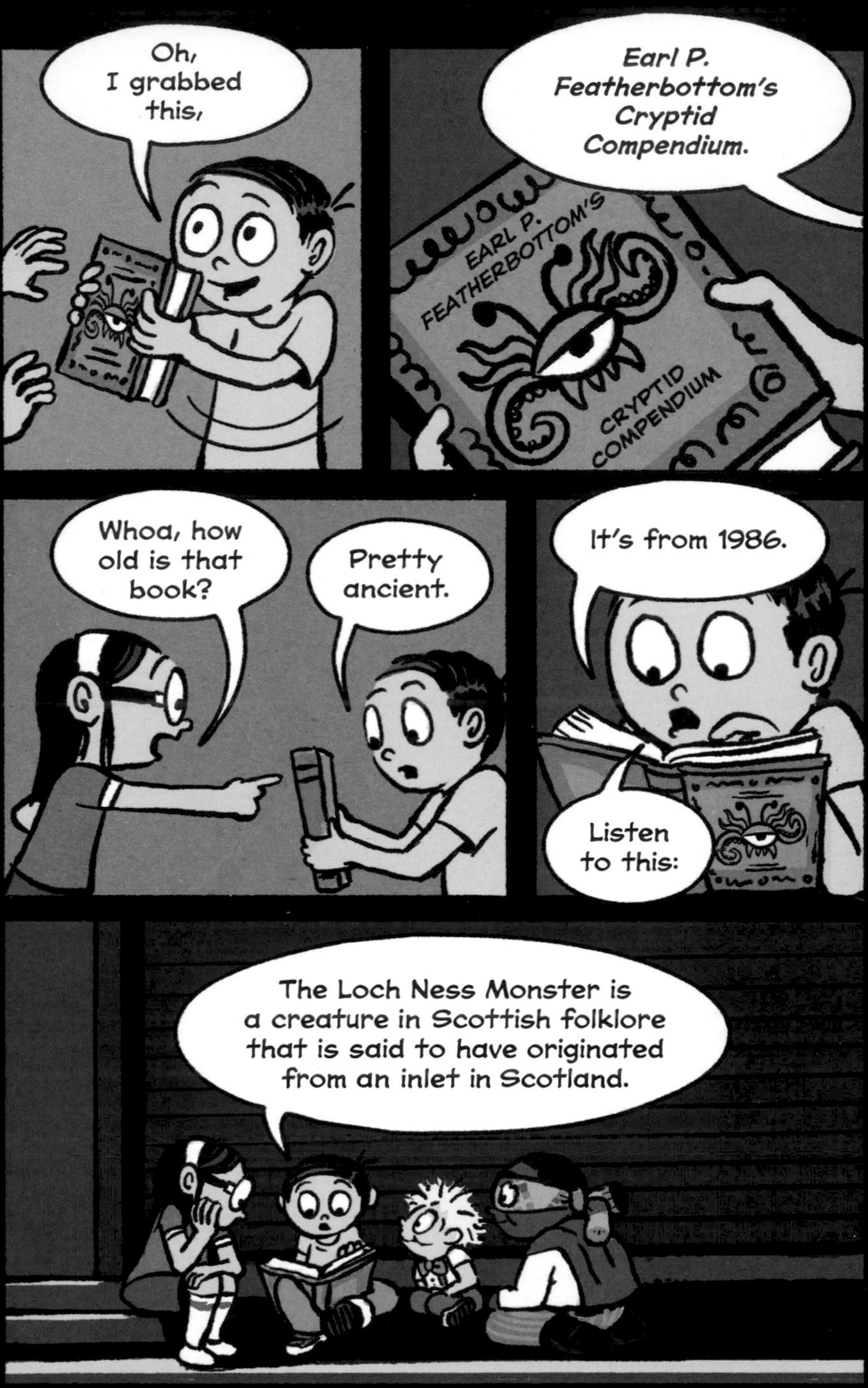

Oh, I grabbed this,
Earl P. Featherbottom's Cryptid Compendium.
EARL P. FEATHERBOTTOM'S CRYPTID COMPENDIUM
Whoa, how old is that book?
Pretty ancient.
It's from 1986.
Listen to this:
The Loch Ness Monster is a creature in Scottish folklore that is said to have originated from an inlet in Scotland.

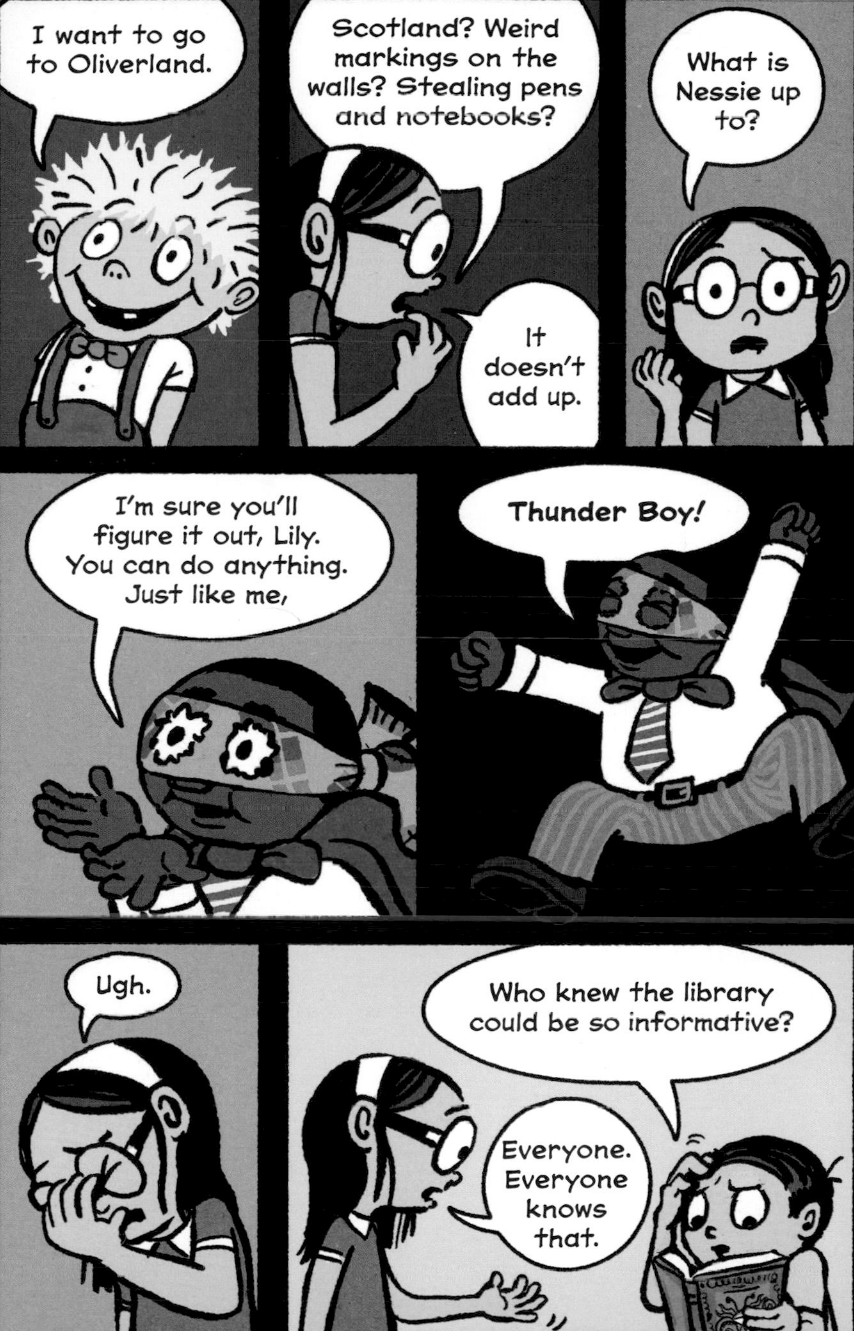
I want to go to Oliverland.
Scotland? Weird markings on the walls? Stealing pens and notebooks?
It doesn't add up.
What is Nessie up to?
I'm sure you'll figure it out, Lily. You can do anything. Just like me,
Thunder Boy!
Ugh.
Who knew the library could be so informative?
Everyone. Everyone knows that.

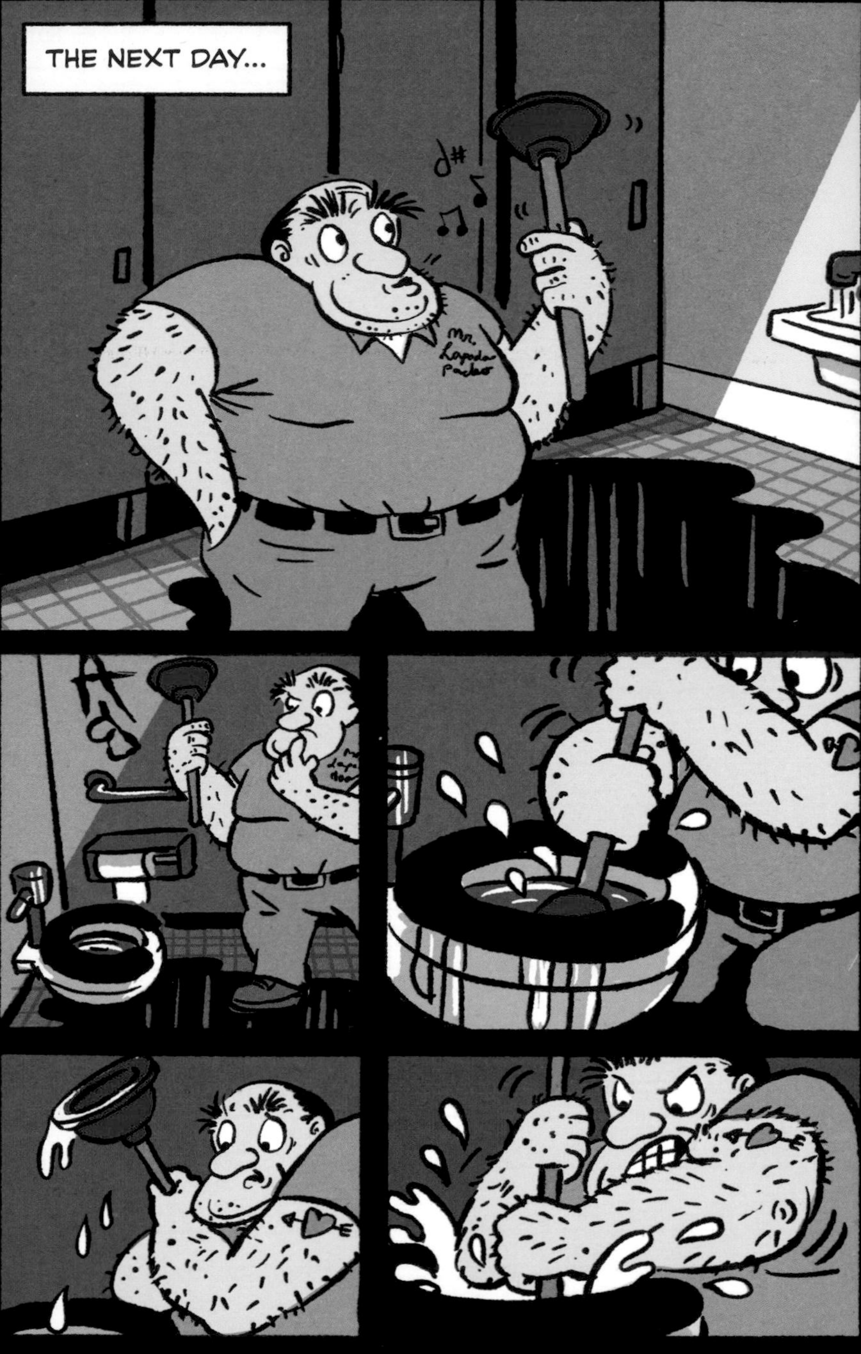
THE NEXT DAY...

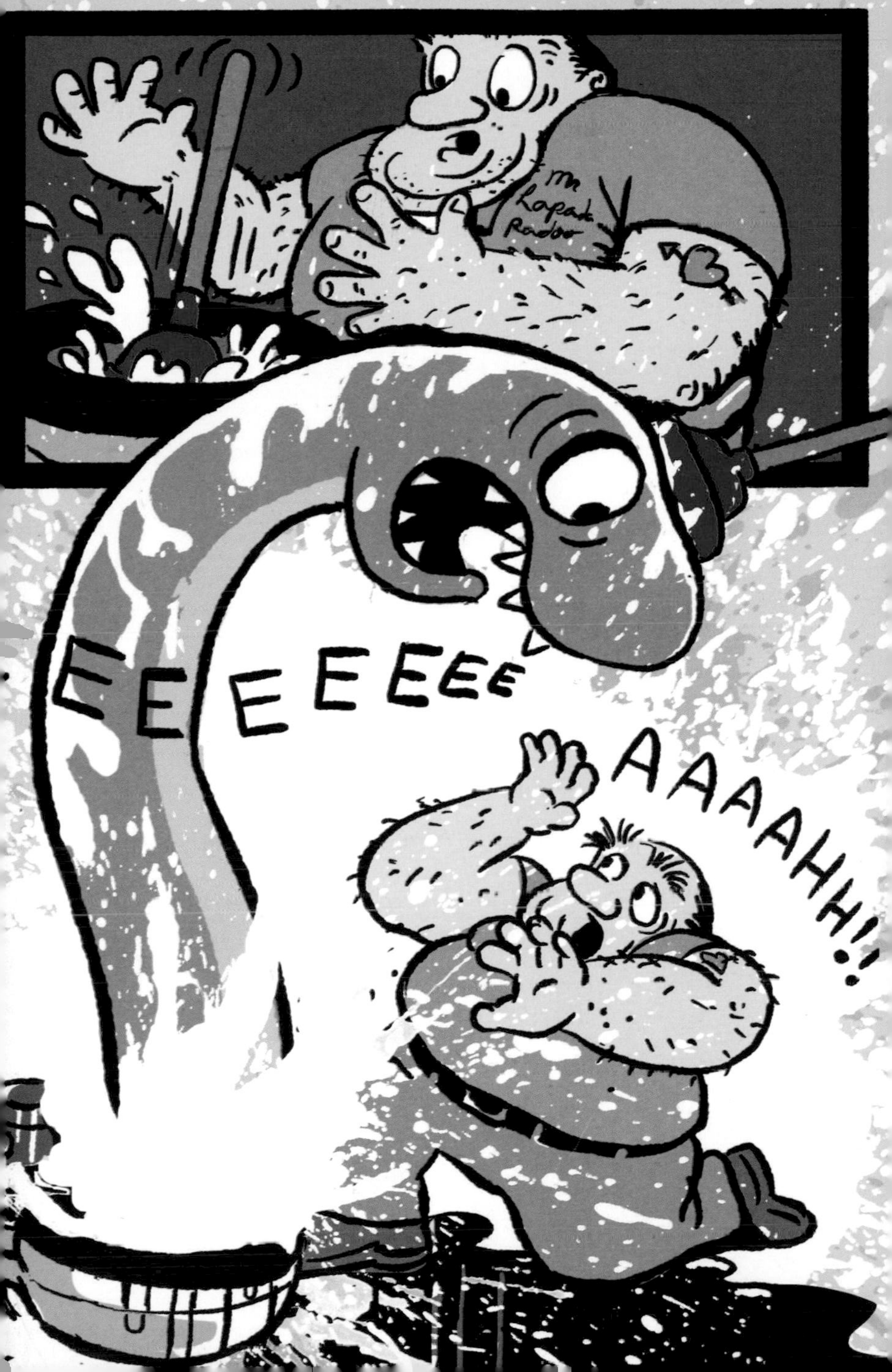
EEEEEEE
AAAAAHH!!

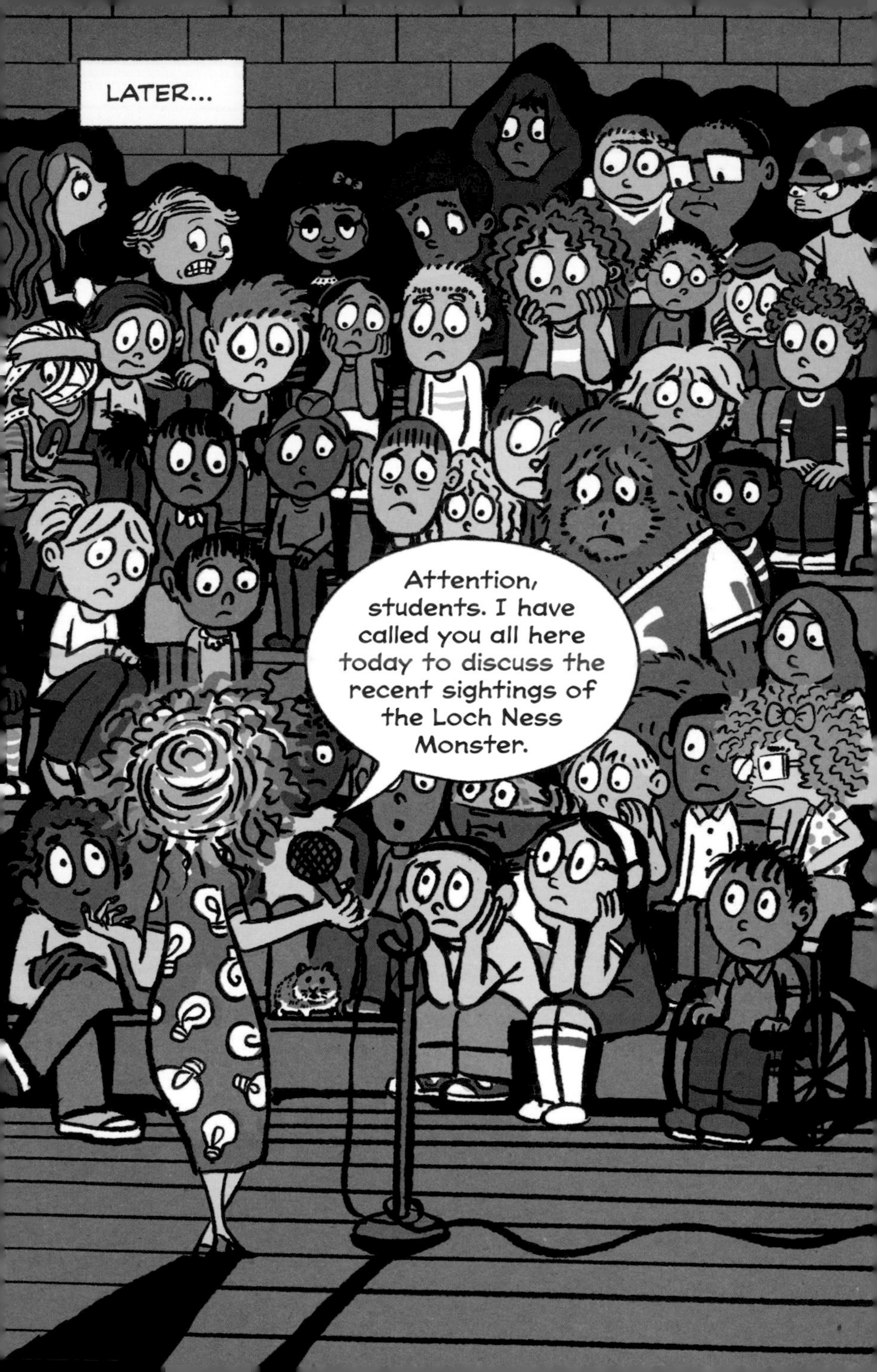
LATER...
Attention, students. I have called you all here today to discuss the recent sightings of the Loch Ness Monster.

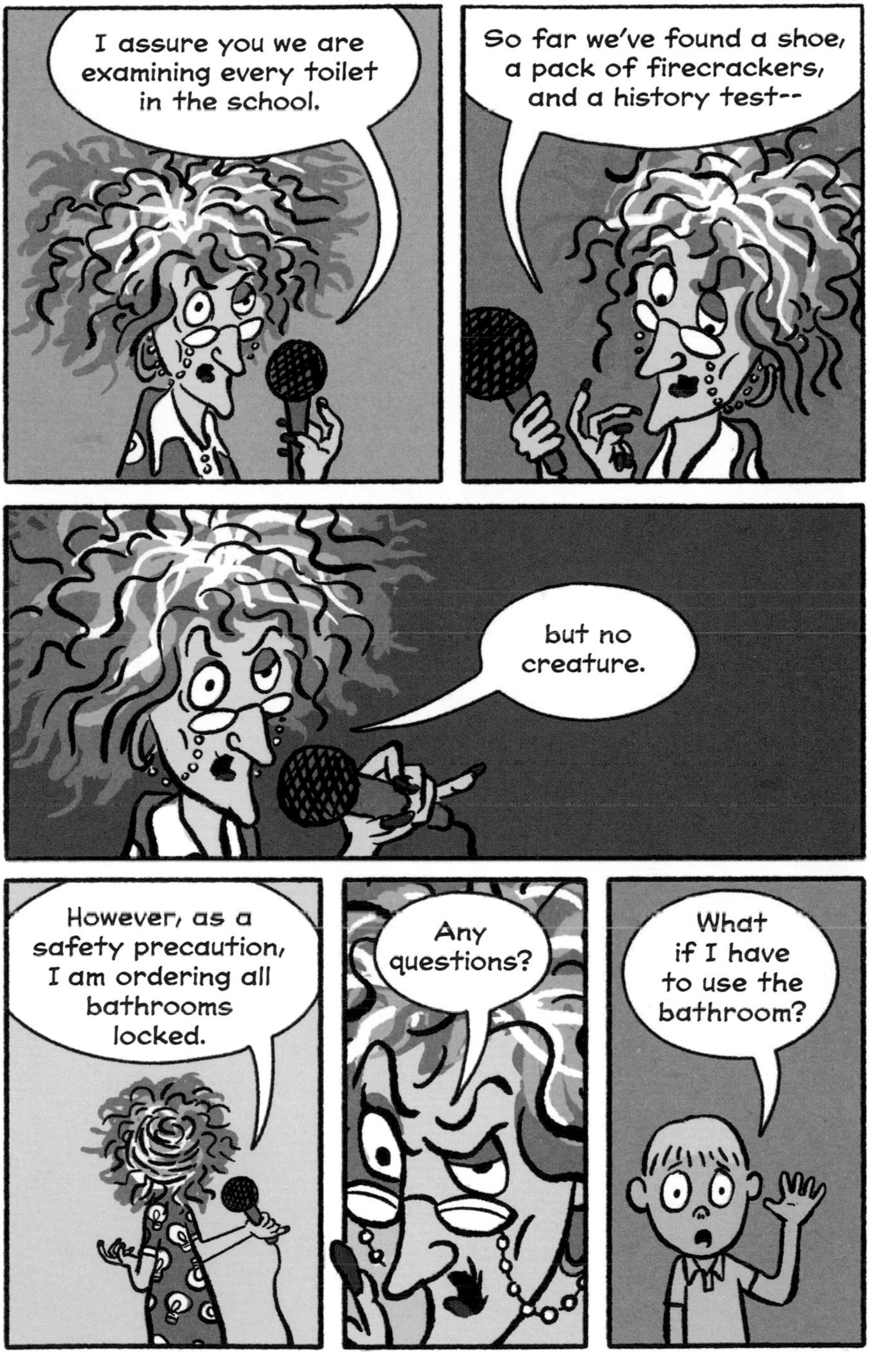
I assure you we are examining every toilet in the school.
So far we've found a shoe, a pack of firecrackers, and a history test--
but no creature.
However, as a safety precaution, I am ordering all bathrooms locked.
Any questions?
What if I have to use the bathroom?

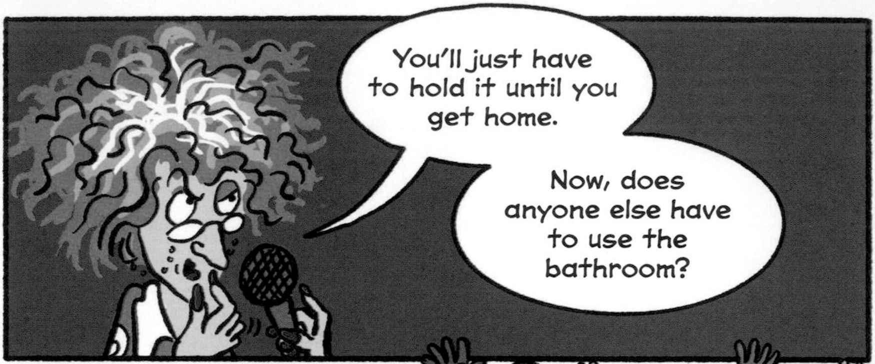
You'll just have to hold it until you get home.
Now, does anyone else have to use the bathroom?

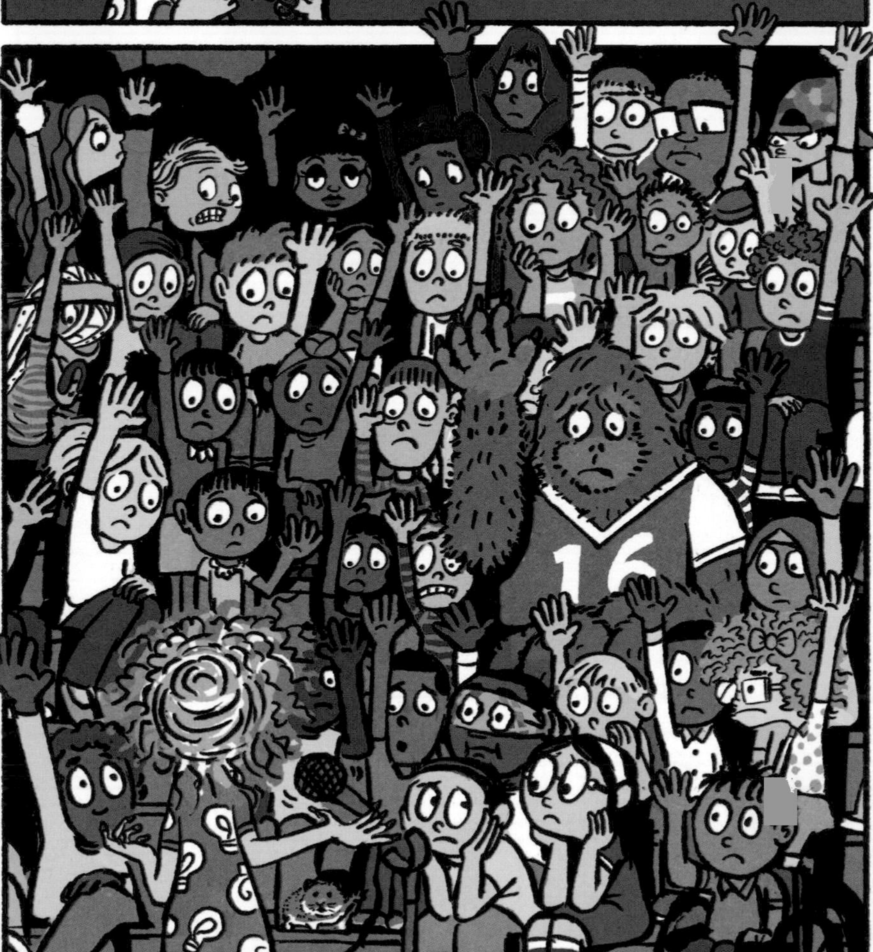
16

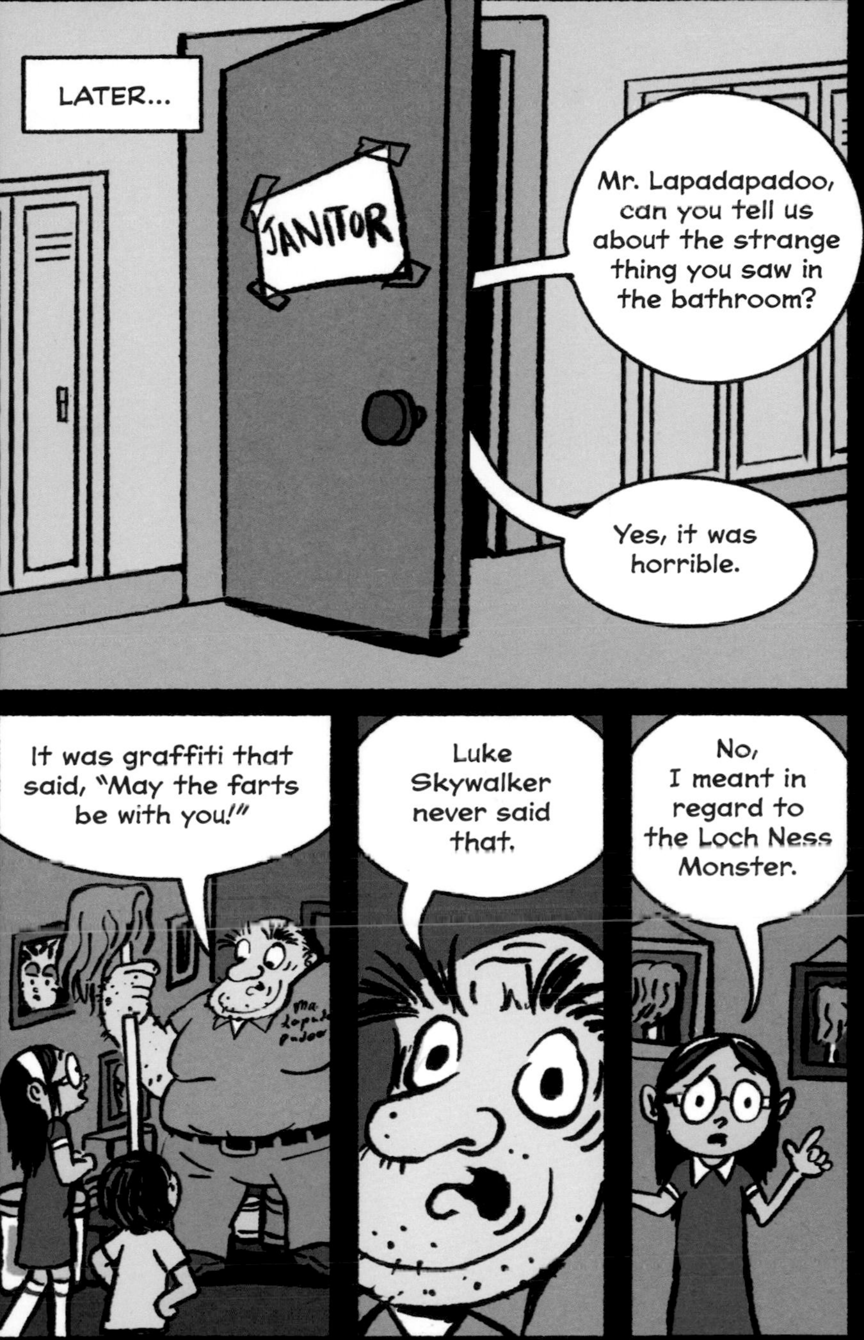
LATER...
JANITOR
Mr. Lapadapadoo, can you tell us about the strange thing you saw in the bathroom?
Yes, it was horrible.
It was graffiti that said, "May the farts be with you!"
Luke Skywalker never said that.
No, I meant in regard to the Loch Ness Monster.

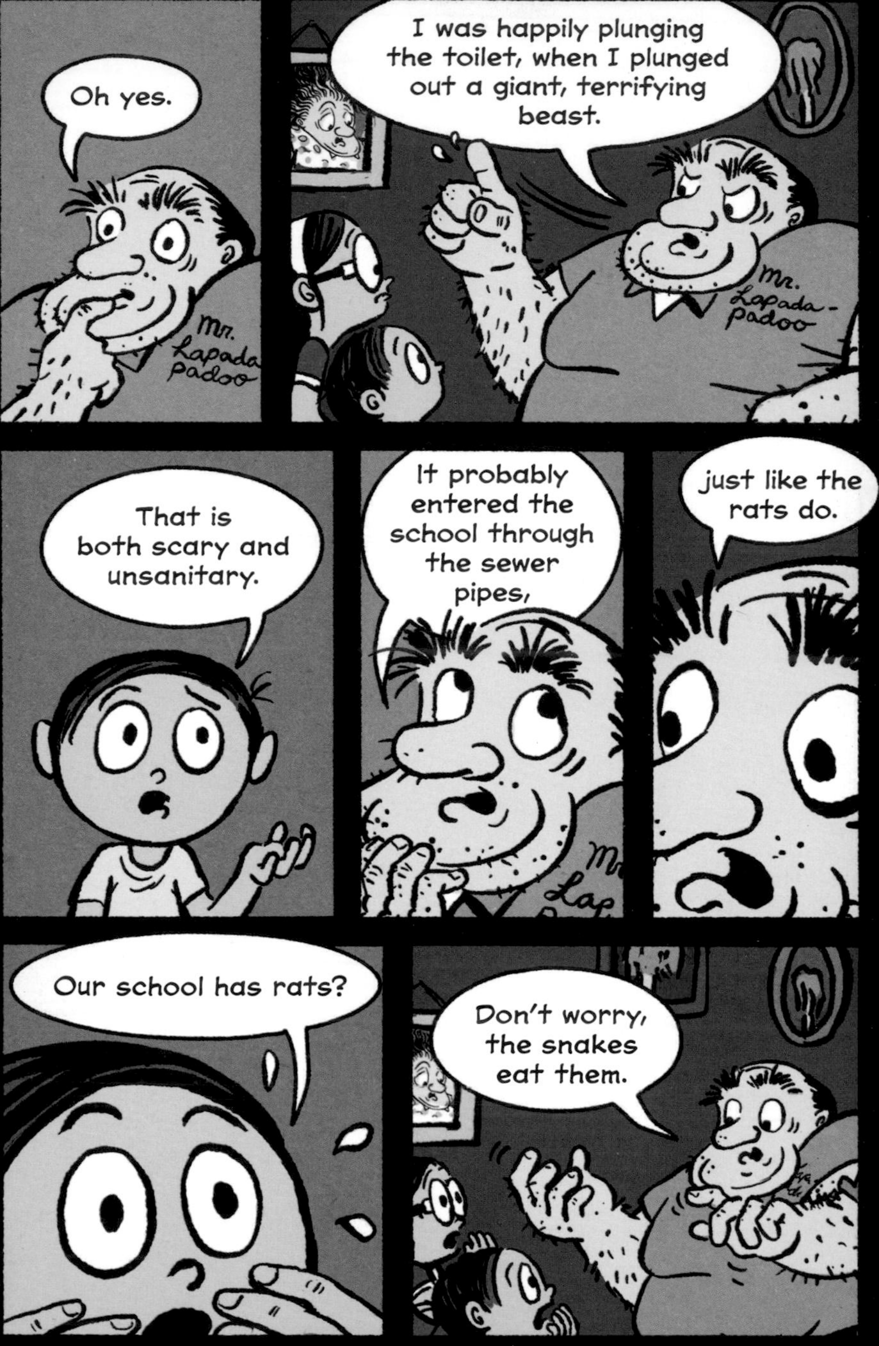
Oh yes.
Mr. Lapada padoo
I was happily plunging the toilet, when I plunged out a giant, terrifying beast.
Mr. Lapada-padoo
That is both scary and unsanitary.
It probably entered the school through the sewer pipes,
just like the rats do.
Our school has rats?
Don't worry, the snakes eat them.

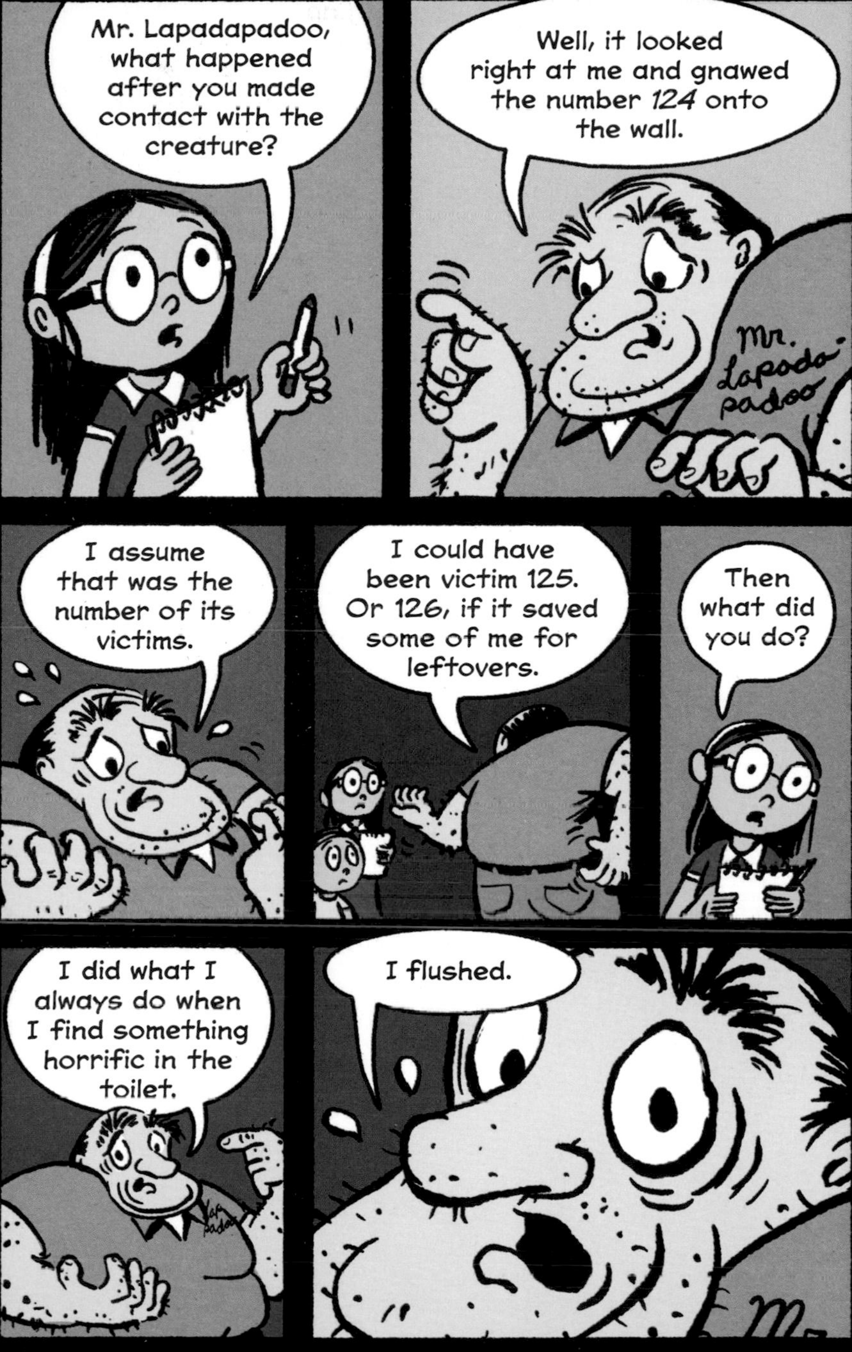
Mr. Lapadapadoo, what happened after you made contact with the creature?
Well, it looked right at me and gnawed the number *124* onto the wall.
Mr. Lapadapadoo
I assume that was the number of its victims.
I could have been victim 125. Or 126, if it saved some of me for leftovers.
Then what did you do?
I did what I always do when I find something horrific in the toilet.
I flushed.

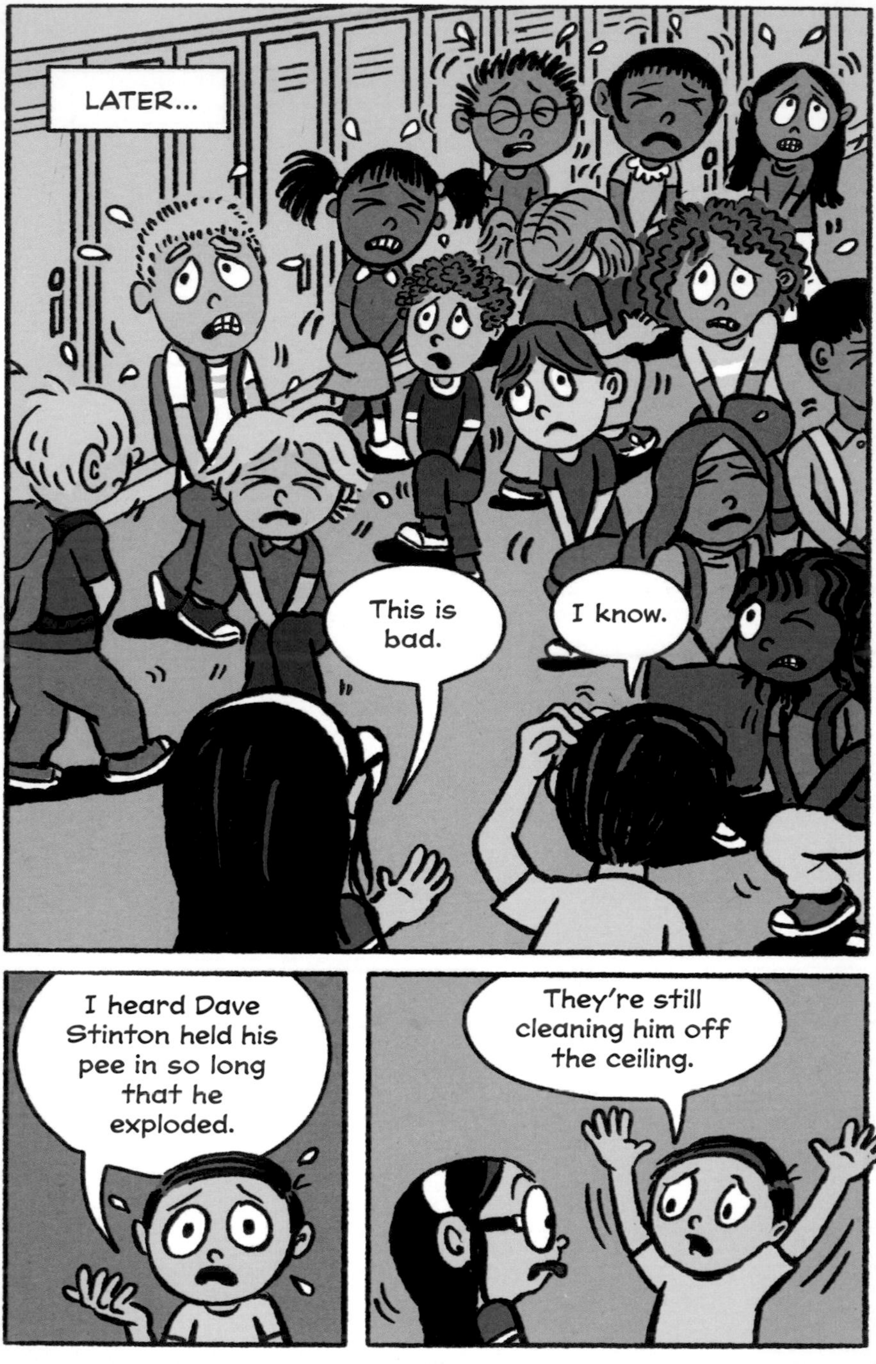
LATER...
This is bad.
I know.
I heard Dave Stinton held his pee in so long that he exploded.
They're still cleaning him off the ceiling.

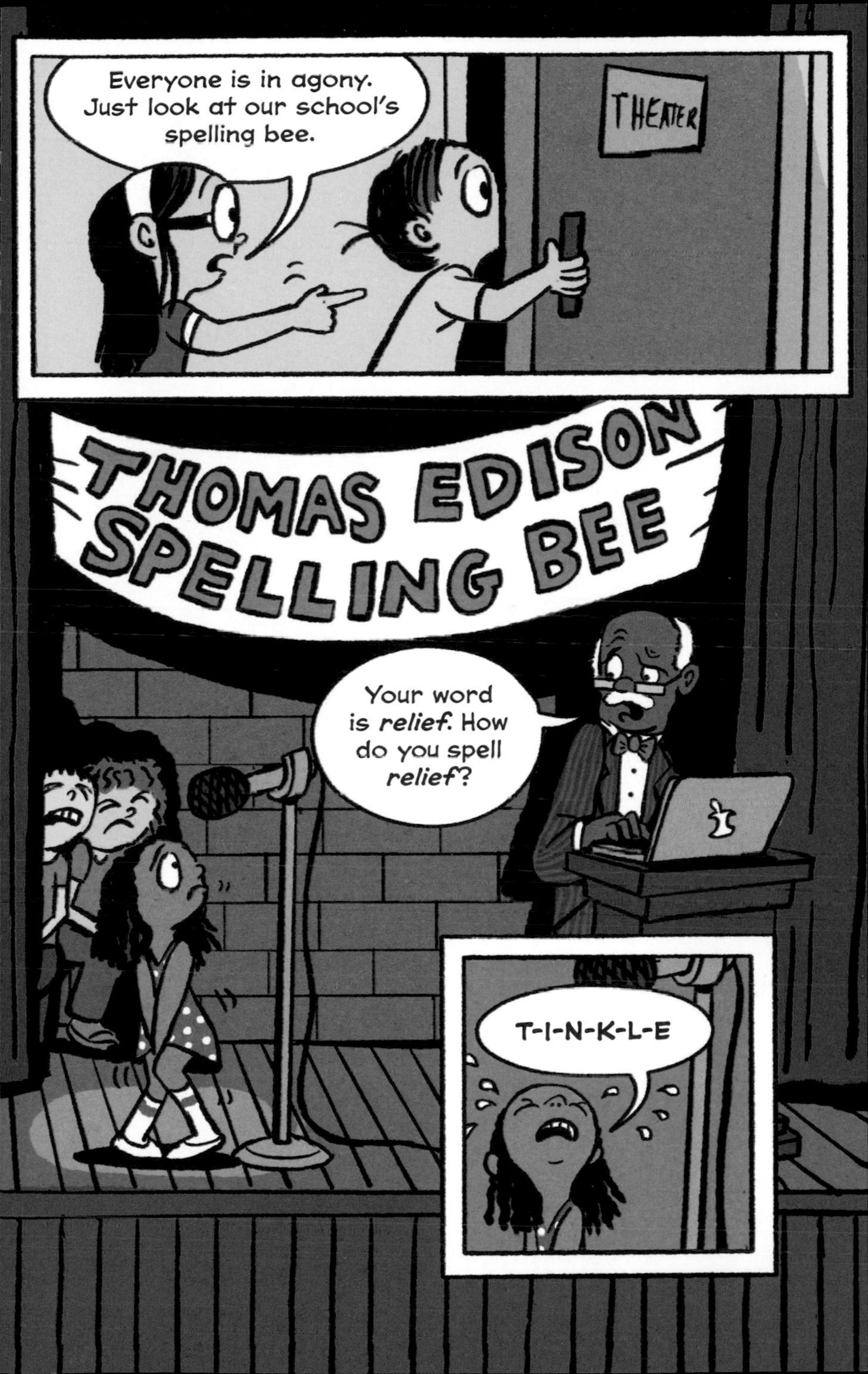
Everyone is in agony. Just look at our school's spelling bee.
THEATER
THOMAS EDISON SPELLING BEE
Your word is *relief*. How do you spell *relief*?
T-I-N-K-L-E

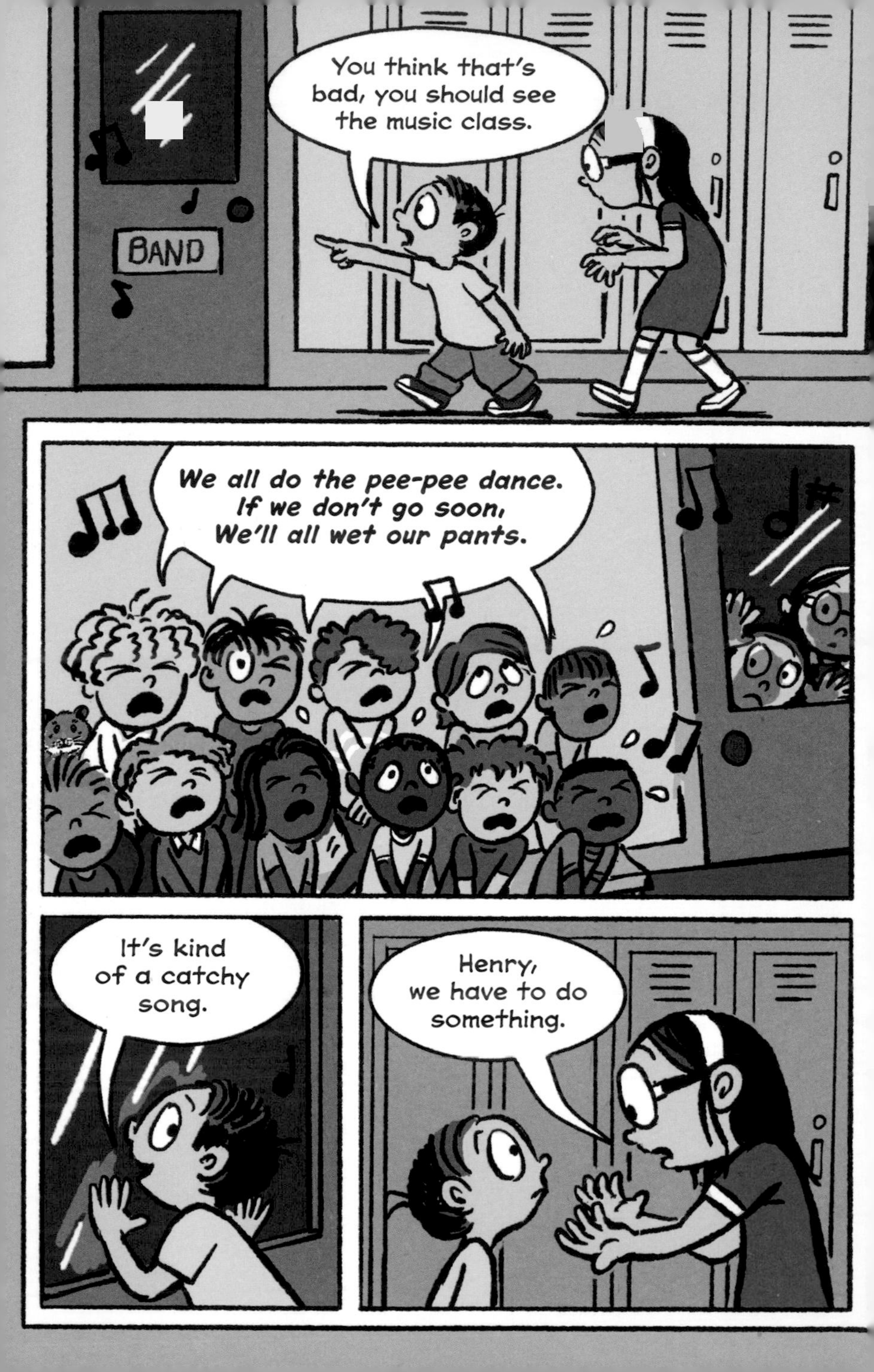
BAND
You think that's bad, you should see the music class.
We all do the pee-pee dance. If we don't go soon, We'll all wet our pants.
It's kind of a catchy song.
Henry, we have to do something.

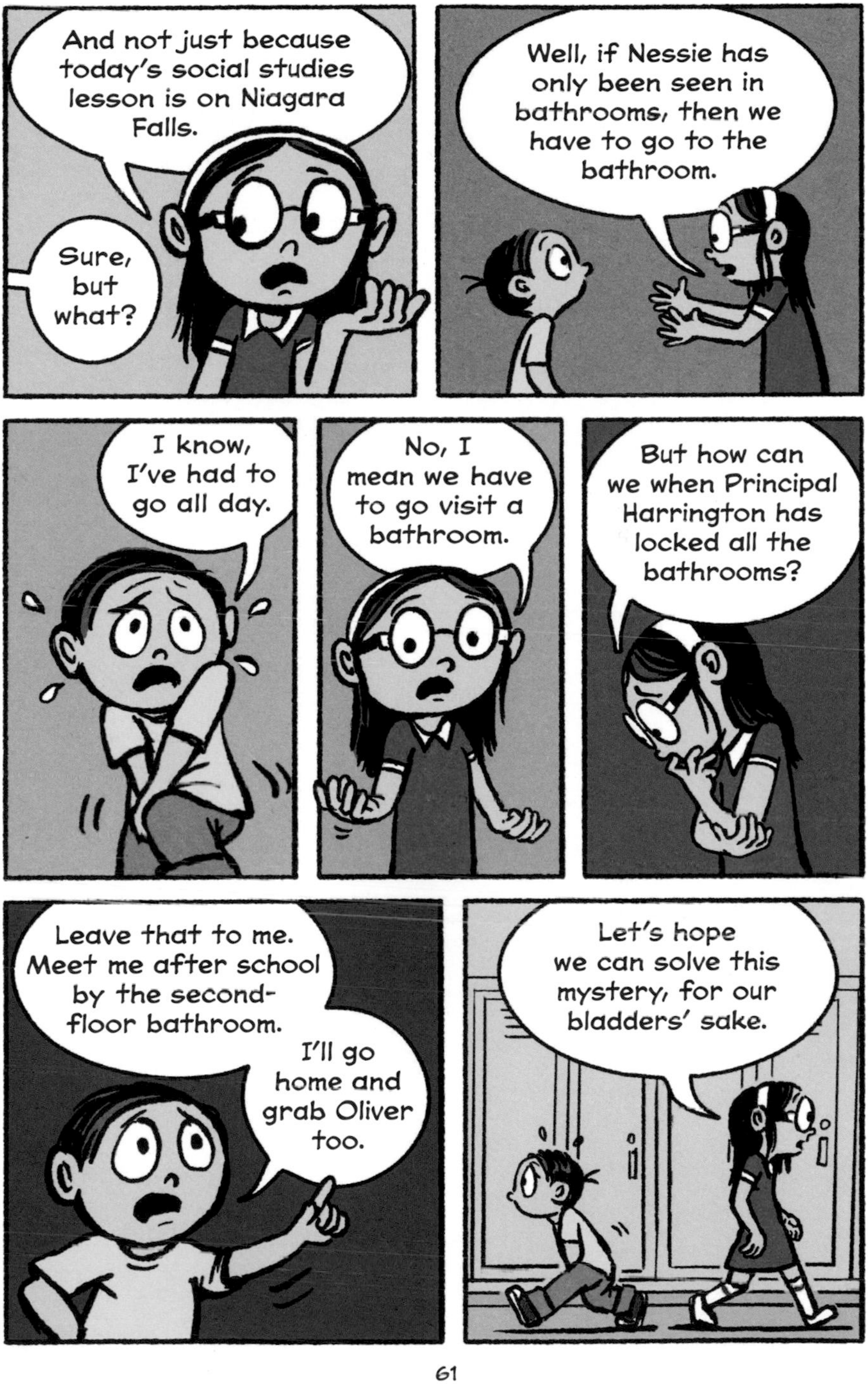
And not just because today's social studies lesson is on Niagara Falls.
Sure, but what?
Well, if Nessie has only been seen in bathrooms, then we have to go to the bathroom.
I know, I've had to go all day.
No, I mean we have to go visit a bathroom.
But how can we when Principal Harrington has locked all the bathrooms?
Leave that to me. Meet me after school by the second-floor bathroom.
I'll go home and grab Oliver too.
Let's hope we can solve this mystery, for our bladders' sake.

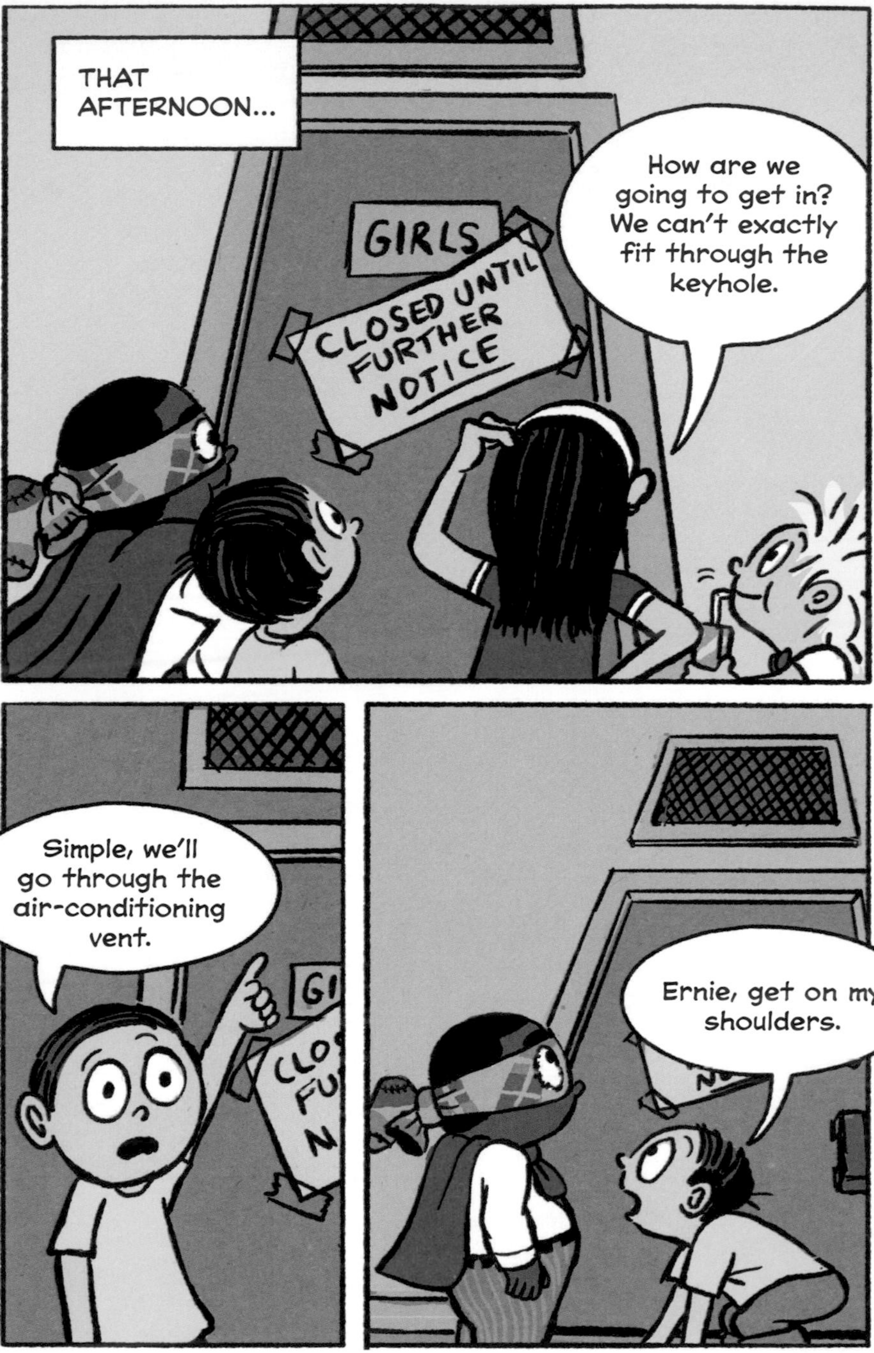
THAT AFTERNOON...
GIRLS
CLOSED UNTIL FURTHER NOTICE
How are we going to get in? We can't exactly fit through the keyhole.
Simple, we'll go through the air-conditioning vent.
Ernie, get on my shoulders.

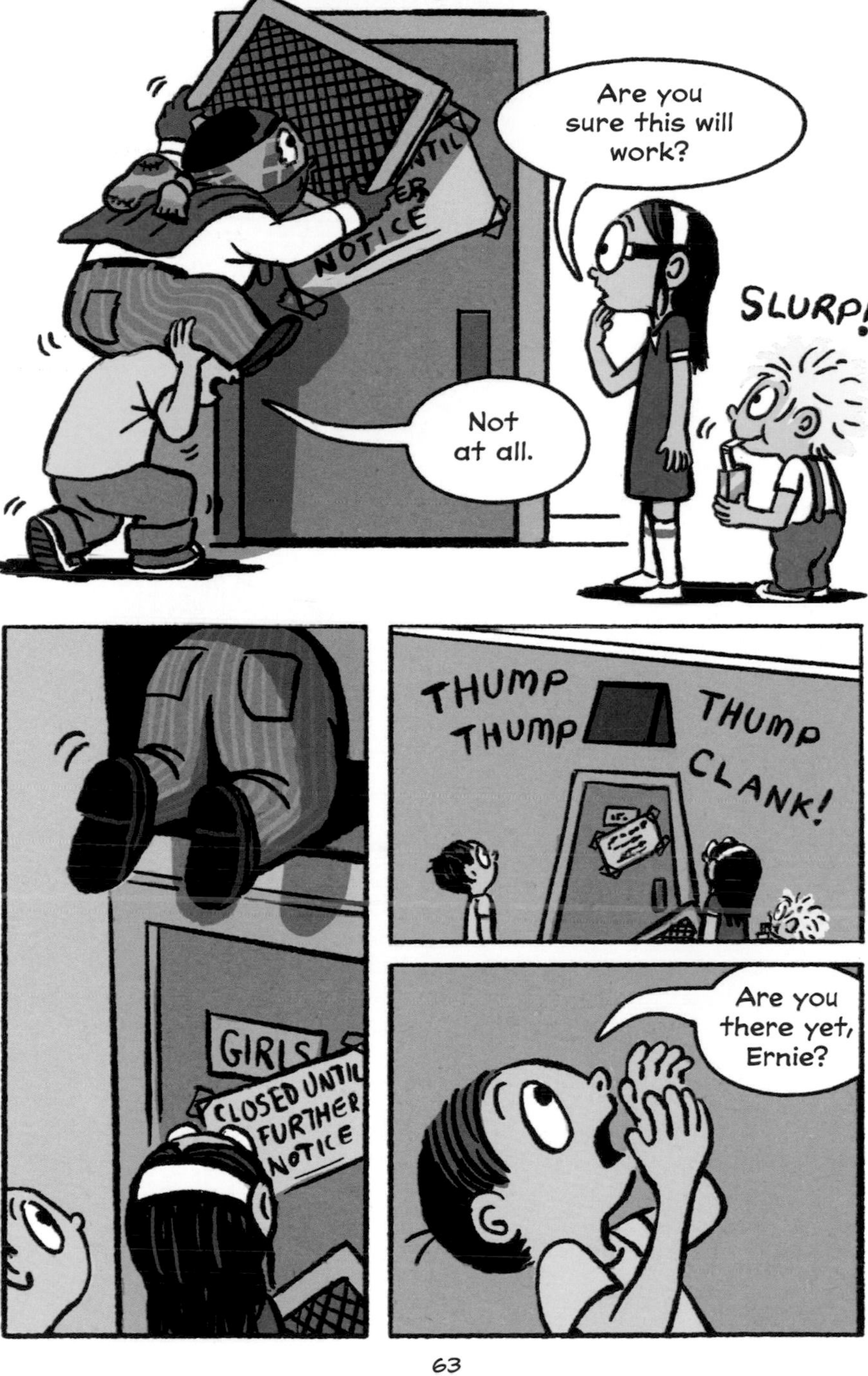
UNTIL FURTHER NOTICE
Are you sure this will work?
SLURP!
Not at all.
THUMP
THUMP
THUMP
CLANK!
GIRLS
CLOSED UNTIL FURTHER NOTICE
Are you there yet, Ernie?

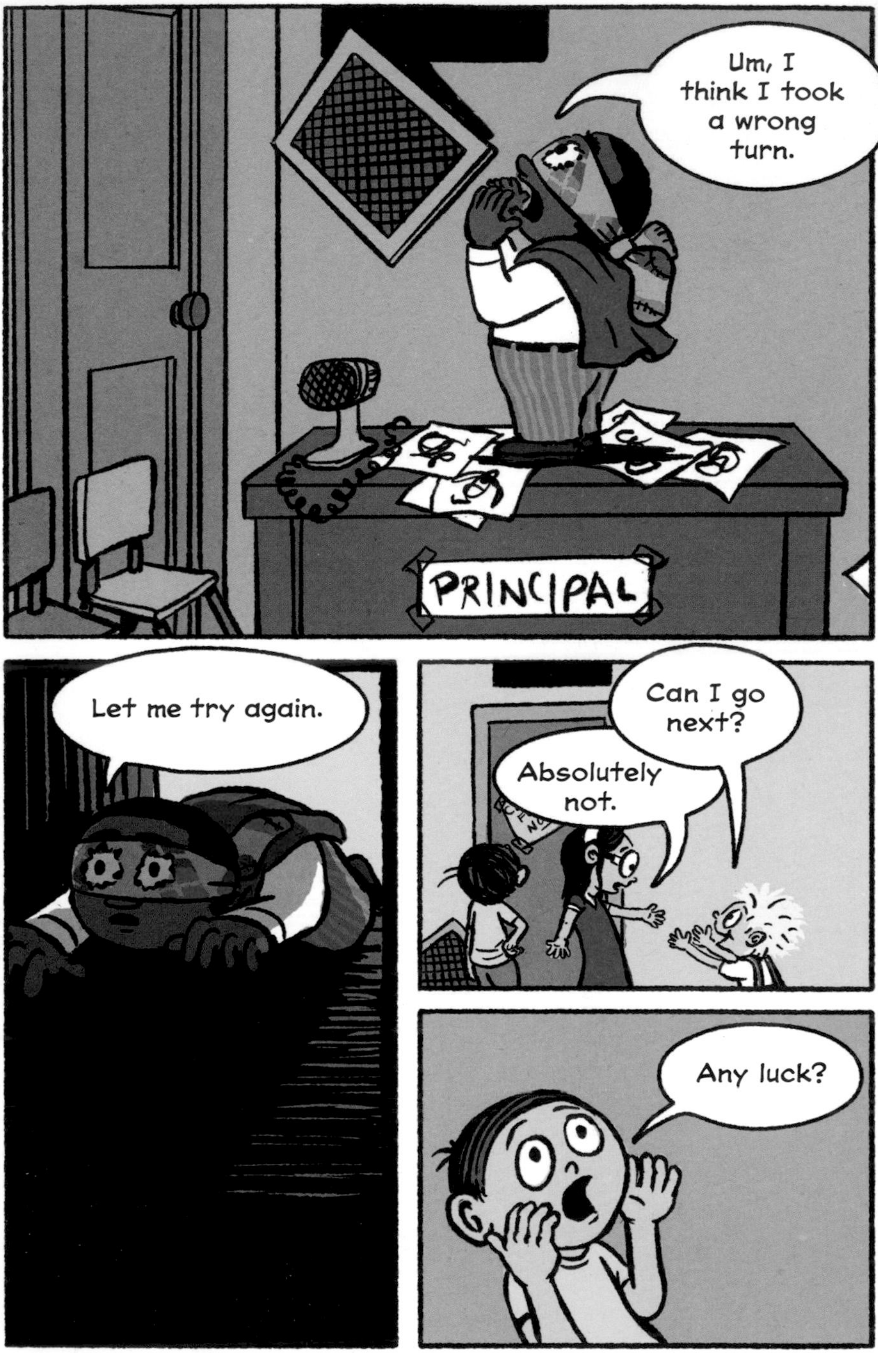
Um, I think I took a wrong turn.
PRINCIPAL
Let me try again.
Can I go next?
Absolutely not.
Any luck?

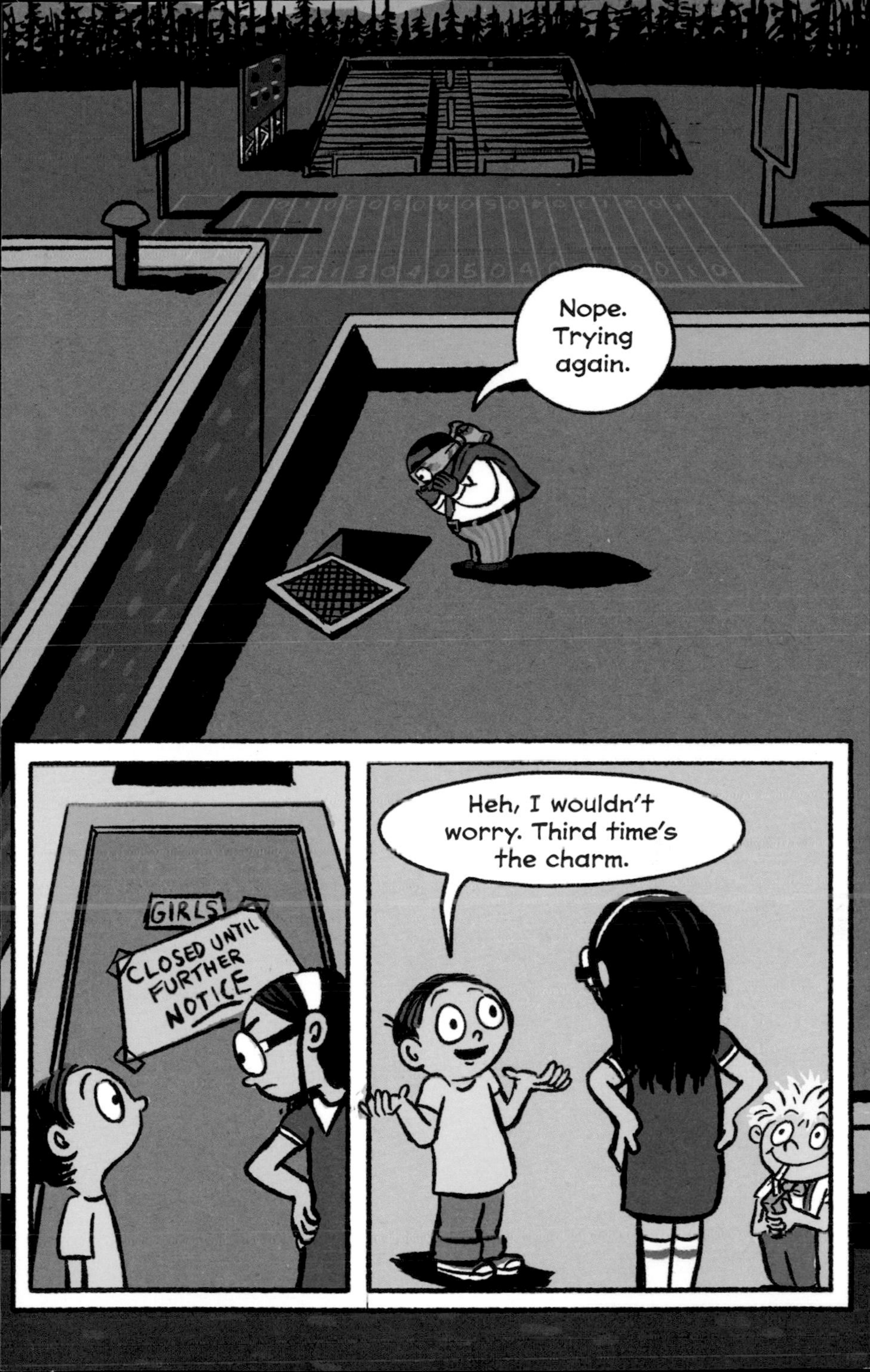
Nope. Trying again.
GIRLS
CLOSED UNTIL FURTHER NOTICE
Heh, I wouldn't worry. Third time's the charm.

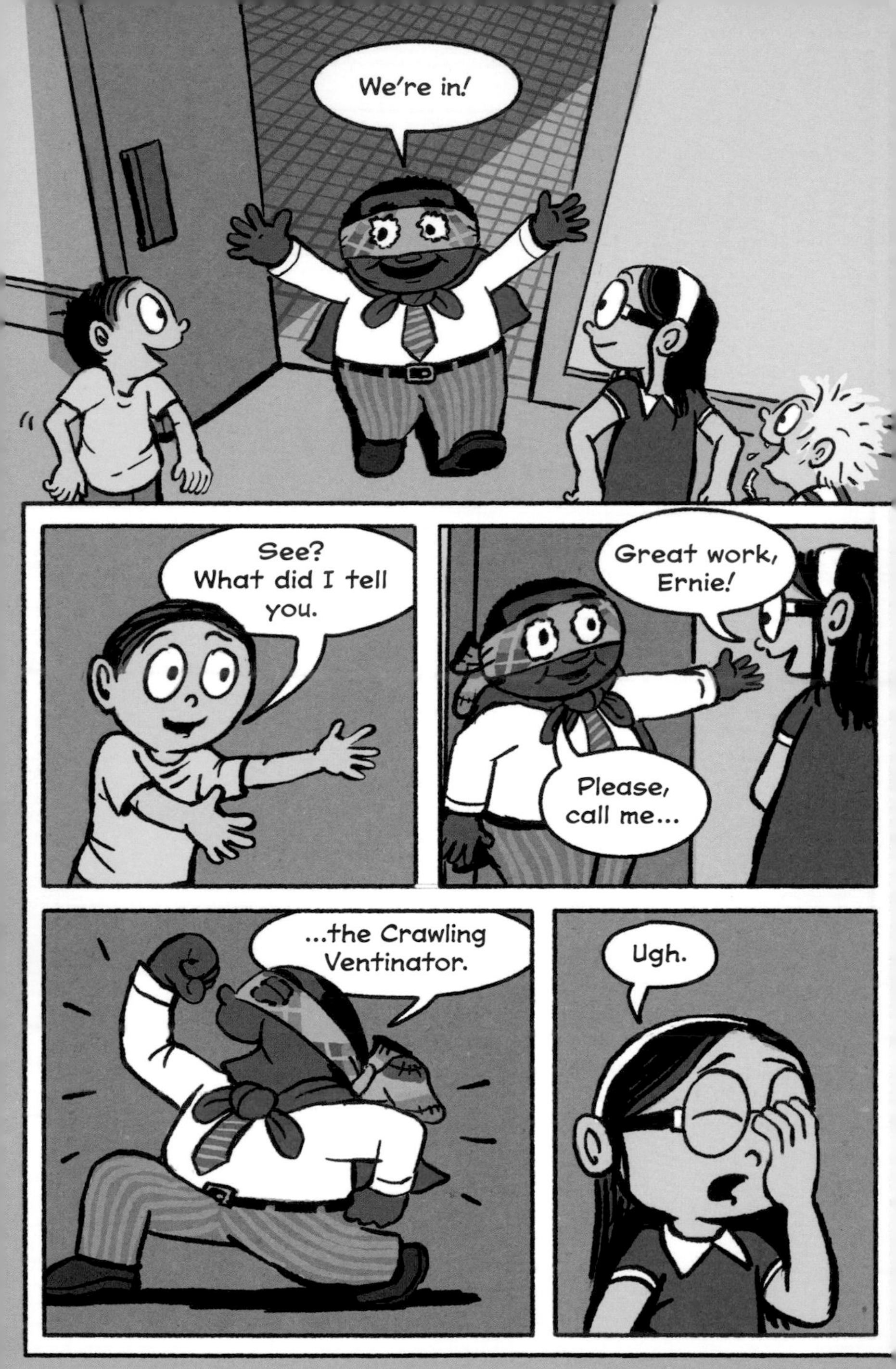
We're in!
See? What did I tell you.
Great work, Ernie!
Please, call me...
...the Crawling Ventinator.
Ugh.

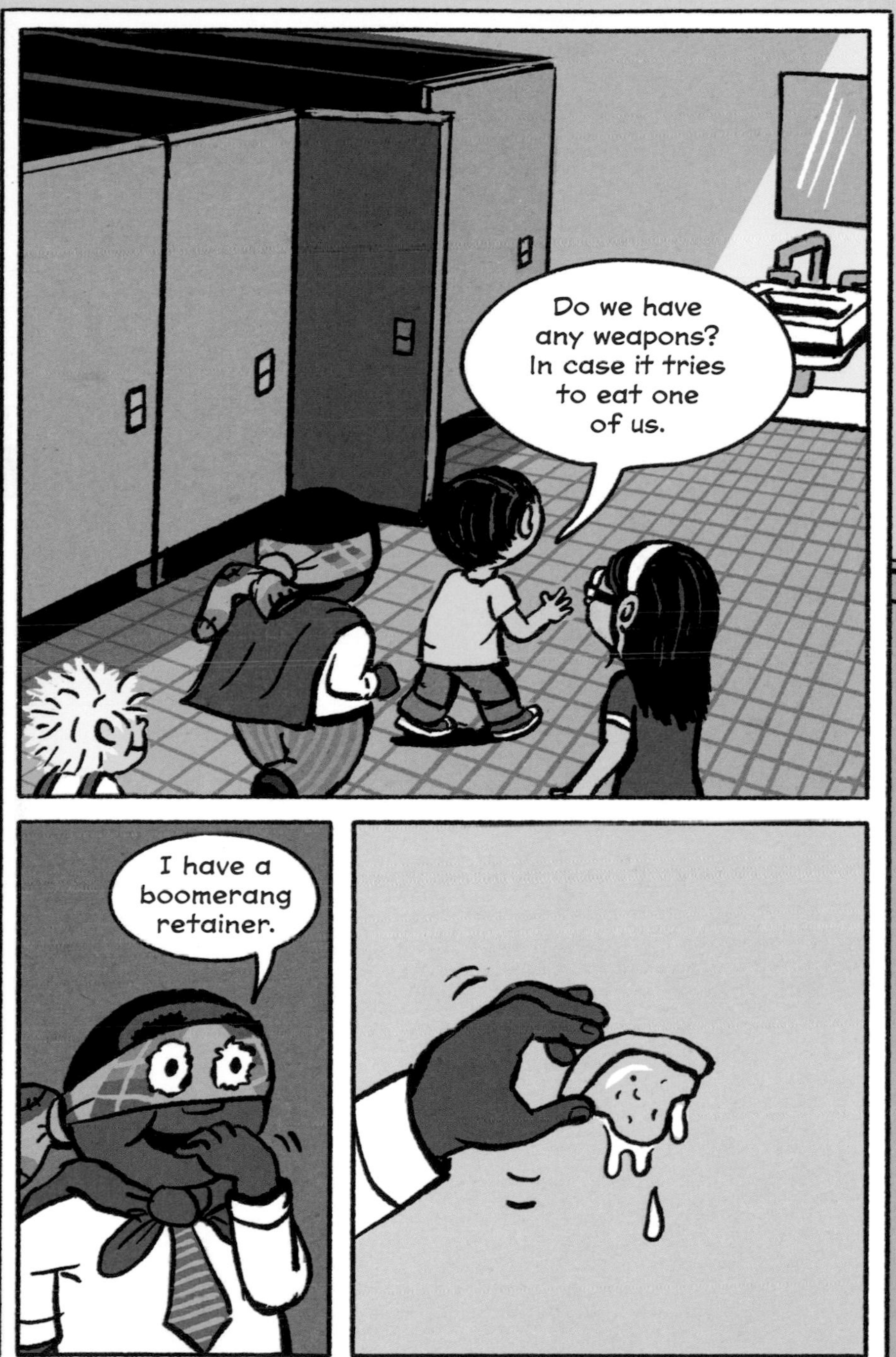
Do we have any weapons? In case it tries to eat one of us.
I have a boomerang retainer.

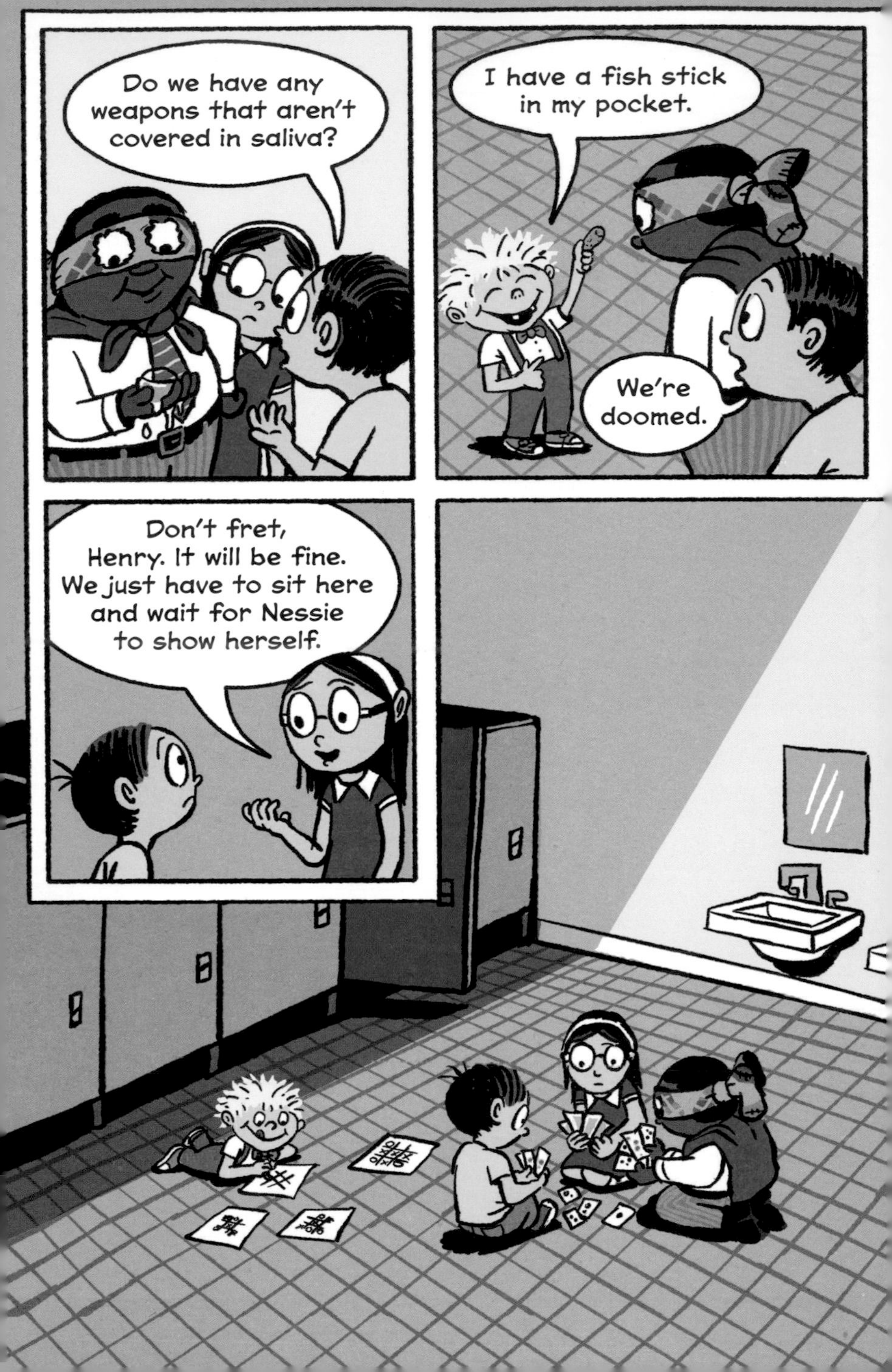

Do we have any weapons that aren't covered in saliva?
I have a fish stick in my pocket.
We're doomed.
Don't fret, Henry. It will be fine. We just have to sit here and wait for Nessie to show herself.

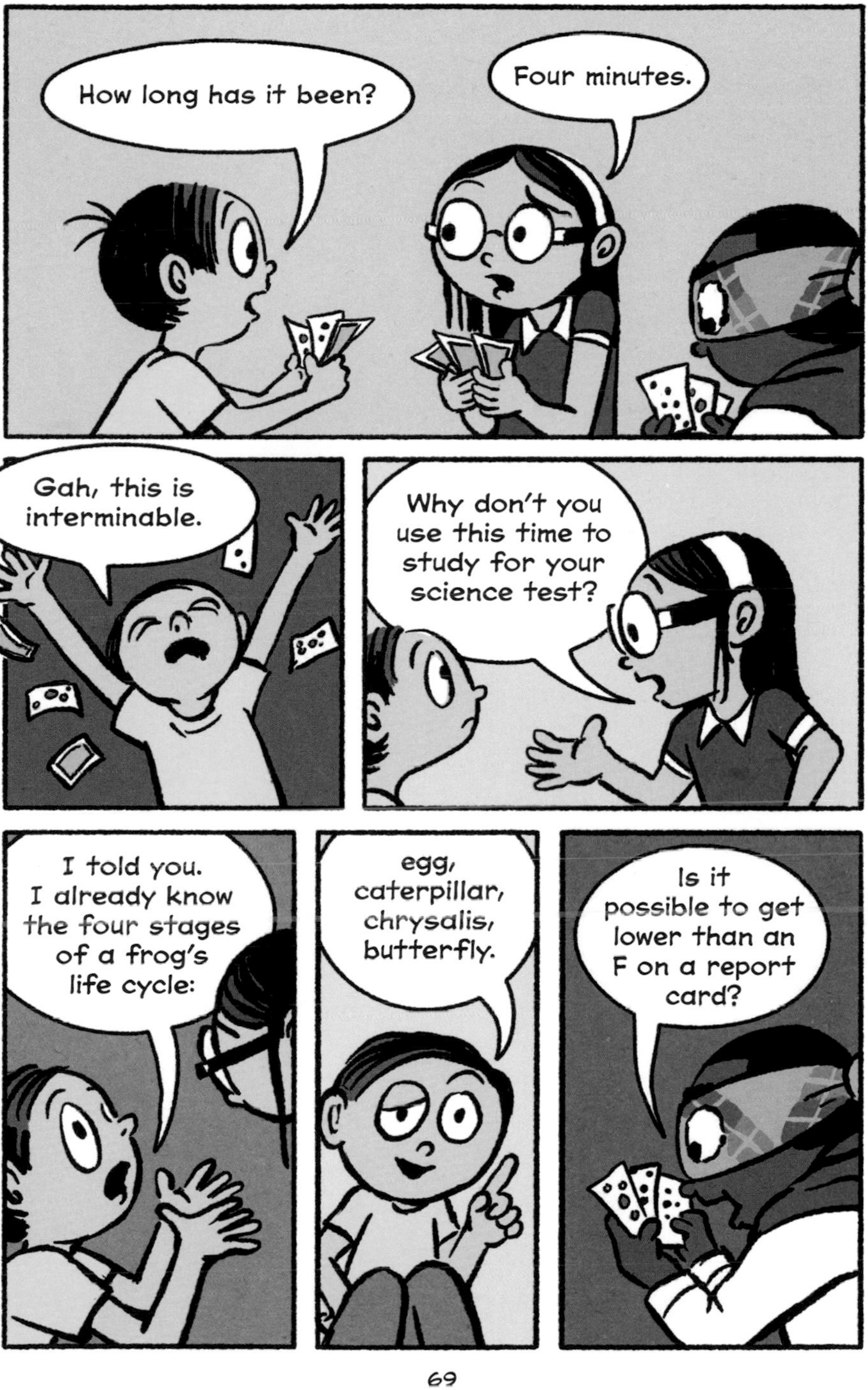
How long has it been?
Four minutes.
Gah, this is interminable.
Why don't you use this time to study for your science test?
I told you. I already know the four stages of a frog's life cycle:
egg, caterpillar, chrysalis, butterfly.
Is it possible to get lower than an F on a report card?

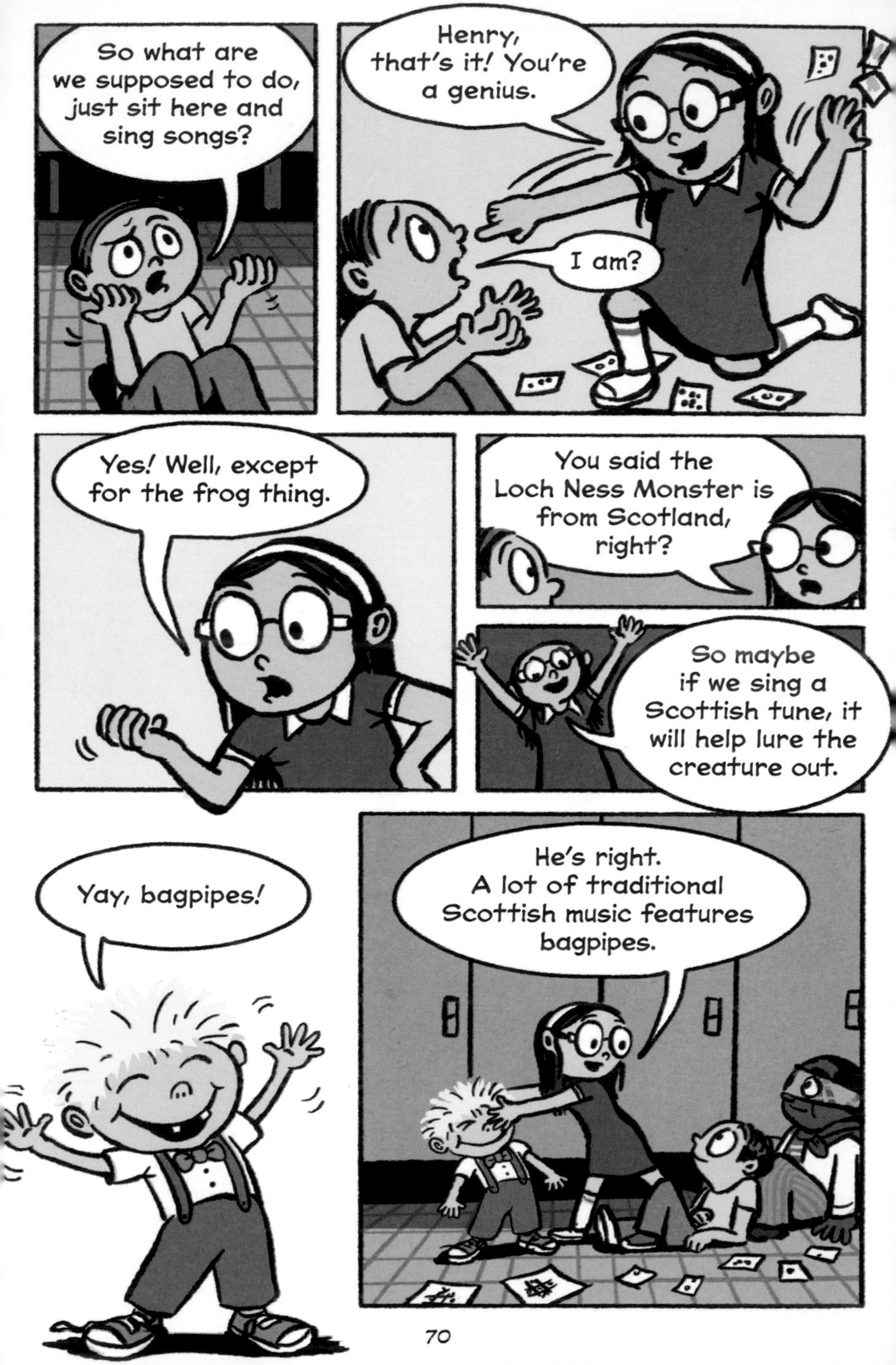
So what are we supposed to do, just sit here and sing songs?
Henry, that's it! You're a genius.
I am?
Yes! Well, except for the frog thing.
You said the Loch Ness Monster is from Scotland, right?
So maybe if we sing a Scottish tune, it will help lure the creature out.
Yay, bagpipes!
He's right. A lot of traditional Scottish music features bagpipes.

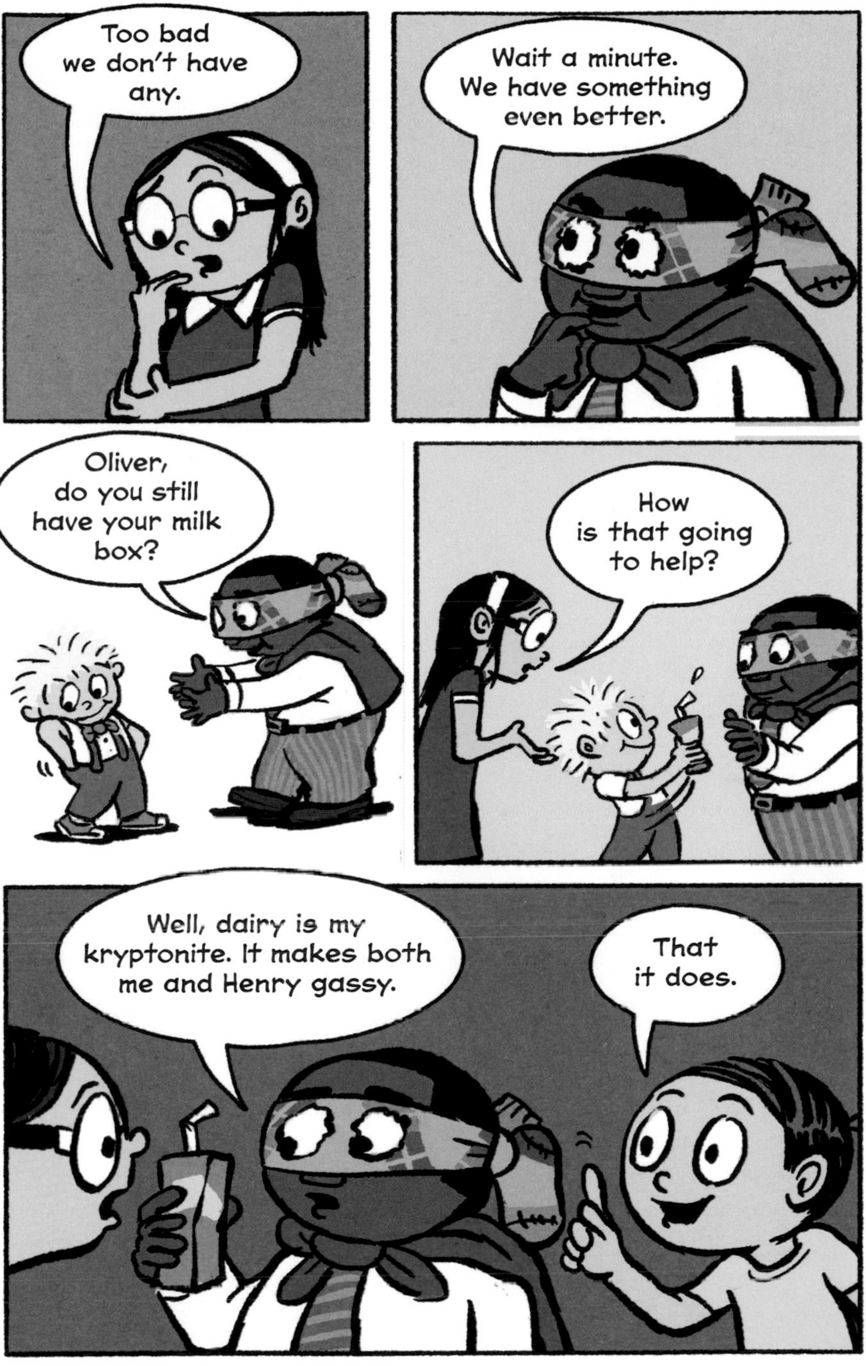
Too bad we don't have any.
Wait a minute. We have something even better.
Oliver, do you still have your milk box?
How is that going to help?
Well, dairy is my kryptonite. It makes both me and Henry gassy.
That it does.

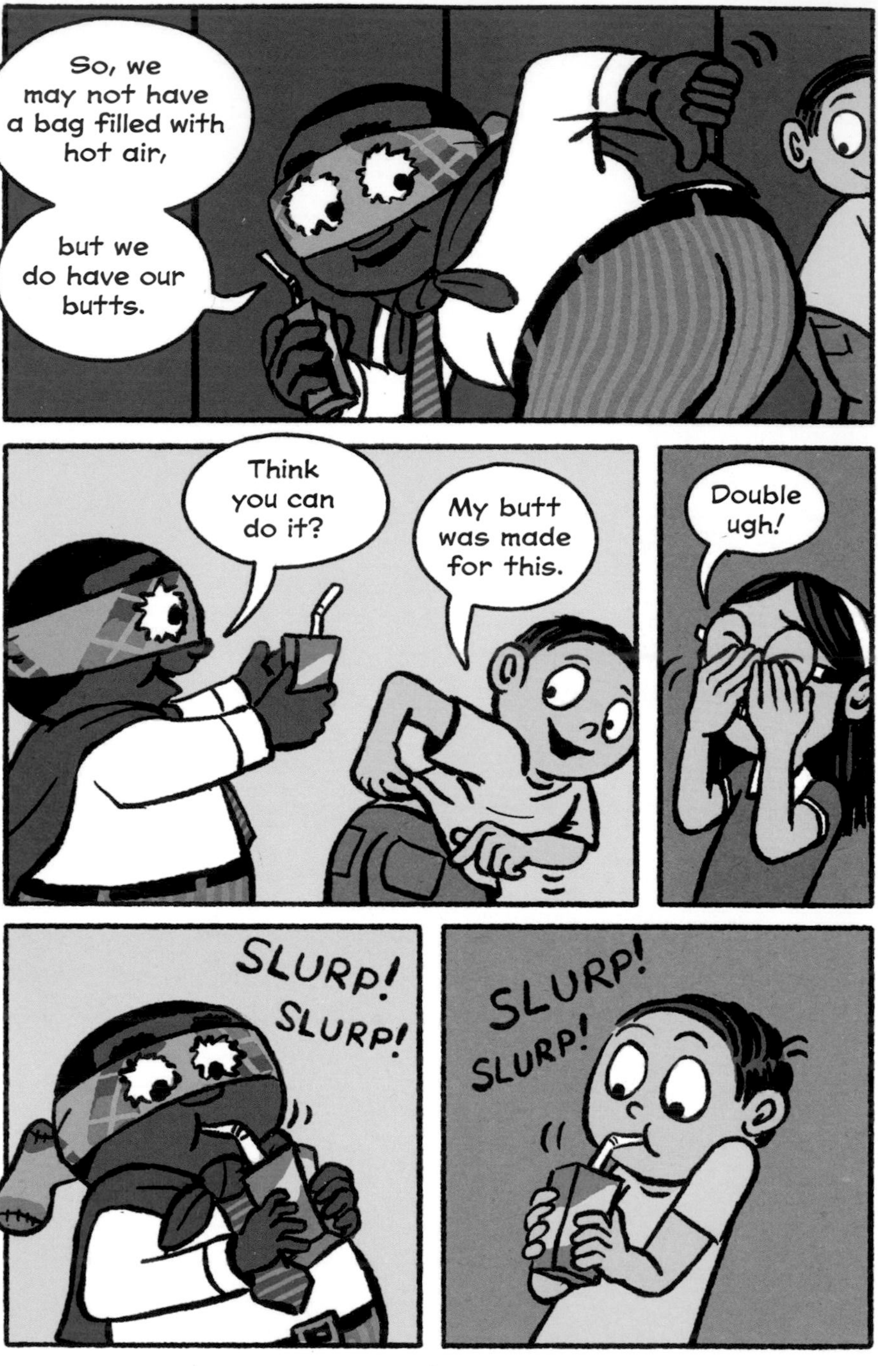
So, we may not have a bag filled with hot air,
but we do have our butts.
Think you can do it?
My butt was made for this.
Double ugh!
SLURP! SLURP!
SLURP! SLURP!

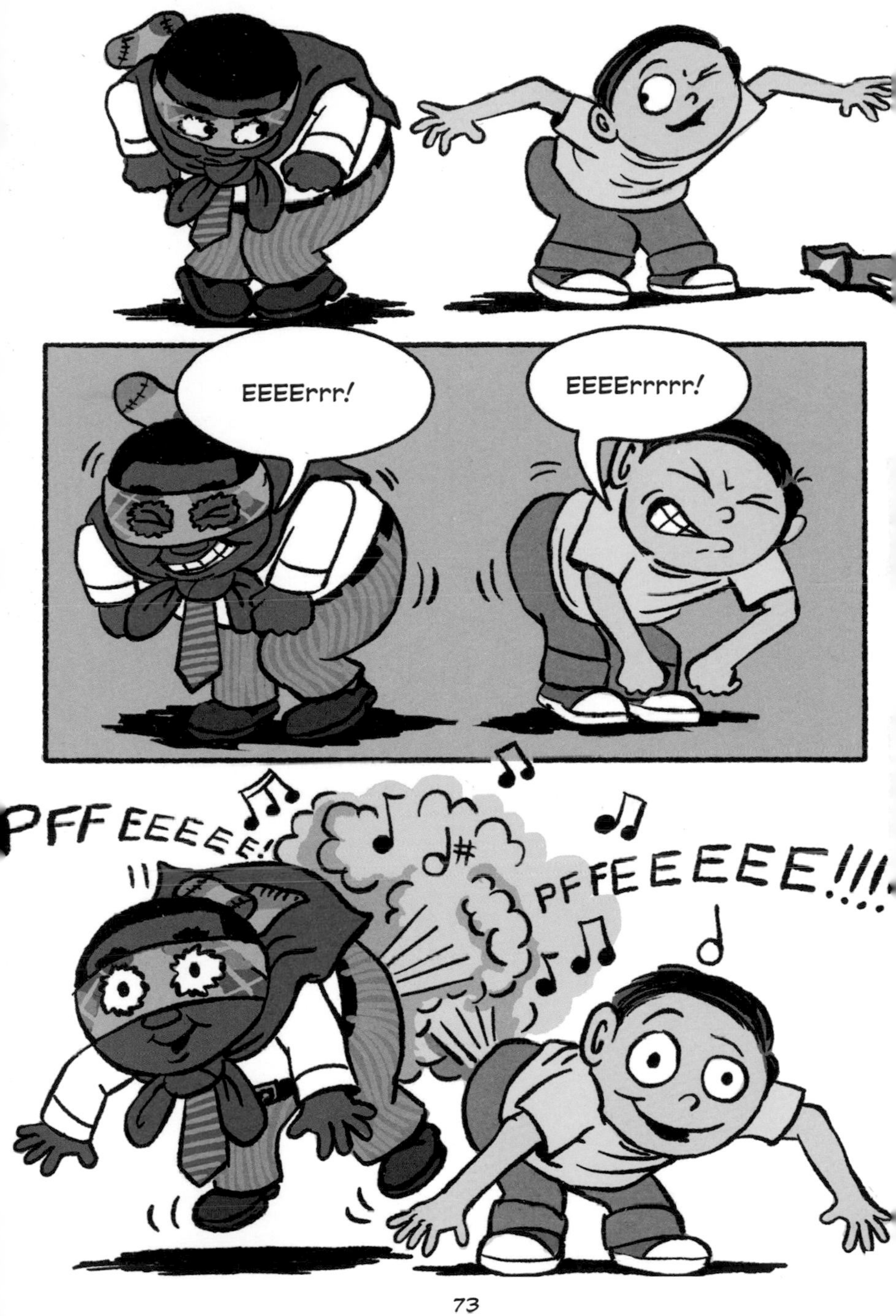
EEEErrr!
EEEErrrrr!
PFFEEEEEE!
PFFEEEEEE!!!!

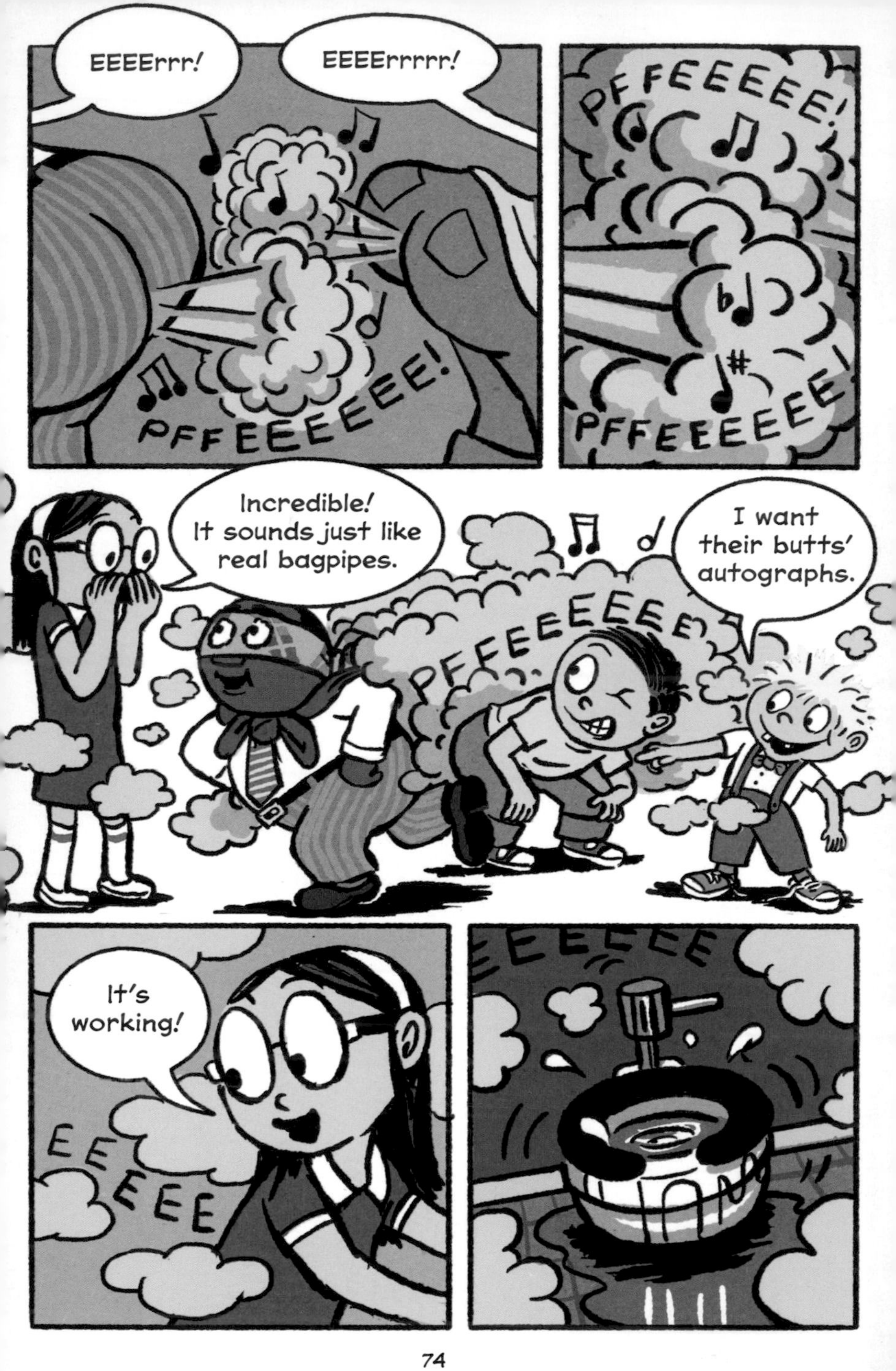
EEEErrr!
EEEErrrr!
PFFEEEEEEE!
PFFEEEEEE!
PFFEEEEEEE!
Incredible! It sounds just like real bagpipes.
PFFEEEEEEEE
I want their butts' autographs.
It's working!
EEEEE
EEEEEE

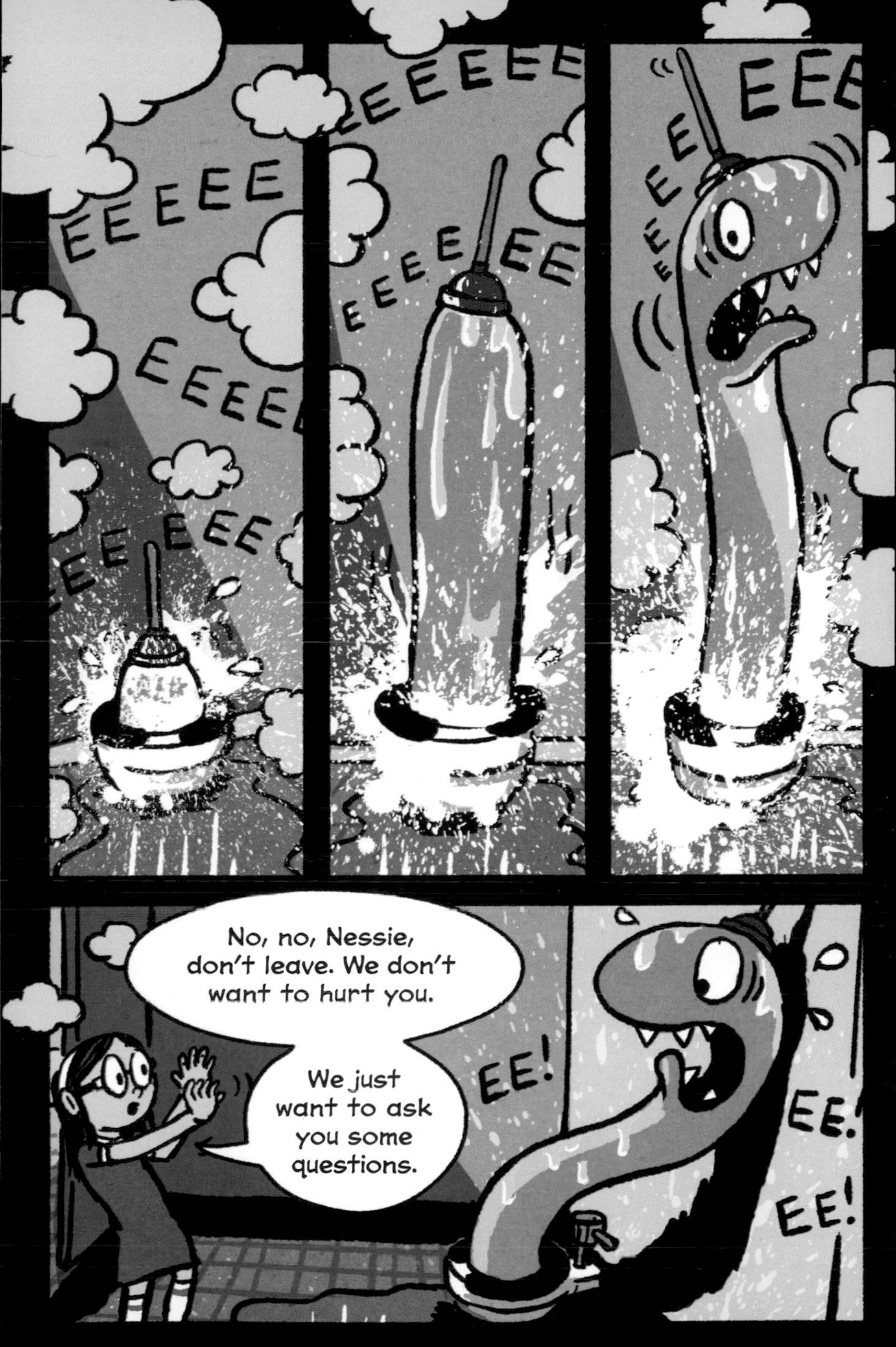
EEEEE
EEEEE
EEEEEE
EEEEEEE
EEEEEEE
EEEEE
EEEEEEE
No, no, Nessie, don't leave. We don't want to hurt you.
We just want to ask you some questions.
EE!
EE!
EE!

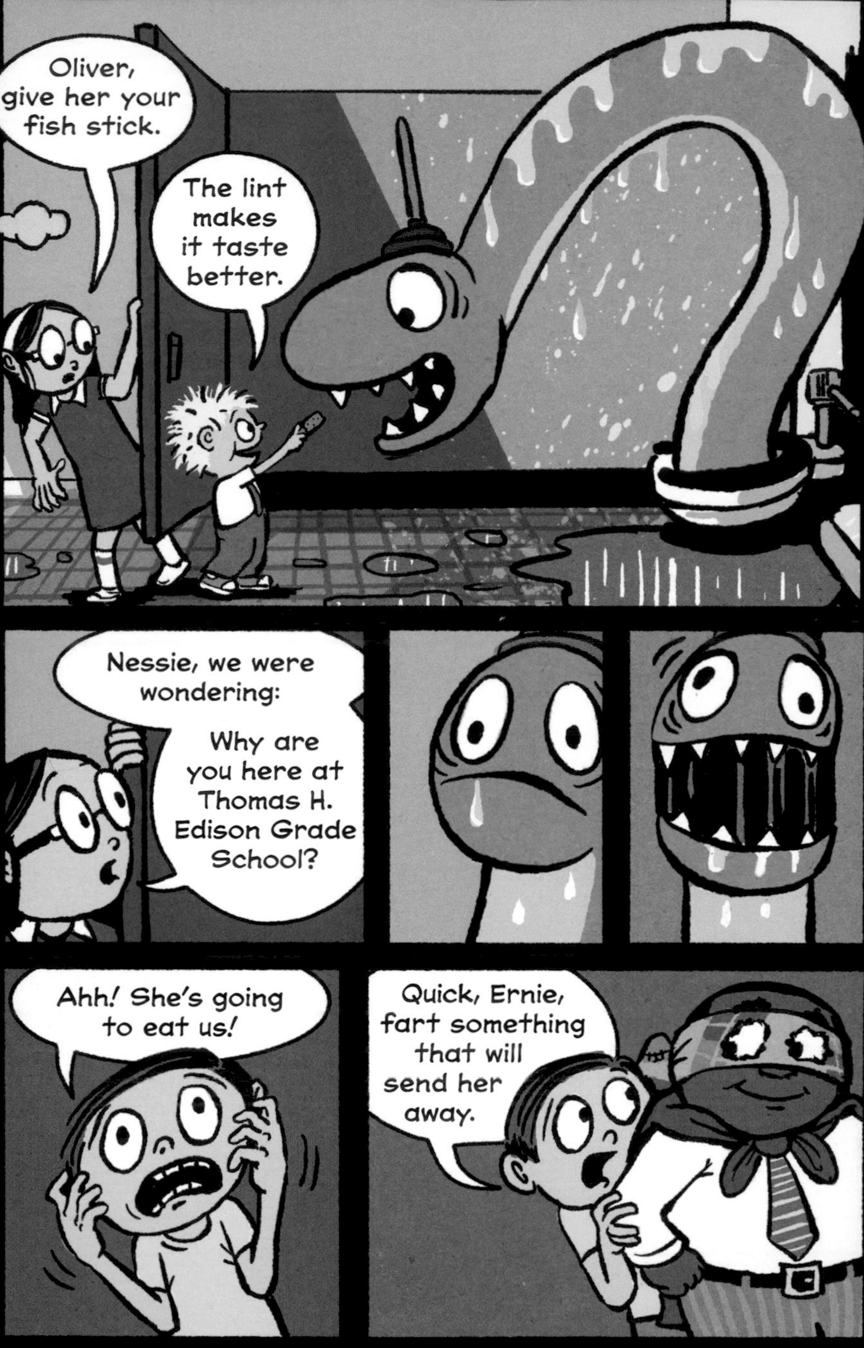
Oliver, give her your fish stick.
The lint makes it taste better.
Nessie, we were wondering:
Why are you here at Thomas H. Edison Grade School?
Ahh! She's going to eat us!
Quick, Ernie, fart something that will send her away.

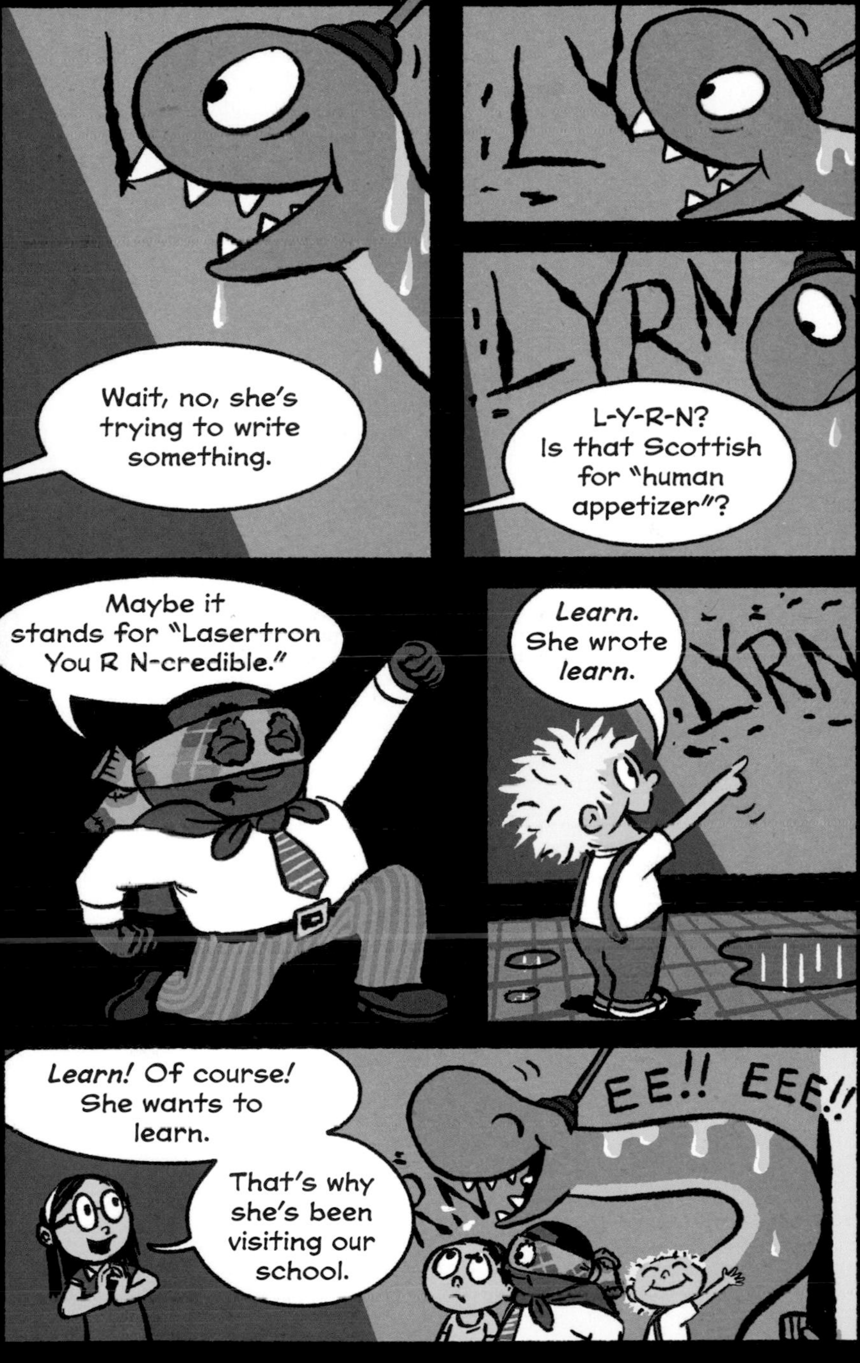
Wait, no, she's trying to write something.
LYRN
L-Y-R-N? Is that Scottish for "human appetizer"?
Maybe it stands for "Lasertron You R N-credible."
Learn. She wrote learn.
LYRN
Learn! Of course! She wants to learn.
That's why she's been visiting our school.
EE!! EEE!!

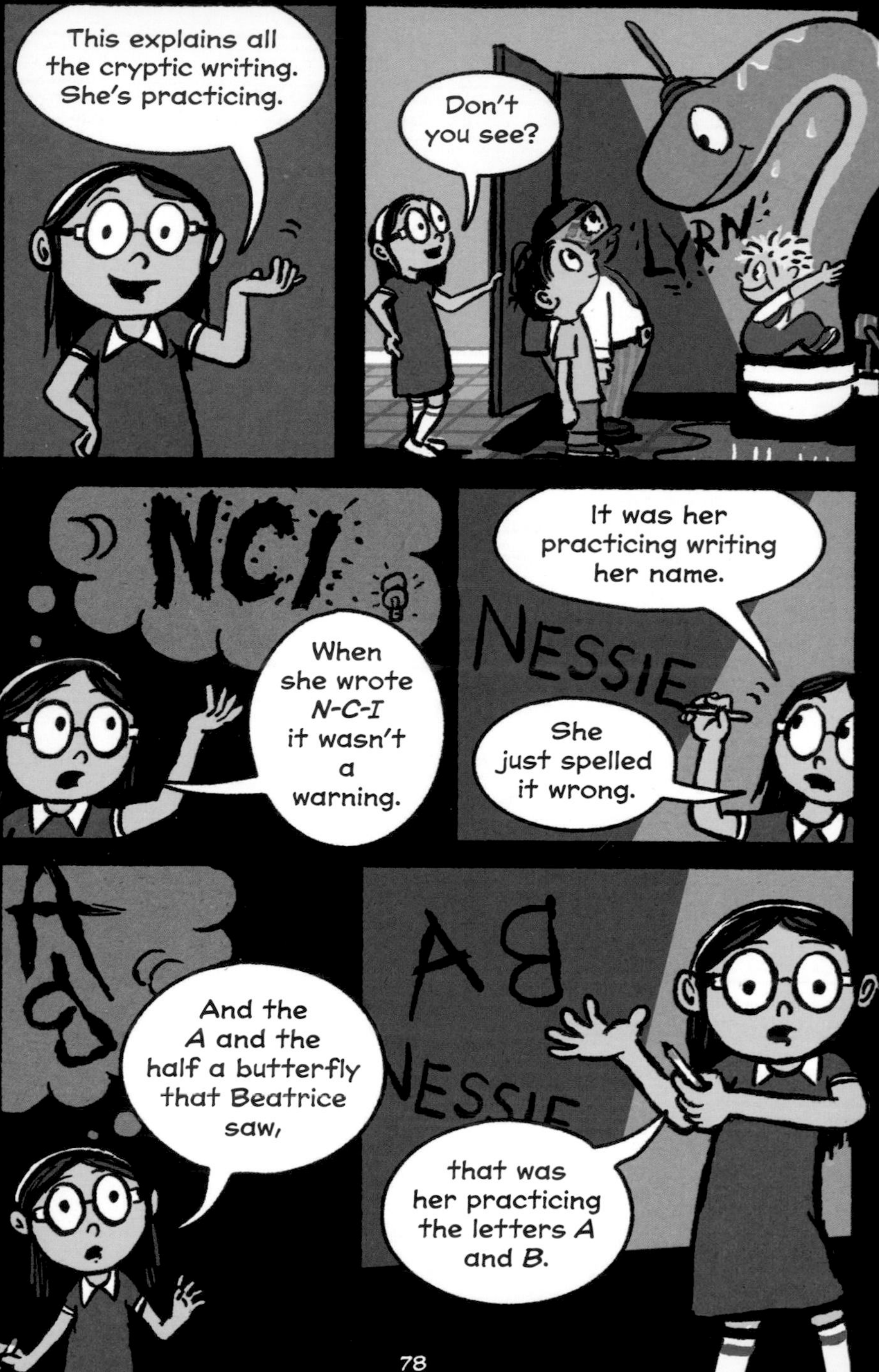
This explains all the cryptic writing. She's practicing.
Don't you see?
LYRN
NCI
It was her practicing writing her name.
When she wrote *N-C-I* it wasn't a warning.
NESSIE
She just spelled it wrong.
And the *A* and the half a butterfly that Beatrice saw,
A B
that was her practicing the letters *A* and *B*.

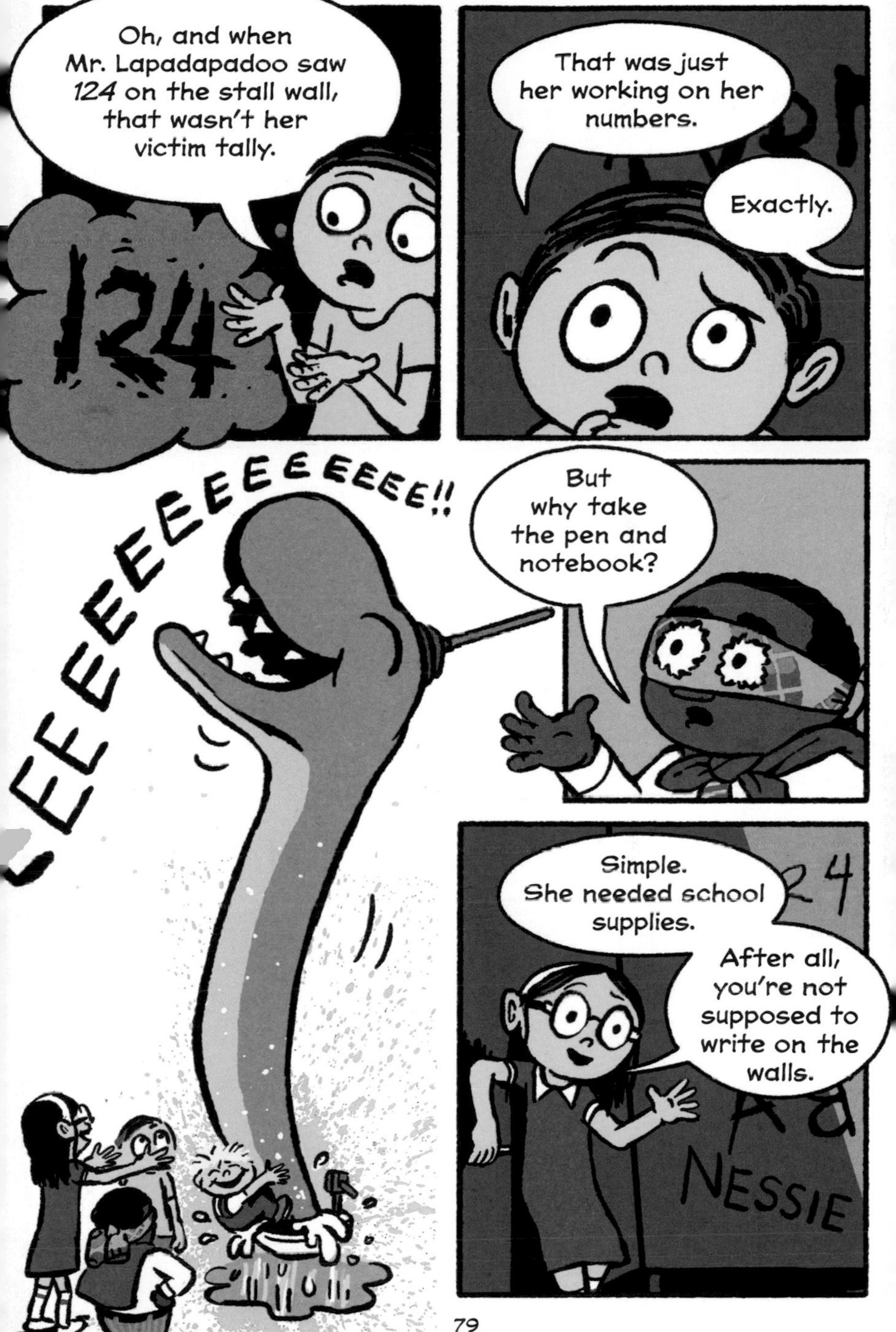
Oh, and when Mr. Lapadapadoo saw 124 on the stall wall, that wasn't her victim tally.
124
That was just her working on her numbers.
Exactly.
EEEEEEEEEEEEEEEEE!!
But why take the pen and notebook?
Simple. She needed school supplies.
After all, you're not supposed to write on the walls.
24
NESSIE

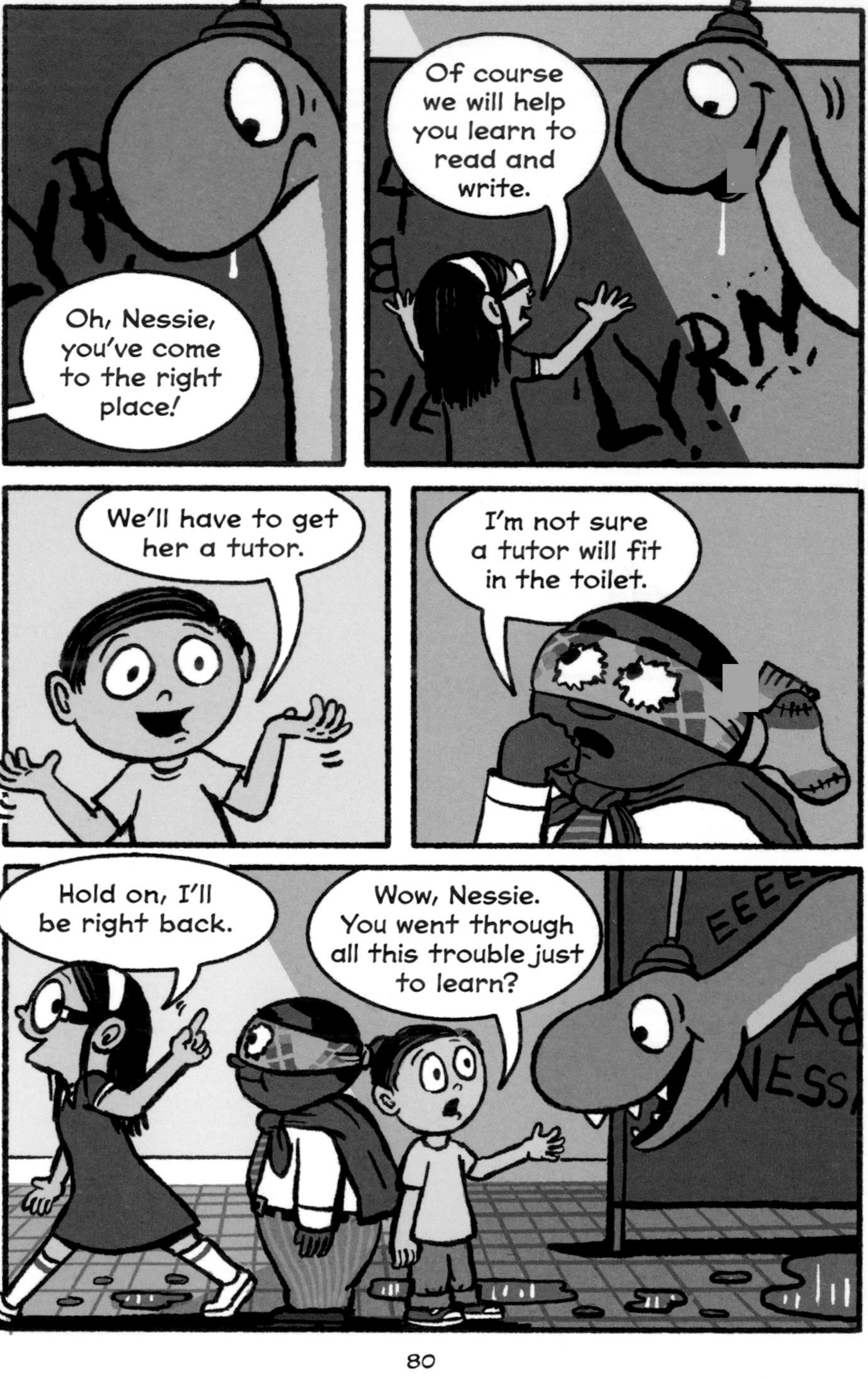
Oh, Nessie, you've come to the right place!
Of course we will help you learn to read and write.
LYRN
We'll have to get her a tutor.
I'm not sure a tutor will fit in the toilet.
Hold on, I'll be right back.
Wow, Nessie. You went through all this trouble just to learn?

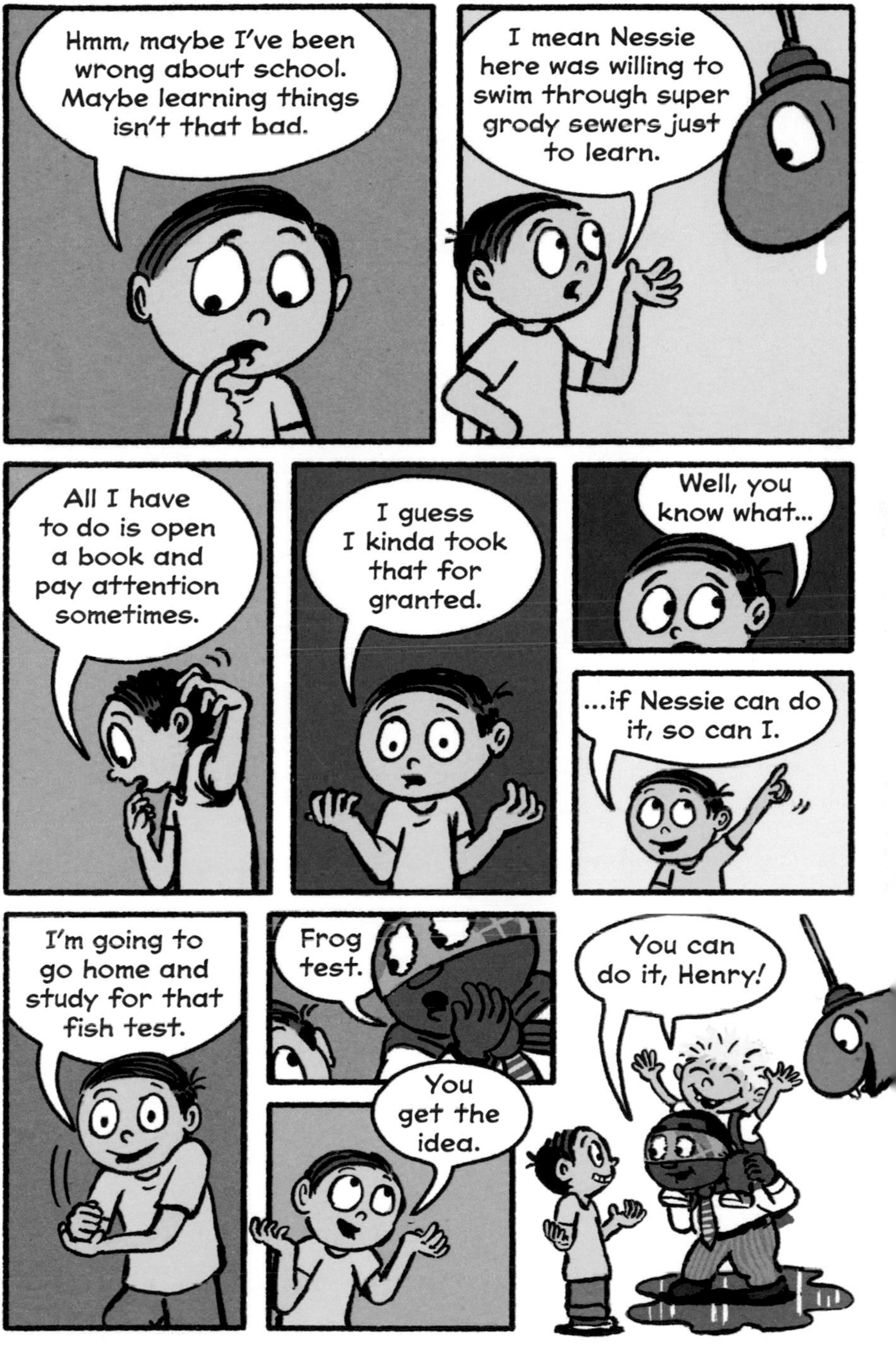
Hmm, maybe I've been wrong about school. Maybe learning things isn't that bad.
I mean Nessie here was willing to swim through super grody sewers just to learn.
All I have to do is open a book and pay attention sometimes.
I guess I kinda took that for granted.
Well, you know what...
...if Nessie can do it, so can I.
I'm going to go home and study for that fish test.
Frog test.
You get the idea.
You can do it, Henry!

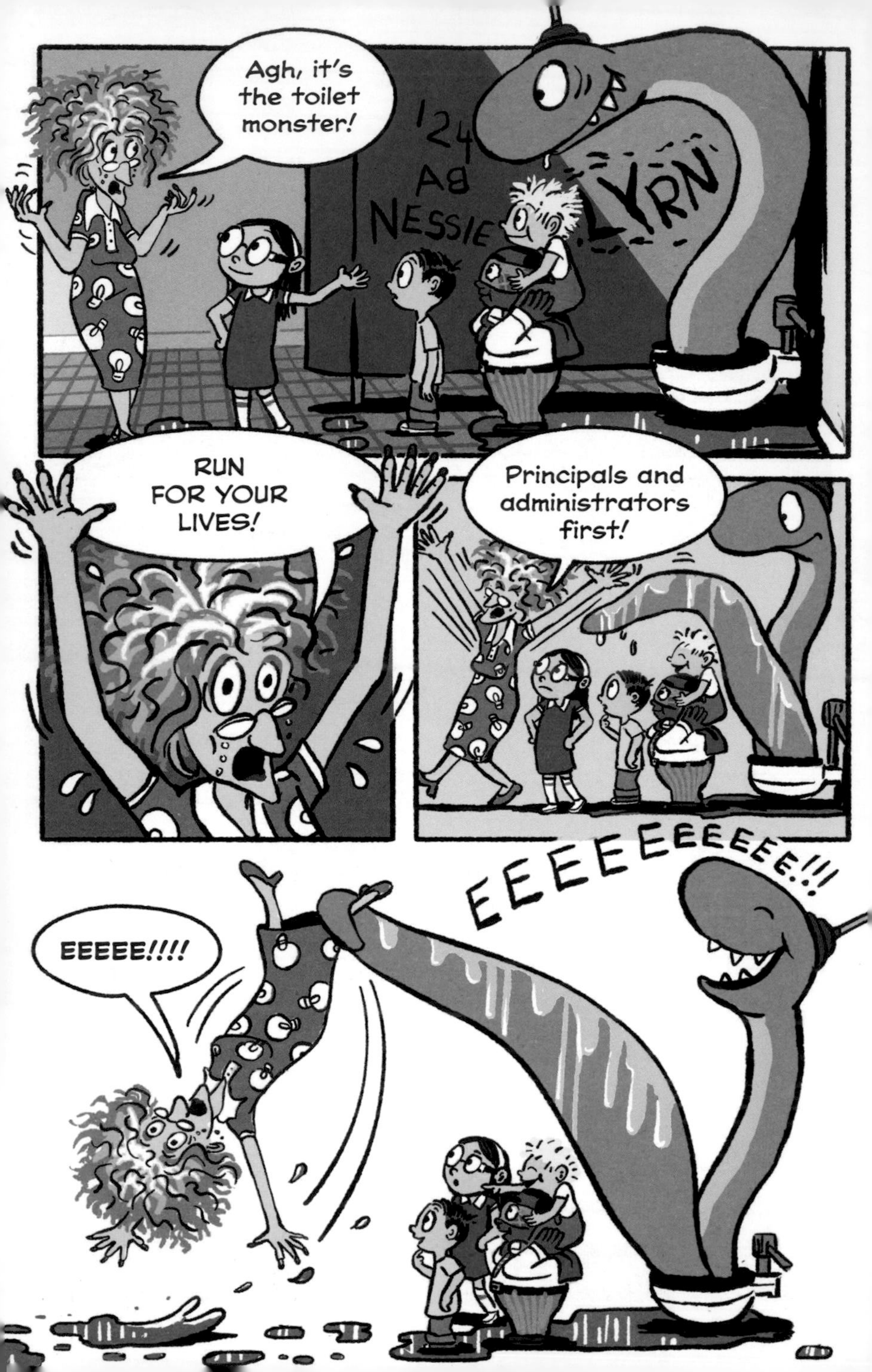

Agh, it's the toilet monster!
124
AB
NESSIE
YRN
RUN FOR YOUR LIVES!
Principals and administrators first!
EEEEE!!!!
EEEEEEEEEEE!!!

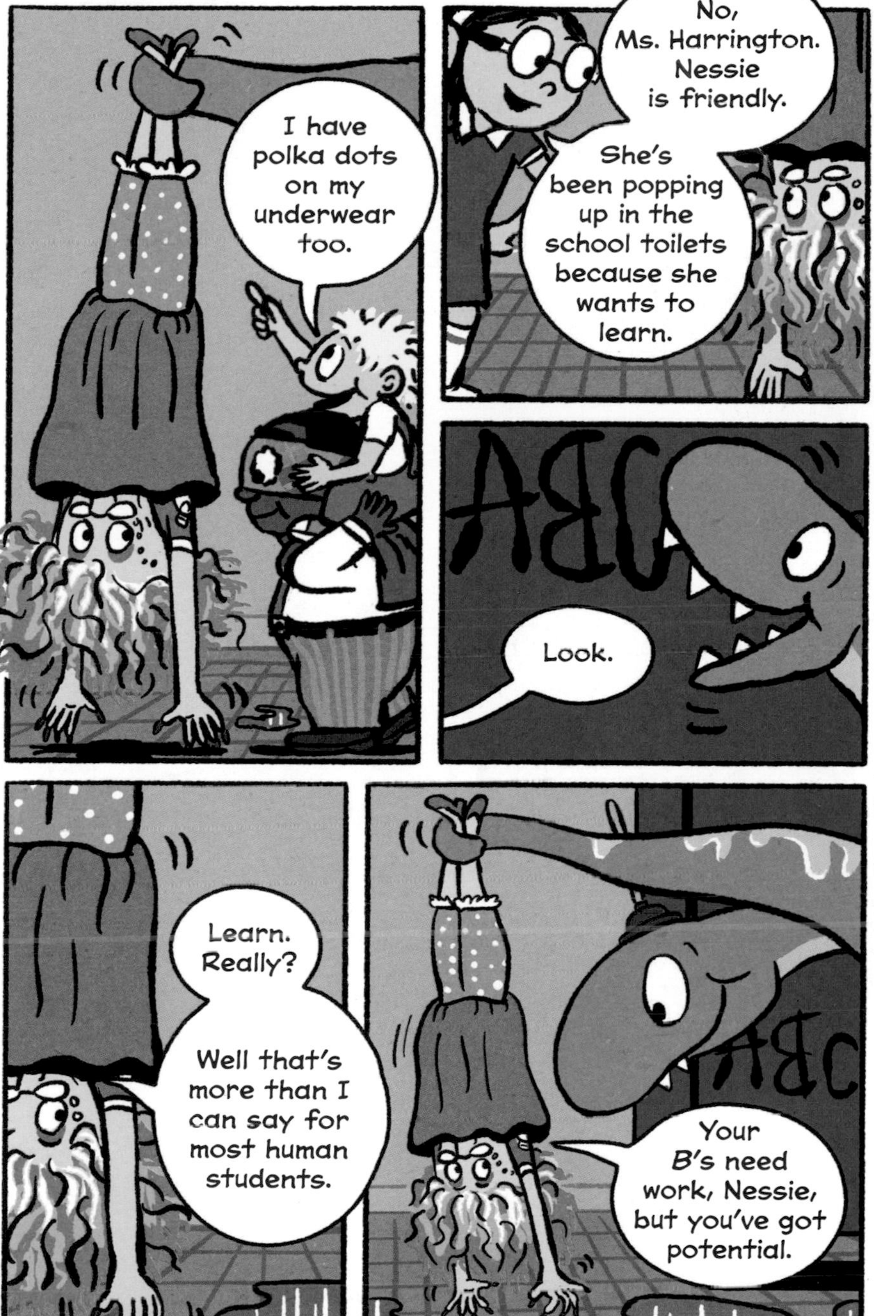
I have polka dots on my underwear too.
No, Ms. Harrington. Nessie is friendly.
She's been popping up in the school toilets because she wants to learn.
Look.
Learn. Really?
Well that's more than I can say for most human students.
Your *B*'s need work, Nessie, but you've got potential.

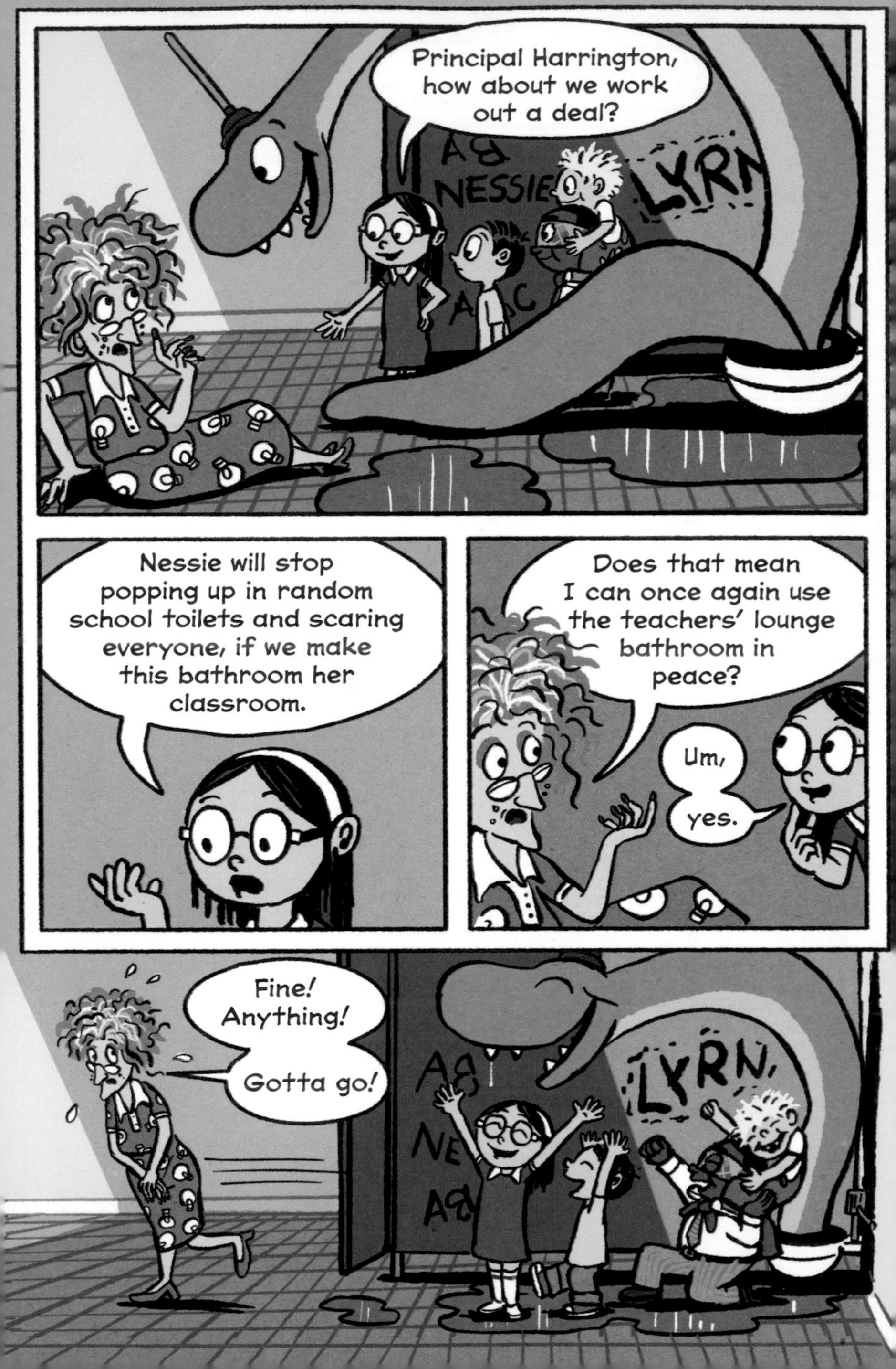
Principal Harrington, how about we work out a deal?
AB
NESSIE
LYRN
AC
Nessie will stop popping up in random school toilets and scaring everyone, if we make this bathroom her classroom.
Does that mean I can once again use the teachers' lounge bathroom in peace?
Um,
yes.
Fine! Anything!
Gotta go!
AB
NE
AB
LYRN

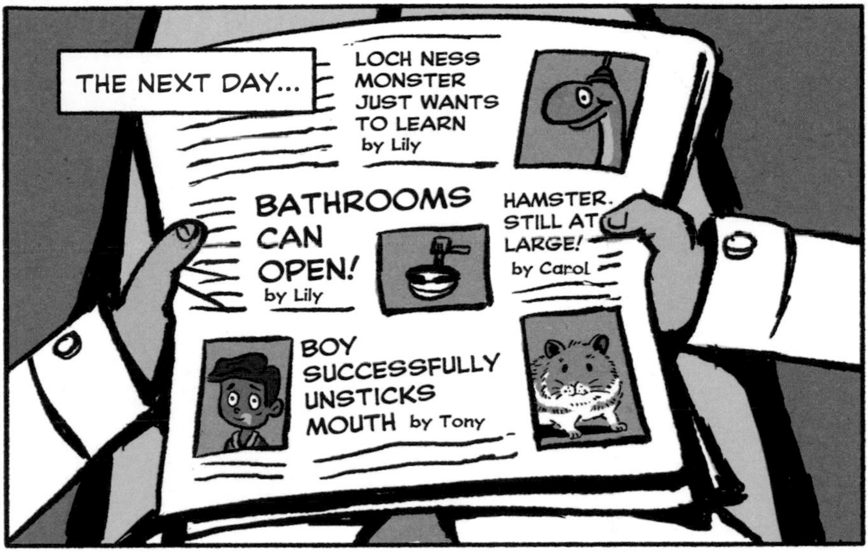
THE NEXT DAY...
LOCH NESS MONSTER JUST WANTS TO LEARN by Lily
BATHROOMS CAN OPEN! by Lily
HAMSTER STILL AT LARGE! by Carol
BOY SUCCESSFULLY UNSTICKS MOUTH by Tony

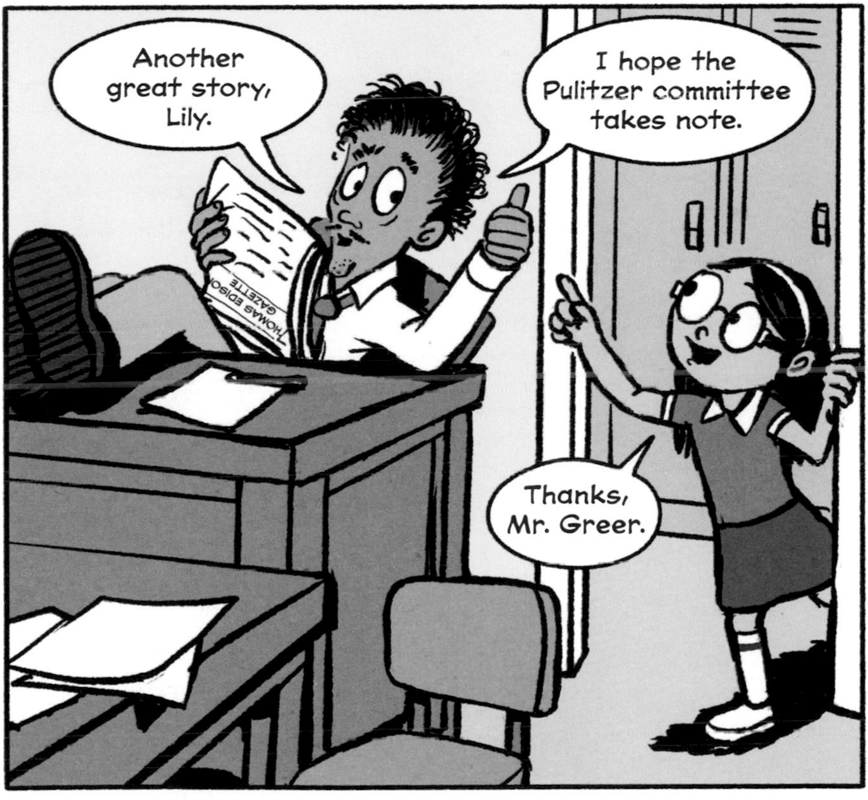
Another great story, Lily.
I hope the Pulitzer committee takes note.
THOMAS EDISON GAZETTE
Thanks, Mr. Greer.

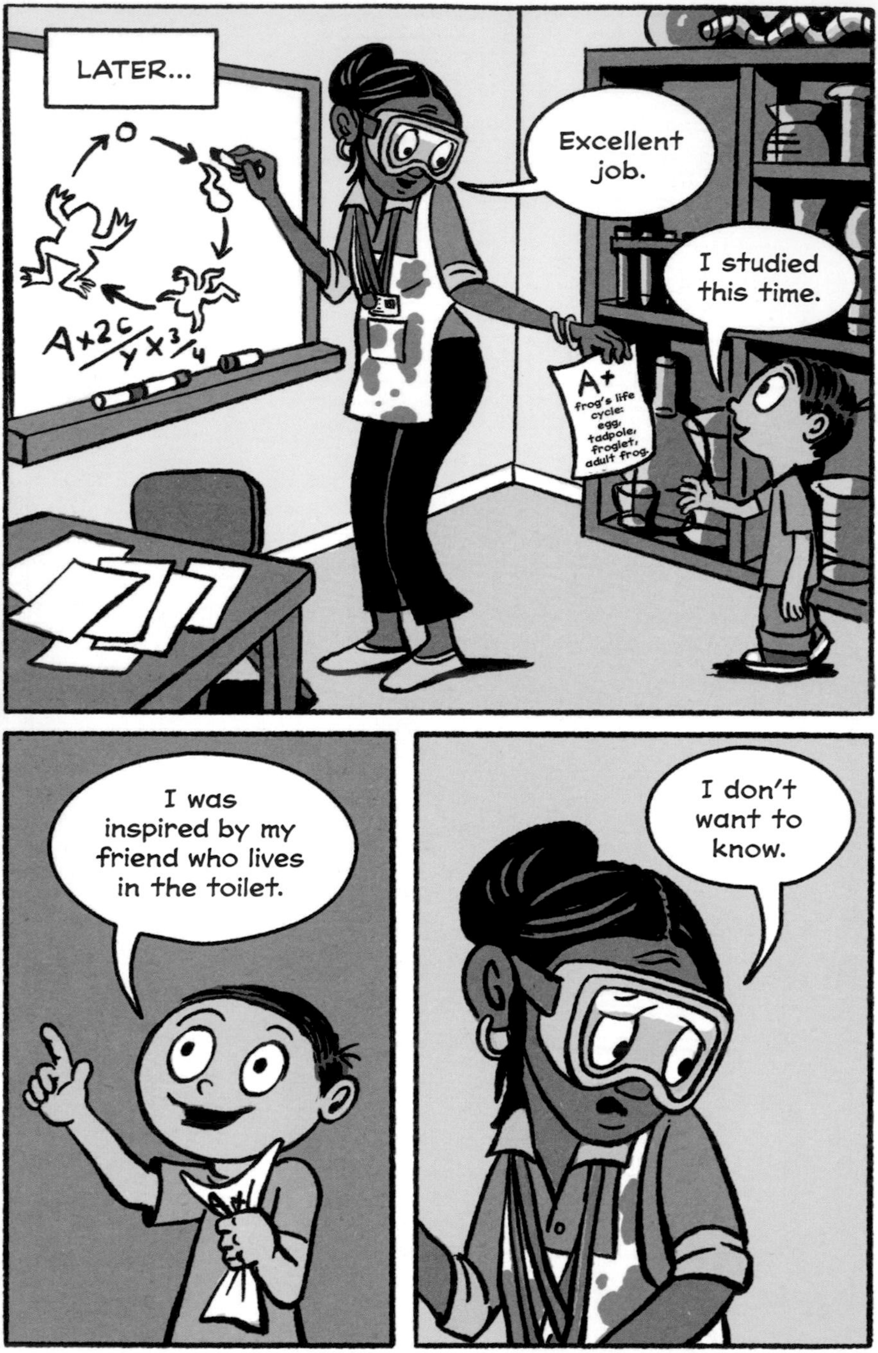
LATER...
Excellent job.
A+
frog's life cycle: egg, tadpole, froglet, adult frog.
I studied this time.
I was inspired by my friend who lives in the toilet.
I don't want to know.

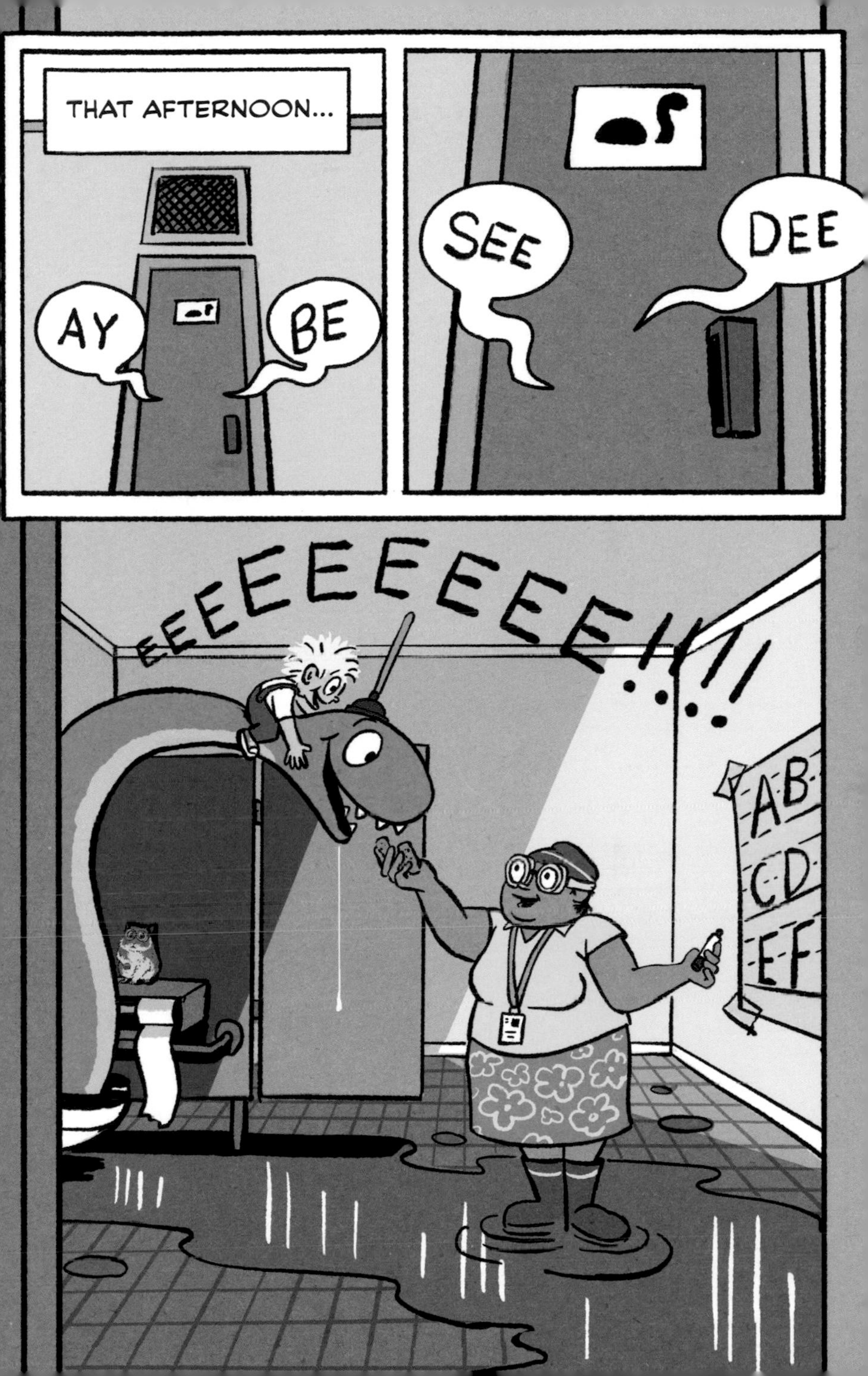
THAT AFTERNOON...
AY
BE
SEE
DEE
EEEEEEEEEEEE!!!!
AB
CD
EF

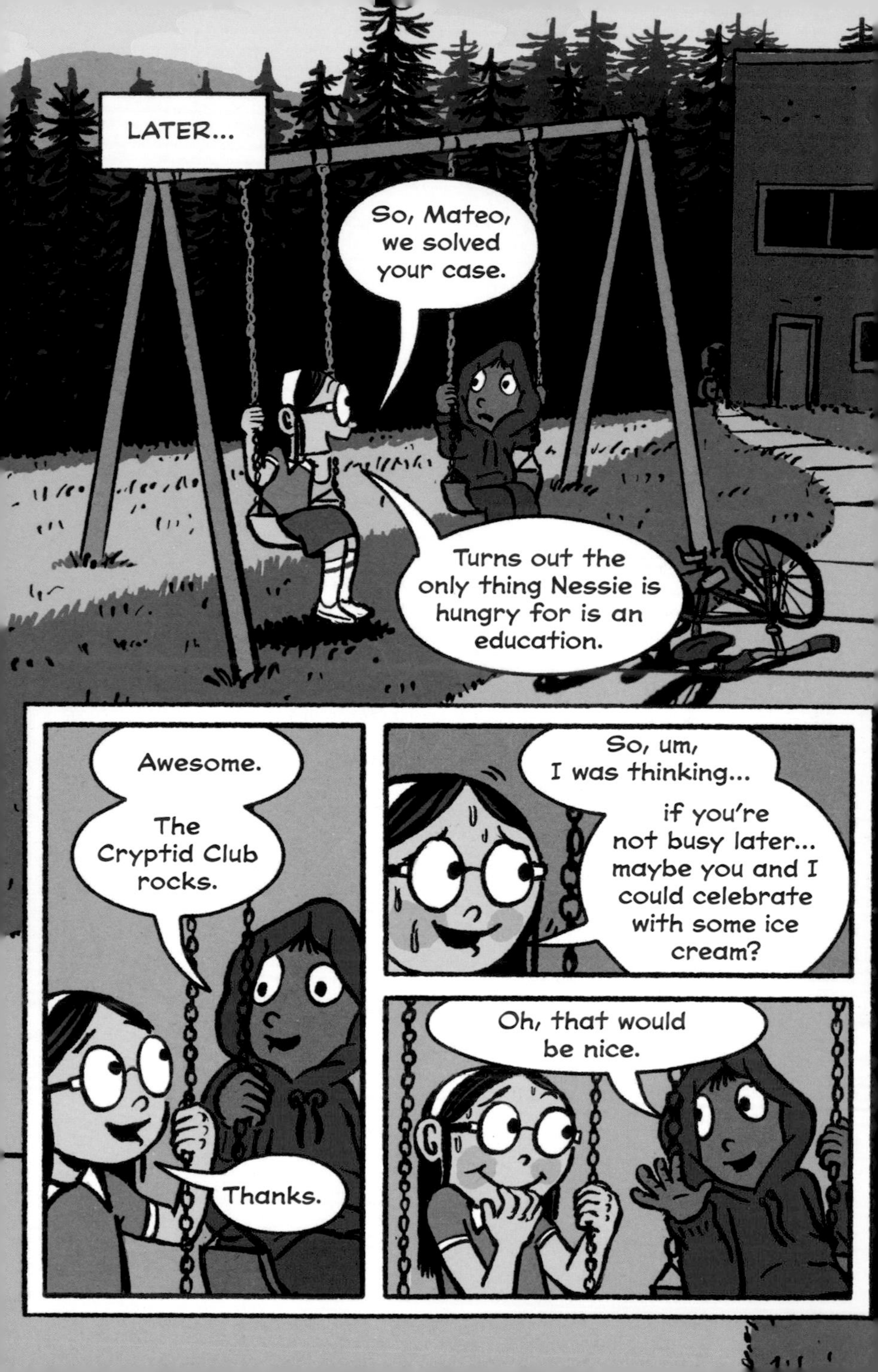
LATER...
So, Mateo, we solved your case.
Turns out the only thing Nessie is hungry for is an education.
Awesome.
The Cryptid Club rocks.
Thanks.
So, um, I was thinking...
if you're not busy later... maybe you and I could celebrate with some ice cream?
Oh, that would be nice.

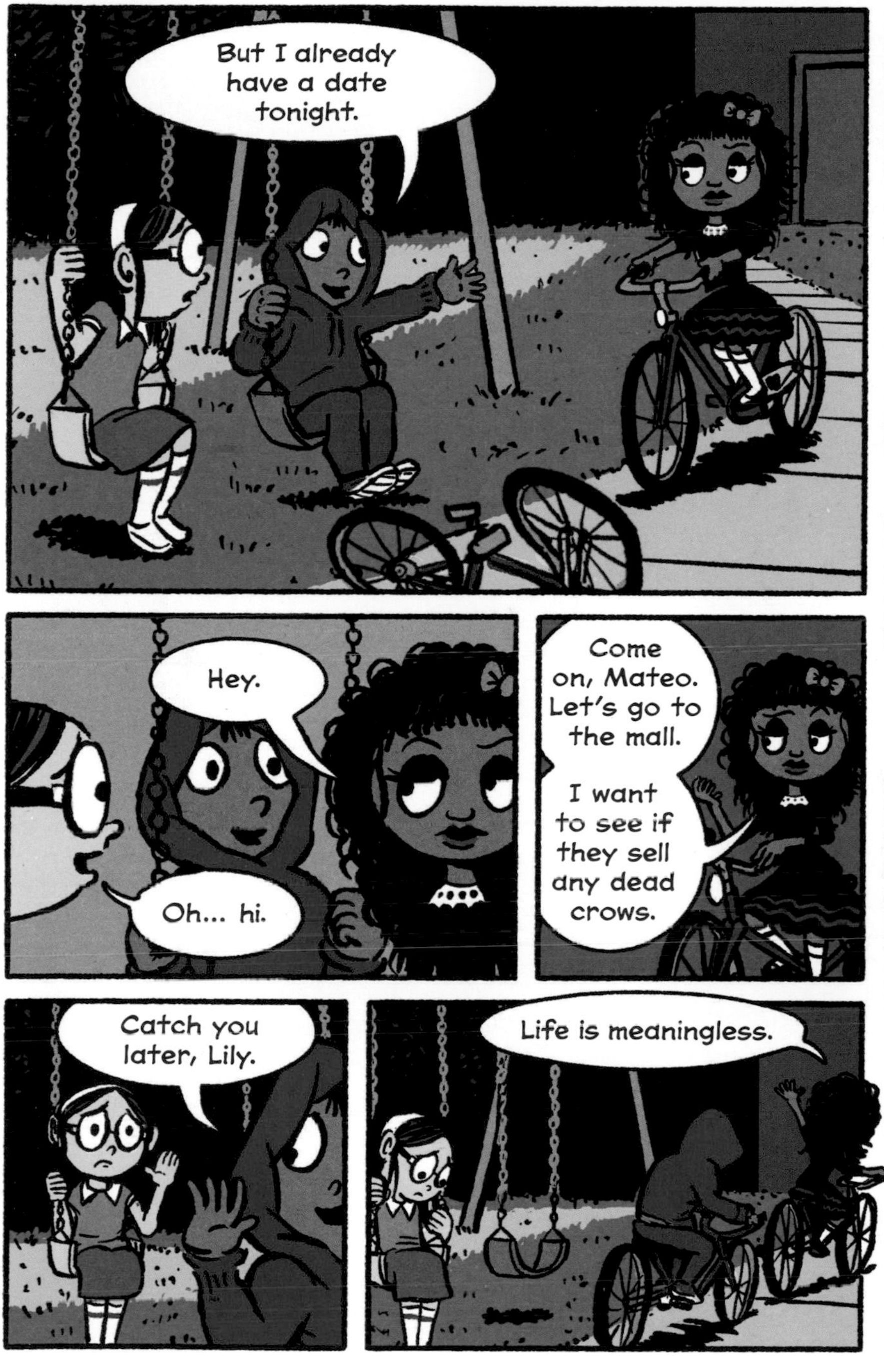
But I already have a date tonight.
Hey.
Oh... hi.
Come on, Mateo. Let's go to the mall.
I want to see if they sell any dead crows.
Catch you later, Lily.
Life is meaningless.

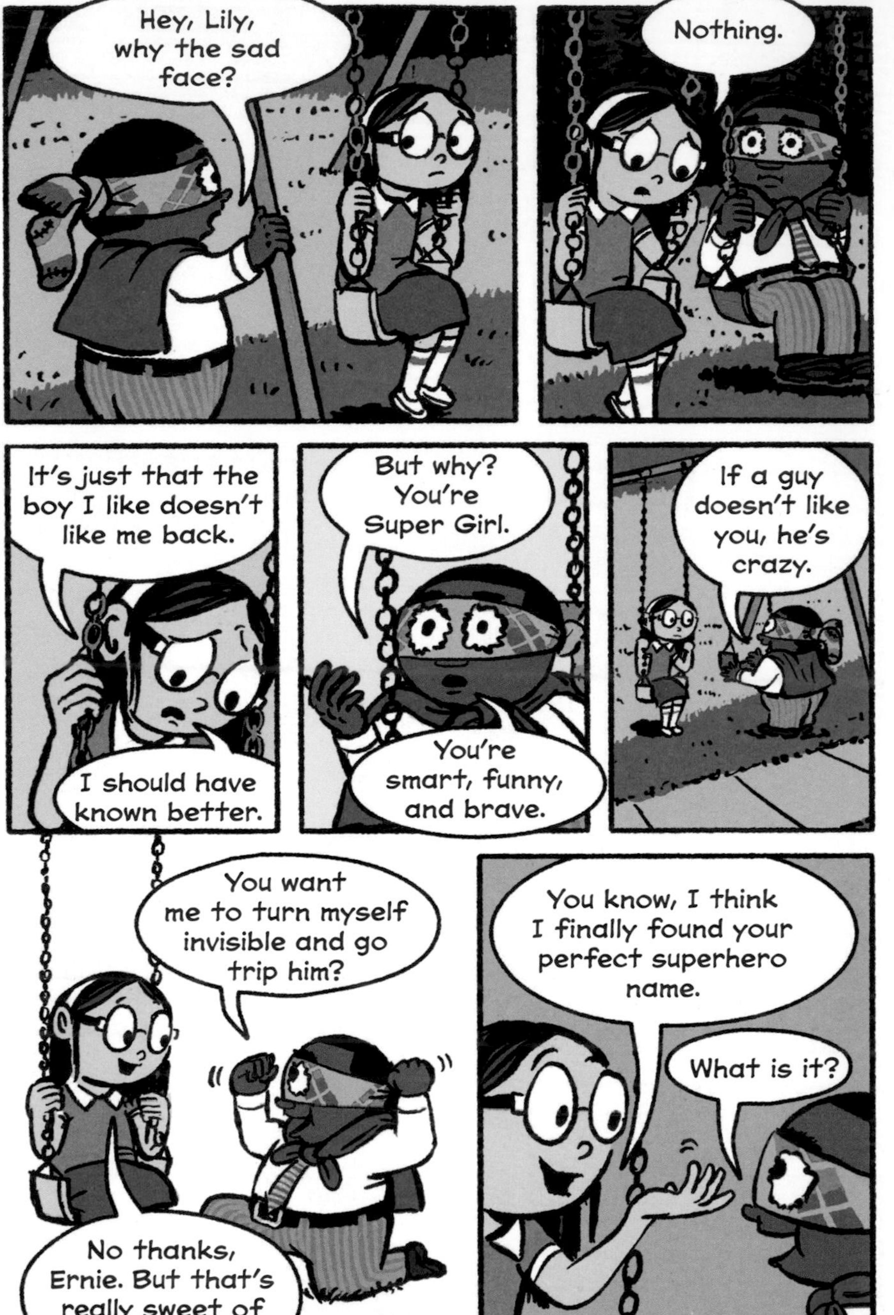
Hey, Lily, why the sad face?
Nothing.
It's just that the boy I like doesn't like me back.
I should have known better.
But why? You're Super Girl.
You're smart, funny, and brave.
If a guy doesn't like you, he's crazy.
You want me to turn myself invisible and go trip him?
No thanks, Ernie. But that's really sweet of you to say.
You know, I think I finally found your perfect superhero name.
What is it?

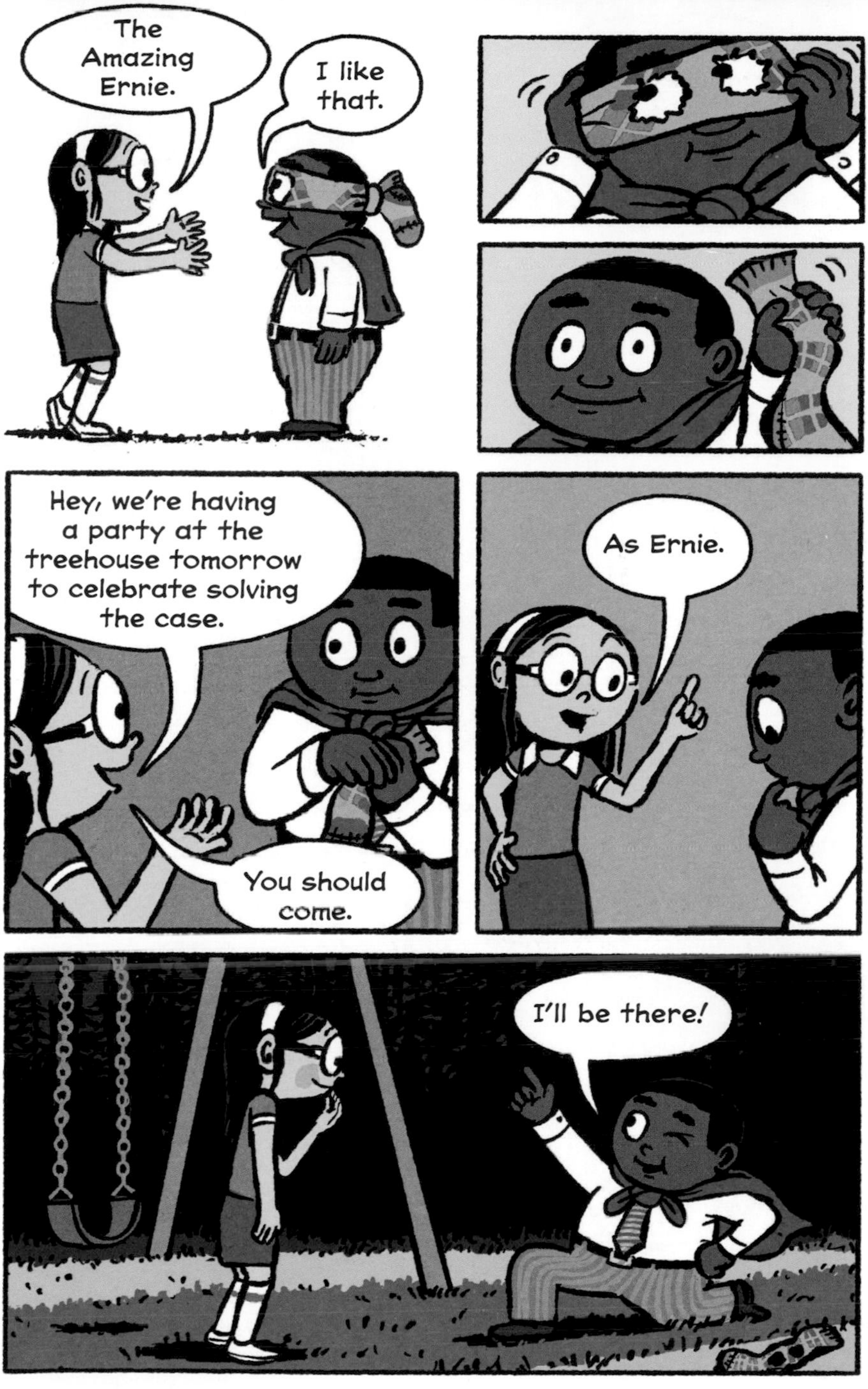
The Amazing Ernie.
I like that.
Hey, we're having a party at the treehouse tomorrow to celebrate solving the case.
You should come.
As Ernie.
I'll be there!

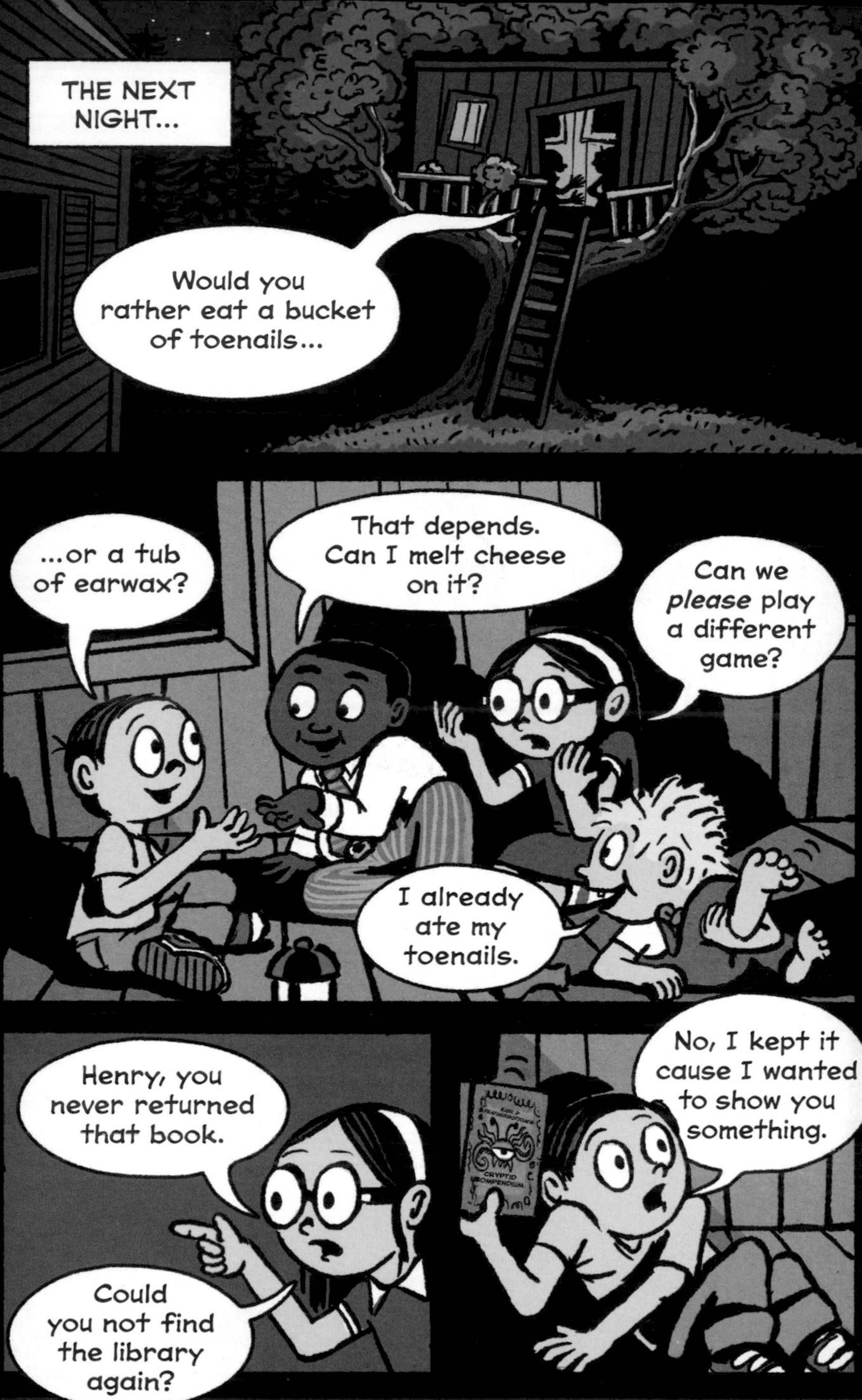
THE NEXT NIGHT...
Would you rather eat a bucket of toenails...
...or a tub of earwax?
That depends. Can I melt cheese on it?
Can we *please* play a different game?
I already ate my toenails.
Henry, you never returned that book.
Could you not find the library again?
No, I kept it cause I wanted to show you something.

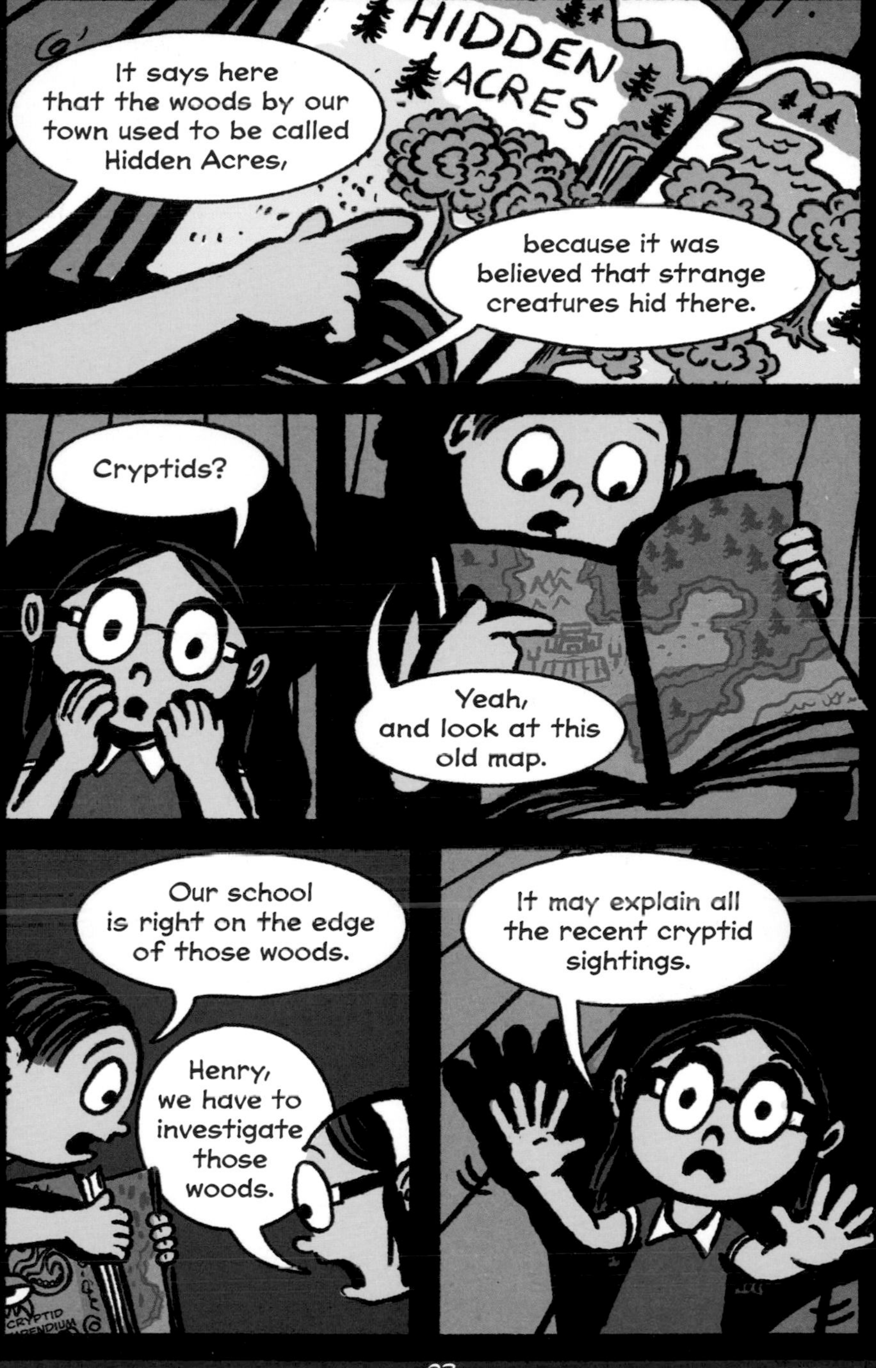
HIDDEN ACRES
It says here that the woods by our town used to be called Hidden Acres,
because it was believed that strange creatures hid there.
Cryptids?
Yeah, and look at this old map.
Our school is right on the edge of those woods.
Henry, we have to investigate those woods.
It may explain all the recent cryptid sightings.
CRYPTID

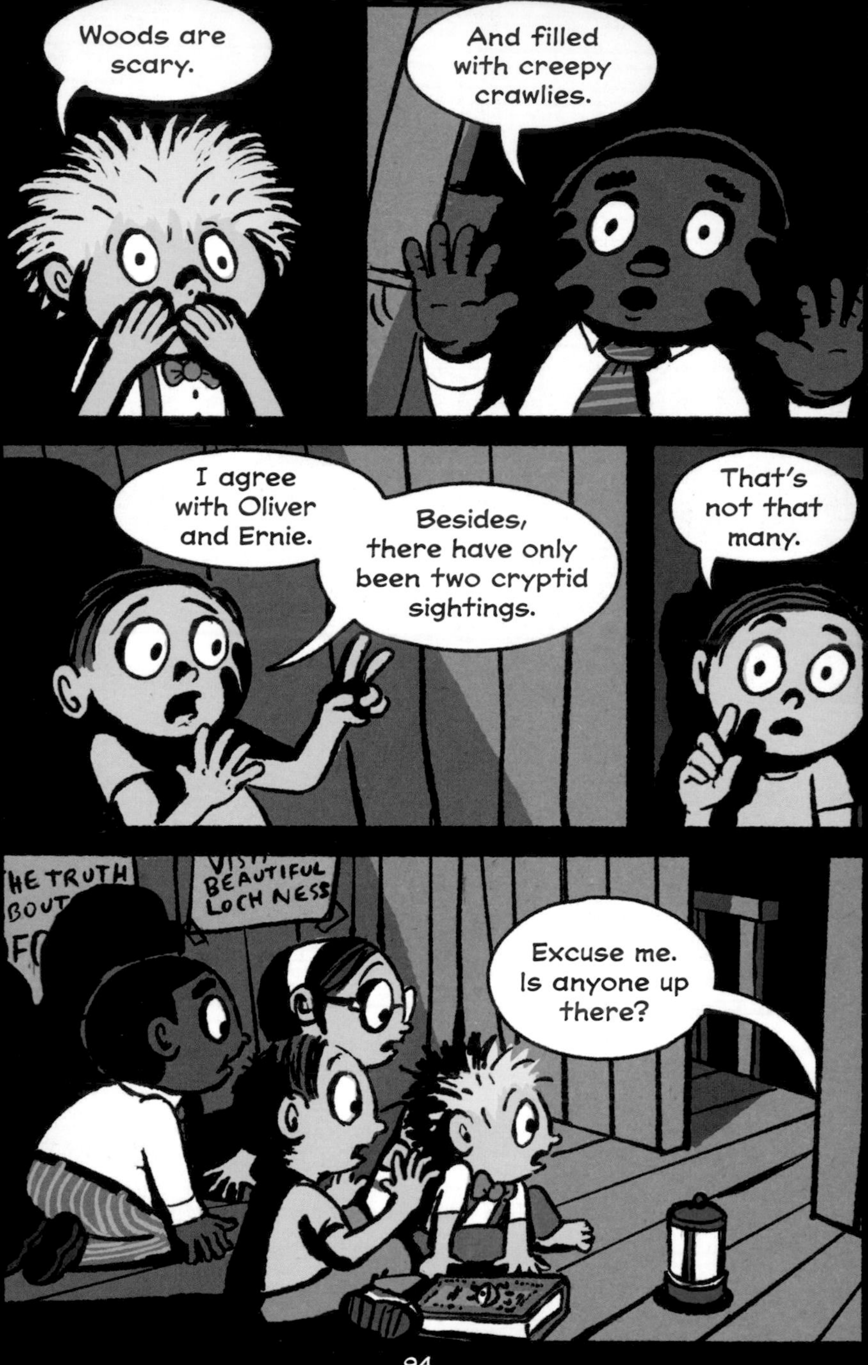

Woods are scary.
And filled with creepy crawlies.
I agree with Oliver and Ernie.
Besides, there have only been two cryptid sightings.
That's not that many.
HE TRUTH BOUT F
BEAUTIFUL LOCH NESS
Excuse me. Is anyone up there?

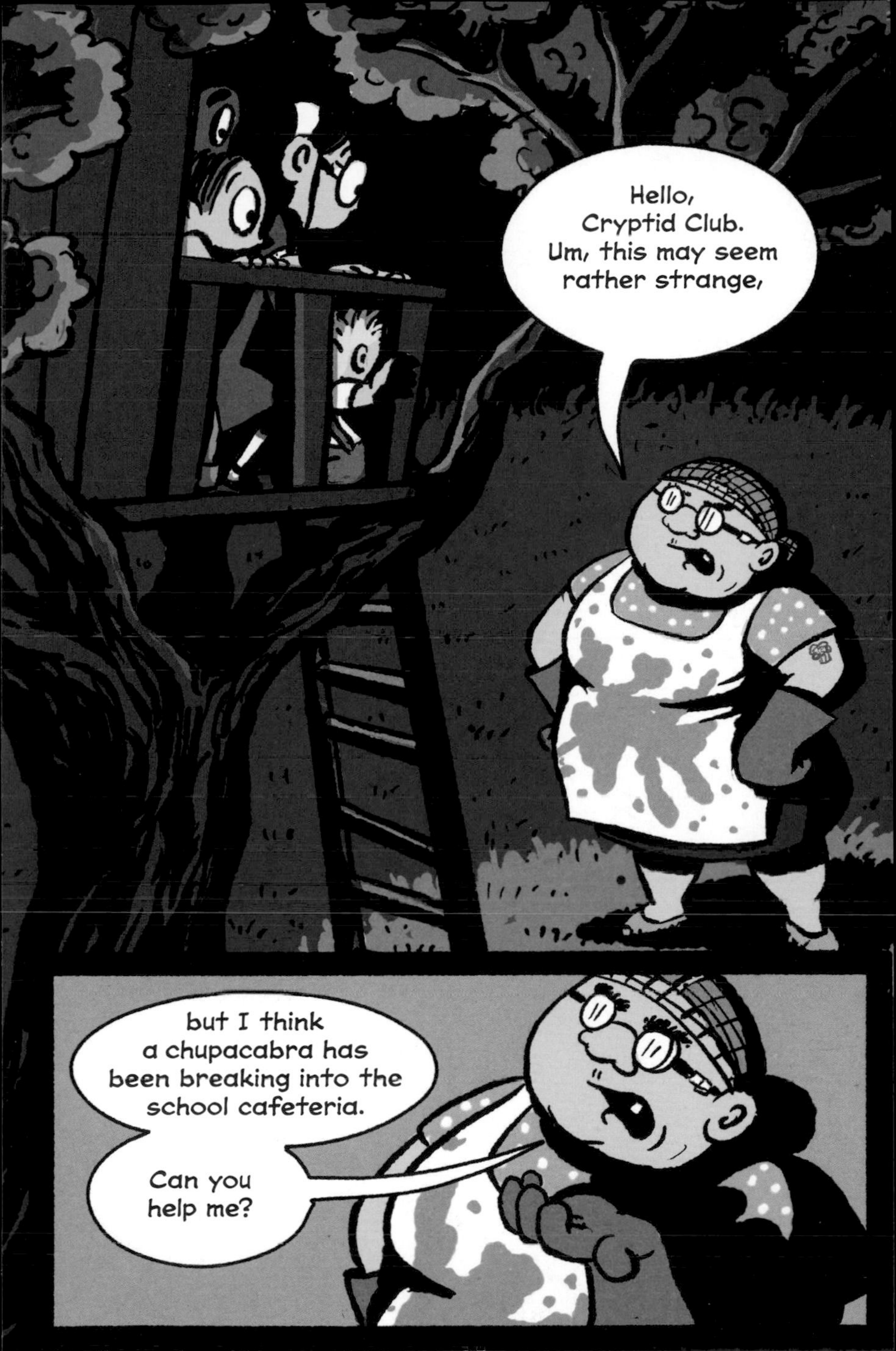
Hello, Cryptid Club. Um, this may seem rather strange,
but I think a chupacabra has been breaking into the school cafeteria.
Can you help me?

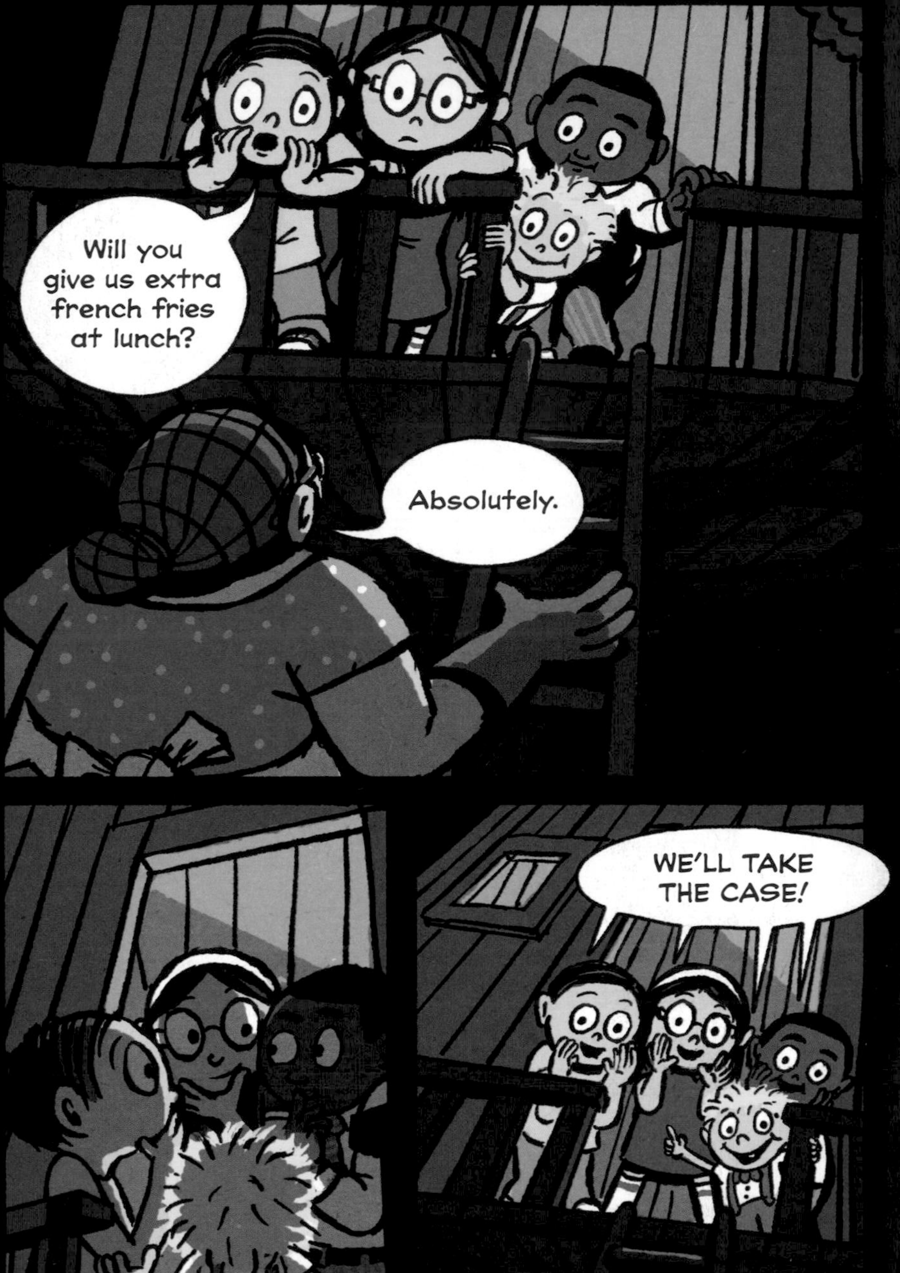

Will you give us extra french fries at lunch?
Absolutely.
WE'LL TAKE THE CASE!